Murder à la Mode

THE HENRY TIBBETT MYSTERIES
BY PATRICIA MOYES

Murder à la Mode

Patricia Moyes

An Owl Book

HOLT, RINEHART and WINSTON
New York

Copyright © 1963 by Patricia Moyes
All rights reserved, including the right to reproduce this
book or portions thereof in any form.
Published by Holt, Rinehart and Winston,
383 Madison Avenue, New York, New York 10017.

Library of Congress Cataloging in Publication Data
Moyes, Patricia.
Murder à la mode.
(An Inspector Henry Tibbett mystery)
"An Owl book."
I. Title.   II. Series: Moyes, Patricia.   Inspector
Henry Tibbett mystery.
[PR6063.09M8 1983]   823'.912   82-23260
ISBN 0-03-063544-6 (pbk.)

First published in hardcover by Holt, Rinehart and Winston in 1963
First Owl Book Edition—1983

Designer: Ernst Reichl
Printed in the United States of America
1 3 5 7 9 10 8 6 4 2

ISBN 0-03-063544-6

Murder à la Mode

1

"I won't do it, I tell you," shouted Patrick Walsh. "I won't! It's obscene. It's hideous. If you give that monster a double spread, I resign. If you as much as run it over the gutter, you can give me my cards, and that's flat." He strode about the room, deliberately clumsy, attempting to tear a handful of shaggy grey hair from the abundant mop that reared like a battered Cossack hat round his large, red face.

"It's the new line and the new length, Patrick," said Margery French firmly. She pushed up the veil of her black straw hat, held the shiny photograph at arm's length, and squinted at it through half-closed eyes. "I see it as a tremendous shock effect, making the point of Helen's copy. I agree it's not conventionally pretty—"

"Pretty!" Patrick stopped pacing and raised his enormous hands to heaven. "Pretty!" he bellowed again. "Who ever said I wanted pretty pictures? I just want something with a little shape to it, that's all. Is it too much to ask?" Suddenly, he lowered his voice to a beguiling Irish whisper. "Look now, Margery darling, you're a lovely girl and you're the boss—but have a little pity on your poor old art editor. I can't make a double spread out of that . . . that plum pudding on stilts."

There was an oppressive silence.

In the office next door, Teresa Manners smiled, wearily.

7

"Uncle's going off the deep end again," she remarked. "He really is impossible. I suppose we'll be here all night." She lit a cigarette and sat down on the desk, dangling her beautiful legs.

"I shall certainly be here all night," Helen Pankhurst replied tartly. "I always am, on these occasions. My work doesn't start until yours ends, if you remember." She blew her nose loudly and put on an enormous pair of spectacles outlined in rhinestone. "Would you mind getting off my desk, Teresa? You're sitting on my justified captions."

The communicating door between the two offices opened, and a precise voice said, "Miss Manners, can you spare the editor a moment?"

"With pleasure, Miss Field," said Teresa. "Here we go. Into battle." She took a long pull at her cigarette and went into the other office.

"Ah, Teresa dear." Margery French's voice came pleasantly and steadily, with no sign of strain. "Patrick is a little unhappy about the Monnier spread. I'd like your opinion . . . "

The door closed behind Teresa. Helen Pankhurst looked at her watch. Half past eleven already, and not a single layout through. Outside, in the lamplit Mayfair street, the commissionaire of The Orangery restaurant, dwarfed under his huge black umbrella, was hailing a taxi; a tired man in a shabby brown overcoat shivered beside a basketful of unseasonable red rosebuds. The road gleamed like black satin in the January rain.

Half past eleven, and the whole long night ahead. Opposite, the houses were uniformly dark above the ground floor, with the exception of the one immediately facing Helen's window. Here, a light still burned in an upper story. For the rest, they had long since been converted from private homes into offices, and the last secretary had hurried home, huddled against the wind and rain, soon after six. In the length of the street, only the tall Georgian mansion which housed the offices of *Style* was still ablaze with light and activity. For this was the night when the Paris Collections number was put to bed; the bi-annual occasion upon which certain members of the staff toiled and bickered until dawn, so that readers all over England could savour, on the appointed release date, pictures and fashion guidance from Paris presented in the authoritative manner of the glossiest of glossy magazines.

The readers in question, who are an ingenuous lot, would have been surprised by this feverish activity, for the delivery date of this particular issue was still three weeks away. They did not appreciate, as Helen did, the immense effort entailed in holding a sixteen-page section for a fortnight beyond its normal press date. They could hardly be expected to know that the superb photographic reproduction, the impeccable colour blocks and fine typesetting of *Style* were the result of weeks of patient work, which, in this exceptional case, had to be telescoped drastically. It was one of the ironies of the business, Helen reflected, that the most important fashion reportages of the year should always have to be produced in this overnight shambles, with little or no time for corrections or second thoughts.

Only that afternoon, the *Style* team in Paris had been perched uncomfortably on miniscule gilt chairs, watching the last show of the Collections. Only at six o'clock had the shutter of Michael Healy's camera clicked for the last time on the skeletal person of Veronica Spence, as she pirouetted on the highest platform of the Eiffel Tower in a top-secret chiffon evening dress by Monnier. Only at nine had Teresa and Michael climbed wearily out of the plane at London Airport, followed by the efficient and imperturbable Rachel Field, private secretary to the editor of *Style*. Only at half past ten had the still-wet prints of Michael's photographs emerged from the darkroom of the *Style* studios into the adjoining office of Patrick Walsh, the art editor.

And now it was half past eleven, and in the editor's office controversy raged as usual, and as usual tempers grew brittle and voices were raised. Which pictures should be used, and how should they be presented? What was the big story? Which trends in the new Collections were valid signposts of fashion influences to come, and which were mere flashes in the pan? Which of the new young designers rated the *cachet* of a page in *Style*? Teresa Manners, lovely and blonde and a semi-illiterate product of the best English private schooling, knew the answers to these questions, for she could feel the flow of fashion in the tips of her slim fingers, as an artist feels colour or a sculptor, form and texture. Teresa knew, but she found it hard to explain articulately. Patrick Walsh knew what would make a striking impact on the printed page. Margery French, as editor, was ultimately responsible. They would be arguing for hours.

Meanwhile, Helen could only sit and wait. Her function was more practical. First, when the completed layouts arrived, she would write the captions—tailoring them carefully to fit the space that Patrick had allotted, and getting from Teresa's scribbled notes *Style*'s views on the significance of Monnier's new Z silhouette and the future of the jagged hemline. Then, from Rachel Field's meticulously typed data, Helen would extract the information that the original fabric was by Garigue or Rodier or the Cumberland Silk Mills, and that this model would be available in March at Harrods or Debenhams. Finally, she had to make sure that, by seven o'clock in the morning, the hysterical confusion of the night had been resolved into neatly typed captions, each with its accompanying layout and photograph, checked and counterchecked and ready for the despatch rider to rush to the printers. It was a hard night's work, and Helen was thankful that it only happened twice a year.

She blew her nose again, and poured herself some tea from the battered red Thermos flask which she always brought with her to the office on Collections night. To her irritation, there was only half a cup left in it. She picked up her house telephone and dialed the number of the darkroom.

" 'Ullo," said a lugubrious voice.

"Ernie, this is Miss Pankhurst. Please come and get my Thermos and make me some fresh tea. At once."

"I'm supposed to be reducin' a print . . . "

"Don't argue," said Helen crossly, and slammed down the receiver. She knew that she had the reputation of being a dragon, but she did not care. It had its uses. Sure enough, in two minutes Ernie arrived, tousle-headed and surly, and removed the precious flask to his cubbyhole off the darkroom, where an electric kettle was installed for "brewing up."

Helen's head ached, and she reflected bitterly that it was just her luck to have caught a stifling cold to add to all the other worries of the night. She felt infinitely older than her thirty-four years, and longed to lie down. Instead, she drank her half cup of tea, and began to study Teresa's ungrammatical but colourful reports.

"Hats like soup plates, v. important . . . sort of bull-fightish colours . . . gorgeous in a maid's-night-out sort of way . . . o.k. for dumpling debs but basically old hat . . . the good old Balenciaga sack hacked round the hem with pruning shears . . . "

It was all vivid and true, and Helen wished she could print it as it stood. Impossible, of course. She began to translate it into *Stylese*. "Discus hats, flat as flying saucers . . . a colour scheme of mantilla black and picador red, spiced with new-minted gold . . . dazzling for the woman who dares . . . classic in the modern manner . . . the slim sheath with the new ragamuffin look . . . " She blew her nose again, and wished she had brought some aspirin. It was nearly midnight.

In the office next door, Teresa and Patrick were on their knees on the deep lilac carpet, groveling among a welter of photographs and experimental layouts.

"Blow it up!" said Patrick, boomingly. "Blow it up enormous, and kill the hat picture."

"No," said Teresa. "No. Honestly. I won't have the hat killed."

"My dear girl, what does it *mean?*"

"It's important." Teresa gestured, a little helplessly. "Without the hat, there's no story. This year, it's the hats that matter."

"All right." Patrick was angry. "Let's have all hat. One great hideous hat right across both pages. Give the spread some guts. Crop the picture here . . . "

The door leading to Patrick's Art Department opened quietly, and Michael Healy came in. He was an immensely tall, thin man, renowned as a dandy. At the moment, he was in shirt-sleeves, his fair hair rumpled, and his long face haggard with fatigue. In a light, biting voice, he said, "I know I'm only a poor bloody photographer, but would you mind telling me what in hell you two are proposing to do to that picture?"

Teresa looked up quickly. "Only cropping it a bit, darling, to show up the hat."

"The point of that photograph," said Michael acidly, "is in the line of the dress carried up to and *through* the hat. If you're going to cut it up into small pieces, I'd be grateful if you took my name off it."

"Now, Michael." Margery French sat back in her swivel chair behind the big desk. The black straw hat was beginning to grow uncomfortably tight around her temples, but she would no more have dreamed of taking it off than of undressing in public. "Let's get this straight. Teresa considers that hats are extremely important this season."

"Well, they are."

"Patrick wants a double spread for the Dior suit."

"It's the only damned picture that . . . "

"Michael feels that this photograph will be ruined if it's cropped, and I quite agree with him."

"Thank you, Margery."

"Well, then. Why don't we give the Dior a double spread, go on to this picture, uncropped, facing a whole-page hat picture, and kill the Monnier chiffon?"

There was a moment of concentrated silence.

"How strongly do you feel about the Monnier chiffon, Teresa?"

Teresa hesitated. "Not desperately," she said, finally. "The Balmain makes the point. I'm for killing it."

"Margery, me darling, you're a genius!" Patrick stood up and bellowed, "Donald!"

Like a rabbit from a hat, the head of a dark young man popped round the Art Department door.

"Take all these bloody layouts and burn them, you miserable Scotsman," cried Patrick, in high good temper, sweeping up a sheaf of papers from the floor. "Then blow up the Dior on the photostat and we'll make a paste-up of . . . "

He disappeared into the Art Department. Margery French smiled—a warm, youthful smile which made it difficult to remember that she was nearly sixty, a formidable brain, and in her own sphere, a very important and influential woman.

"That should give us ten minutes' peace," she said. "I think I'll go and freshen up in the rest room. Call me there, Miss Field, if anyone needs me before Mr. Walsh gets back." She stood up, very erect, not a blue-rinsed hair out of place. "I hope you've sent Ernest home, Michael. Surely all the darkroom work is done by now."

"He left ten minutes ago, Margery."

"Good. He's been looking rather tired lately." Margery smiled again, but this time it was a little forced. She swayed slightly, and put out a hand to her desk to steady herself. "Well, see you in ten minutes."

As the door closed behind Margery, Michael Healy said, "I hope to God she's O.K. I've never known her . . . "

Teresa yawned and stretched. "She's not superhuman, darling, even though lots of people seem to think she is. She gets tired like everybody else, although she won't admit it. She depends an awful lot on Helen these days. Unfortunately."

The silence that followed was broken by the sharp tapping of a typewriter, a necessary reminder to Teresa and Michael that they were not alone. Indeed, they could have been forgiven for forgetting that there was a third person in the room. Rachel Field was the acme of all that a private secretary should be. Neat, unremarkable, precise, soft-spoken, dauntingly efficient. Teresa knew that Miss Field (as she always called her) was considered by the junior staff to be a terrifying martinet, but she personally had never been able to see it. Miss Field simply wasn't there unless one needed her. It never occurred to Teresa that it was only her own privileged position as fashion editor that protected her from the more ruthless aspects of Rachel's nature.

As for Rachel, she regarded Miss Manners (as she always called her) with carefully concealed dislike and exasperation. Miss French—now there was someone a person could be proud to work for; kind—sometimes too kind, in Rachel's opinion—but efficient, decisive, and with a proper respect for files and an orderly office system. But Miss Manners . . . well . . . scatter-brained and irresponsible and spoilt were the epithets that Rachel, privately, applied to her. Miss French said that Miss Manners had a flair for fashion, and if Miss French said so, Rachel supposed it must be true. Personally, she failed to understand the fuss that people like Miss Manners and Mr. Walsh made about which picture was to be used, and how. To hear them go on, you'd think they were talking about something important. Rachel considered it remarkably indulgent of Miss French to put up with their silly temperaments the way she did. And to think that Miss Manners and that man Michael Healy could go gossiping about Miss French behind her back, in her own office . . . Rachel hit the keys of her typewriter viciously, in loud, unspoken criticism.

Michael said, "Oh, well. If you're going to use the Paulette hat picture big, I'll make another print of it. This one's too dark." He picked up a photograph from the floor and studied it. "God, that girl, Veronica Thing, has wonderful bones. A young Goalen. I could do something with her."

"I'm sure you could." Teresa sounded slightly mocking.

"Not what you mean, darling," said Michael. He kissed the top of her ash-blonde head and went out, whistling. In the art department, he passed Patrick Walsh and Donald MacKay, enmeshed in festoons of sliced-up photostats and Gripfix.

"I hope you two boys aren't playing any nasty, messy games," he said severely.

"Go to hell," said Patrick.

"My dear Uncle, I've been there for years," said Michael lightly, and went on into the quiet dusk of the darkroom, his own domain. It was half past twelve.

Margery French lay on a day bed in the rest room and fought against feeling old and tired and ill. For years—more years than she cared to be reminded of—she had reveled in these all-night sessions. Even up until last year, she had been able, effortlessly, to run the younger members of the staff off their feet and still emerge, smiling and serene, to face the next day's business. This tiredness frightened her more than she would admit.

She was thankful for Helen and Teresa. Poor Helen. A fine brain, a good writer, but no fashion flair at all. Of course, it wasn't often that fashion sense and executive ability were fused in one person, as they were in Margery French. Margery was not a fool, and, without being conceited, she acknowledged this fact to herself. The question that bothered her now was the choice of her successor. Margery was shrewd and clear-minded, and she knew that she must soon retire. Who would take her place— Teresa or Helen? On the face of it, Teresa would never make an editor. She was inefficient, tactless, irresponsible, and rather lazy —and yet she had what *Style* needed—fashion sense—the one quality without which the magazine would die. Helen was the obvious choice, and Margery knew that the Board of Directors favoured her, and yet . . . Helen would not have known, instinctively, that hats were important this season. She would probably have gone all out for the jagged hem line, which was certainly showy and amusing, but which Teresa had quickly dismissed as a mere gimmick, good for a mention and one photograph but no more. Then there was another thing. Margery knew that Helen was devoted to the magazine, and would work cheerfully and loyally under Teresa's editorship; but she also knew that Teresa had made it plain that she would not stay on if

Helen were appointed. No, it must be Teresa, with all her faults. Margery closed her eyes and relaxed, as the doctor had told her. It was then that she became aware of the insistent tapping of a typewriter somewhere close at hand.

In an instant, she was awake. That couldn't be Miss Field— her office was too far away. It was coming from next door. Olwen's office. Irritated, Margery got up from the couch, put on her hat, and went out into the passage. Yes, without a doubt. There was a light under Olwen's door. Margery opened it and went in.

Olwen Piper, the features editor of *Style,* presented a bizarre sight. Dressed in an unbecomingly bright orange evening dress, she was sitting at her typewriter with large horn-rimmed spectacles on her nose and her rather ugly face bent earnestly over her work. Her stockinged feet were placed solidly and inelegantly on the floor, beside a pair of kicked-off brocade shoes and a carelessly discarded white mohair stole. She did not even hear the door opening, and when Margery said, "Olwen!" sharply, she looked up dazedly, as if coming out of a dream.

"Olwen." Margery's black hat quivered. "What are you doing here at this time of night?"

Olwen was confused. "I'm sorry, Miss French. I didn't mean . . . "

"Some of us have to be here for the Collections issue," said Margery, "but surely you're not so overworked that you have to come to the office after midnight in those extraordinary clothes?"

Olwen flushed. "No . . . no, of course not. It's just that . . . well . . . I've just come from the first night of *Lucifer* . . . the new play at the Court, you know . . . "

"I know." Margery was brusque.

"It was so exciting . . . " Olwen took off her glasses. Without them, she was slightly short-sighted, which gave her an attractive air of vagueness. She forgot her embarrassment, and glowed with enthusiasm. "It's a great moment in the English theatre, Miss French. A real breakthrough which ought to start a whole new movement. The most important thing in two decades. I just had to come in and write it all down while it was in my head."

"You don't imagine you're going to get it into the March issue, do you?"

"Oh, no." Olwen was quite undaunted. "But I was going to ask you for more space in April. I want Michael to go down there and photograph John Hartley in the second act in that marvellous make-up, and I want to face it with . . . "

"The April issue is already planned."

"But, Miss French, I saw Hartley afterwards, and he's promised to do us a piece on the play from his standpoint as an anti-Brechtian actor. You know he's always refused to comment on his own work before. The dailies have offered him thousands and—"

"That's very good work, Olwen. Congratulations." Margery forced her voice to sound warm and friendly. "I'm sure we'll be able to find room for it in April. But I do think you should go home, dear. You'll exhaust yourself."

"Oh, no. I love working."

Margery French looked at the young, serious face, the hopelessly dowdy dress—now defiled by an inkstain—and the rather square feet liberated from their fashionable shoes. In a painful moment of truth, she recognized her twenty-two-year-old self, just down from Cambridge with a first-class degree, and passionately involved in the eternal realities of art. On the far wall, her own reflection in the mirror mocked her, mercilessly. Blue-rinsed, chic, corseted, wearing a hat in the office.

"Fashion is an art, too," she said, aloud.

Olwen looked surprised. "Of course it is, Miss French," she said politely.

Margery did not trust herself to smile. "Goodnight, dear," she said. She went quickly down the corridor towards her own office.

Half past one. The tension had ebbed out of the atmosphere, leaving only exhaustion. Slowly, acrimoniously, the final layouts had been approved, and the photostat machine shrouded decently for what remained of the night. Donald MacKay mopped his brow and put on his jacket. Patrick Walsh took a well-earned swig of Irish whisky from the flask which he always kept, discreetly, in the bottom drawer of his desk, and whistled tunelessly to himself. He had had a splendid evening, full of the great, bombastic, good-tempered fights in which he reveled: what was more, he had won most of them.

Teresa Manners powdered her exquisite nose in the rest room. Michael Healy combed his lank fair hair and noted with regret that the carnation in his buttonhole was drooping. Margery

French adjusted her black straw hat and asked Rachel Field to telephone for a taxi. Then, with a slight feeling of guilt, she went into Helen's office.

Helen was sitting at her typewriter. Her desk was invisible under a disorderly pile of papers and layouts. Her dark hair was untidy and her sharp, rather long nose glistened almost as brightly as the rhinestones in her spectacle frames.

"I really don't like leaving you all alone, Helen dear," said Margery. "Are you sure you wouldn't like me to stay and help you?"

"I'm perfectly all right, thank you, Margery," said Helen, in the crisp voice which her secretaries knew and feared. "Once you've all gone, I can get down to some work in peace."

Margery accepted this for what it was—not rudeness, but a simple statement of fact. "Very well," she said, "but I insist that you take tomorrow off."

"I can't possibly," said Helen. "The early form for April closes tomorrow."

"We can manage without you."

"I'd rather be here. I'll just go home and take a bath and breakfast, and come back."

"Well . . . see how you feel in the morning . . . "

"Thank you, Margery. Goodnight."

"Goodnight, Helen."

With a certain reluctance, Margery went back to her own office. Helen ran a fresh sheet of paper into the typewriter, and wrote: "The Beggar's Opera has come to town. Ragged Robin is running the hedgerows of Paris in the most sophisticated tatters since . . . " She frowned, turned the paper up, and started again. "Paris says . . . rags and tatters for spring. Gamines and gutter-snipes swagger jauntily through the Collections in a riot of gaudy colour . . . "

It was at that moment that Godfrey Goring arrived.

Godfrey Goring, the managing director and chief shareholder of Style Publications Ltd., was a shrewd, affable man in his early fifties. Grey-haired and distinguished, he looked exactly what he was—a businessman, pure and simple. He had bought himself a controlling interest in Style some years before, when the magazine had been in rough financial water, and it was common knowledge that he had sunk a considerable amount of his own

17

money in the venture of pulling *Style* out of the doldrums and setting it firmly on its feet. The fact that Goring had been successful was chiefly due to the fact that he did not hamper his staff in any way. He knew that fashion was big business, and he prided himself on engaging the greatest experts in that ephemeral art, and leaving them to get on with it. He tolerated their tantrums and temperaments, and allowed their zaniest ideas free rein. Their success or failure he gauged, very simply, by the amount of advertizing revenue which flowed into the company from high-class manufacturers—the kind whose garments sell at upwards of twenty guineas. Privately, Godfrey always thought of clothes as garments, but he would not have dreamed of using the word in front of Patrick or Teresa; just as he would not have confided to them that *Style's* celebrated standard of good taste was to him not so much a sacred trust as a moneymaking proposition. Only if revenue appeared to be falling off in one direction or another did he presume, in the discreetest possible way, to make a suggestion to his editorial staff.

Fortunately, it was very seldom necessary. There was an ever-increasing public interest in good taste and gracious living; the commodities which Goring had to sell. Nevertheless, without his gentle but firm guidance, the magazine might well have slipped back into the unhealthy economic state in which he had found it. Of all his subordinates, only Margery French was fully aware of these realities. She was, as Goring frequently remarked, one of *Style's* greatest assets. Her fashion sense was sound and true, and yet at the same time he had not hesitated to leave administrative and financial affairs in her hands when he had gone to America, just a year ago, to study transatlantic methods of printing and presentation. Godfrey Goring had a great respect and affection for Margery.

He also appreciated the unrewarded devotion to duty that inspired the *Style* staff to these late-night working sessions, and this evening he felt a generous urge to recompense them. He had just concluded a most successful business dinner at The Orangery with Horace Barry, the resourceful owner of Barrimodes Ltd., to whom he had succeeded in selling a number of four-colour pages of advertizing in forthcoming issues. Over coffee, they had been joined by Nicholas Knight, the brilliant young dress designer (reputed a likely candidate for promotion to the Big Ten), whose salon, workrooms, and private apartment were above The Orangery, in the house which faced *Style*'s offices.

At half past one, the restaurant showed signs of closing, and Godfrey suggested that the other two should go back with him to his house in Brompton Square for a nightcap. It was when he was already on the rain-drenched pavement that he noticed the lights still burning in the *Style* building. Then the front door opened, and Donald MacKay came out, turning up the collar of his raincoat with a shiver.

Goring recognized him at once, and went over. "How's it going?" he asked.

"Very well, sir. We've just finished—all except for Miss Pankhurst, of course. It went very smoothly, considering," he added, not quite truthfully.

"Ah, good, good. Well, goodnight, MacKay."

Donald hurried off, and Godfrey went back to his car. It was then that he conceived the typically unconventional and warm-hearted gesture of inviting those of the staff who were still there to join his party. The big glass entrance doors had slammed firmly behind Donald, but Goring had his own key. He let himself in and took the lift to the fourth floor.

His entrance could not have been better timed. Margery, Teresa, Michael, and Patrick were all in Margery's office, and Miss Field had just reported no success with the fifth taxi rank. They were talking about getting a hire-car and sharing it. Godfrey descended on them like a *deus ex machina*.

"My dear, hard-working people," he said, "you shall all come with me in my car to Brompton Square. We will drink champagne, and then Barker shall drive each and every one of you home. No argument."

His eye swept quickly round the room, calculating. Barry and Knight had gone ahead in Knight's car. That meant, besides himself, one, two, three, four, five people . . . five . . . ? He counted heads again, and realized with mortification that he had, as usual, overlooked Miss Field.

"And Miss Field, of course. You will come, won't you, Miss Field? I know how much work Collections mean for you. Our unsung heroine."

"I don't think I should, Mr. Goring, thank you very much. I ought to be getting home. And in any case, I came straight here from the Paris plane. I've still got my suitcase, and that makes it . . ."

"Crikey," said Teresa, inelegantly. "So have Michael and I. I'd forgotten all about them. They're in the darkroom, aren't they, darling?"

Godfrey Goring frowned. "I don't think we have room for luggage as well as people," he said. "The boot of the car is full of dog baskets, of all things, that my wife made me buy. Why don't you leave your cases here and pick them up tomorrow? Yes, that's the best thing. Come along now, everybody . . . you, too, Miss Field. I insist. I positively insist."

A couple of minutes later, all six of them were packed, not uncomfortably, into the dark grey Bentley which stood purring outside the front door. Godfrey slipped her into gear and moved smoothly off down the wet, shiny street—but not before he had earned the undying gratitude of the flower-seller by buying the last three bunches of red roses at an inflated price, and presenting them to Margery, Teresa, and Rachel.

In The Orangery, tired waiters put up the shutters and counted their tips. In her office, Olwen Piper glanced at her watch and found it hard to believe that it was ten minutes past two. She got out her big dictionary and checked on the exact meanings of "neoterism" and "profulgent," and was gratified to find that she had used them both correctly. It was a hard struggle for a dramatic critic to dig up words which had not been used too often by other people.

At the other end of the corridor, Helen Pankhurst finished her lead-in blurb to the Collections feature. She had heard Godfrey Goring's voice, and was profoundly thankful that he and the others had departed, leaving her in peace. She started on a caption.

"Roger Leblanc, at Monnier, takes a swathe of aubergine silk (by Garigue), adds the sparkle of tiny diamonds (by Cartier), whips them into a featherweight meringue of a hat . . . " She sniffed, blew her nose again, and was suddenly aware that she was very cold indeed, in spite of the central heating. There was an electric fire beside her desk, and she got up and switched it on. In doing so, she stumbled on something, and saw to her annoyance that it was a suitcase—shabby but of good leather—with R.F. in faded gold embossed on the lid. One of the catches had sprung open, and a piece of tissue paper slipped from the over-stuffed interior. Dutifully, Helen tried to refasten the lock, but only succeeded in opening the other one as well. The lid sprang up, and several things fell out of the case onto the floor. The fact of the matter was that it was much too full, and Helen had neither the time nor the energy to waste on closing it. She left it as it was and went back to the featherweight meringue of a hat.

Some time later, pausing in the middle of a caption to think up yet another synonym for "white," Helen remembered that Ernie had never brought back her recharged Thermos, and went down the corridor to the darkroom to collect it. On entering the small storeroom, however, her attention was immediately caught by two suitcases which stood incongruously under the sink. One of them was of fine pigskin, and bore the initials M.H. The other was of white leather, with a large pink label on which was scrawled, *Teresa Manners, Crillon, Paris.* Helen hesitated. She suspected that one of those suitcases contained something which she was particularly anxious to lay hands on. Quickly, she tried the catch of the case in question. It was not locked. She opened it, found what she wanted, and closed it again. Then, the Thermos forgotten, she went back to her office.

It was shortly after this that she heard footsteps in the corridor, and was only mildly surprised to see, through her open office door, that Olwen Piper was making her way towards the lift.

Olwen called, "Goodnight, Helen. See you in the morning."

Helen did not answer. She was by now immersed in Monnier's deceptively simple little black dress in silk and mohair mixture (by Ascher), available at Marshall & Snelgrove in late March. A little later, she was vaguely aware of the sound of the lift, and registered mentally that Olwen must have finally gone home.

It was some hours later, with many captions still to write, that Helen found herself yearning for a cup of tea, and went once again in search of her Thermos. Stiffly, still reading the sheaf of notes in her hand, she walked down the passage to the dark-room, where the Thermos stood, reassuringly, beside the electric kettle. She picked it up and, absorbed in her notes once more, carried it back to her office and put it on the desk. She poured out a mugful of tea.

Thoughtfully, Helen ran a piece of paper into the machine, and started typing a caption. She paused for a second to consider a word, and, without taking her eyes off her work, reached out her right hand and picked up the mug. She drank, avidly. It was half past four.

The young despatch rider from Pictorial Printers Ltd. was growing impatient. It was a miserable, dark, drizzly morning, and he had been outside the offices of *Style* since seven o'clock, as ordered. It was now nearly a quarter past seven, and the glass entrance doors remained firmly locked, the vestibule dark and unrevealing. He rang the night bell again. It wasn't as if there was nobody there. He could see a light burning in one of the fourth floor windows. He was not only cross, but puzzled, for he had been doing the *Style* run for a couple of years, and it was one job that always went like clockwork. Had to, what's more. The compositors were waiting, down at Sydenham, and there wouldn't half be a dust-up if the stuff was late. Eight o'clock deadline, the foreman compositor had said. He didn't see how he'd make it now, not with the morning rush-hour traffic.

"Bloody woman's probably fallen asleep," he muttered to himself. He tried to decide what to do for the best. He knew that Alf, the doorman, did not arrive until a few minutes before eight, in time to let in the battalion of cheerful charladies who cleaned and swept the offices before the staff arrived at nine thirty.

The despatch rider left his motor bike by the pavement, stepped back into the road, and let out a piercing whistle. The only effect of this was to attract the attention of a bored, cold policeman, who came up amiably and said, "What's up, then, mate?"

"Urgent lot of stuff to pick up here at seven prompt, and they're all asleep."

"Still, mustn't wake the whole neighbourhood, you know," said the policeman, affably. "Tell you what. There's a phone box in the mews at the back. You go and ring them. That'll wake 'em up. I'll mind your bike."

"Thanks, chum."

The young man disappeared like an eel into the misty darkness. Soon, the policeman heard the shrilling of a telephone inside the building. For two minutes it rang continuously. Then the despatch rider returned, disconsolate.

"Reckon there's nobody in there," said the policeman.

"Must be. The light's on. Besides, there's the stuff to collect . . ."

"I'm afraid I can't help you, son." The policeman was genuinely regretful. "Best wait until someone turns up with a key." He grinned, and ambled off in search of crime.

It was a long wait. At half past seven the despatch rider telephoned Sydenham, and was much aggrieved to be sworn at roundly by the foreman compositor. As if it was *his* fault . . . At ten to eight, when the whole street was beginning to stir and stretch and collect its milk bottles, Alf arrived, grumbling at the weather and his rheumatism.

"Don't you worry," he said, encouragingly. "I'll go up and see what's what. You come in and wait in the warm." He fumbled with his key, and the door swung open. Alf got into the lift. "Shan't be more than a minute," he said.

It was, in fact, a minute and a half later that the lift was down in the hall again. Alf came out of it like a rabbit out of a trap, ashen-faced and trembling. He grabbed the young man by the arm. "Quick! Police! Doctor! Quick!"

"But what's up?"

"Miss . . . Miss Pankhurst . . . something awful . . . I think she's dead . . ."

"And where's my envelope?"

"To hell with your envelope!" Alf was recovering. "Get a policeman, boy! I tell you, she's dead!"

2

Monday

Dearest Aunt Emmy,

Just a line to tell you what a super-terrific time I'm having, but, gosh, I've never worked so hard! To think I once imagined that modeling would be nothing but standing around in gorgeous dresses!! We've been up the Eiffel Tower most of the day (lucky I've got a good head for heights), and straight from there to the studios, which are screaming chaos. I'm so tired I can hardly stand.

But what fun! And what clothes! You've no idea. I'm much luckier than some of the other girls, because the *Style* people are so sweet. Miss Manners isn't a bit frightening and Michael Healy is a POPPET. Remember how scared I was at the thought of working for him? And Miss Field has been terribly kind—she's a sort of super-secretary and scared the wits out of me at first, but she's a marvellous organizer—without her we'd never get the clothes out of the salons, sometimes she has to FIGHT for them!

Do you know, I actually met Pierre Monnier himself!! And he said he might be able to use me one day if I learned to walk! I nearly died!

I wish I could stay on and see a bit of Paris, but we fly home tomorrow evening and I've got another job with *Style* on Wednesday morning—some Young Style clothes with Beth Connolly on Hampstead Heath (Or in the studio if wet. I hope it's wet.)—and an evening dress retake with Miss Manners.

Lots of love to you and a big kiss for Uncle Henry. Can I come and see you when I get back?

Ronnie

P.S. I really think Michael Healy likes me. He said I had bones like a young giraffe!

Emmy Tibbett smiled to herself as she read the letter. She had always been specially fond of her goddaughter—her sister's youngest child—and she had, with affection and pride, watched Veronica grow from a tubby schoolgirl into a raving beauty. In fact, it was Emmy who had championed the girl when, on her seventeenth birthday, she had announced her passionate desire to become a fashion model.

Emmy's elder sister, Jane, had married a farmer named Bill Spence, and the family lived in a quiet Devonshire village, where the greatest excitement of the year was the Vicarage Flower Show. Not unnaturally, Veronica's parents had been taken aback by their daughter's exotic ambition, and had appealed to Emmy, as a Londoner and the most sophisticated person they knew, to "talk all this nonsense out of the girl's head."

This, Emmy had not done. Instead she had been strictly practical. "Listen, Jane," she said. "Ronnie's never going to be a great scholar. Let's face it, she's pretty average dim. What'll happen to her? She'll take a secretarial course like a million other girls, and rot in some boring office until she marries."

"I know, Emmy, but *modeling* . . . "

"Modeling is a perfectly respectable profession, and very hard work," said Emmy, her eyes twinkling with laughter. "You surely don't still think it means posing in the nude for disreputable artists, do you?"

Jane blushed. "Well . . . I suppose not . . . but all the same, it doesn't seem quite . . . "

"Why not let her come to London and take a course?" suggested Emmy. "Henry and I haven't room to put her up, but we'll find her a bed-sitter nearby and keep an eye on her. If she's no good at the job, she'll soon find out, and it will have got it out of her system. If she *is* any good, she'll have a splendid time and make lots of money."

"Well . . . if you *really* think so, Emmy . . . "

So it was that Veronica Spence was launched on her career. It had taken very little time to establish that she was good. Within six months, her engagement book was satisfactorily full of appointments at photographic studios, and now, at nineteen, she had achieved the supreme distinction of being picked to go to Paris and model clothes for *Style*. Within the last six months, she had moved out of her room in Sydney Street and into a pretty flat in Victoria Grove, which she shared with another model, a girl called Nancy Blake, who had jet-black hair, the largest green eyes in London, and the disposition of an agreeably spoilt kitten.

Veronica herself was all honey-coloured—spun-gold hair, a delicate skin which never seemed to lose its country tan, and wide-open, nut-brown eyes. She was everybody's dream of the girl next door, redolent of sweet, simple country fare and the smell of hay, honeysuckle, and home-baked bread, and she was exactly what the photographers were looking for.

Parkinson had launched her once and for all when he photographed her, roaring with laughter, standing knee deep in a village pond surrounded by ducks and small boys. It had ruined the dress she was modeling, but since the picture was instrumental in selling thousands of copies of that particular design, nobody minded. Then Henry Clarke had plunged her up to her neck in a haystack for his famous colour shot advertizing the new make-up range, "Hayseed Honeypink." Vernier had shot her underwater in the Dolphin Square swimming pool in a Mermaid swimsuit, and Dormer had perched her precariously in the open doorway of a helicopter fifty feet above the tower of Canterbury Cathedral. At nineteen, Veronica was earning nearly twice as much as her distinguished uncle, Chief Inspector Henry Tibbett of the C.I.D.

For all this, Veronica had remained, to Emmy's delight, simple and enthusiastic and unspoilt. She never forgot that she owed her exciting life to Emmy's intervention, and so it was that she had found time, in the swirling bedlam of the Paris Collections, to scribble a note to her favourite aunt.

Emmy read the letter again. Returning Tuesday. Today was Wednesday, so Veronica must be home already. Perhaps she should ring her up later on and ask her round for a drink. The thought in Emmy's mind was cut short, like a broken dream, by the telephone ringing. At the first peal of the bell, she knew quite certainly that it was Veronica, and she felt a moment of mild surprise that the child should be ringing at half past ten in the morning, when she should be in the middle of her job for *Style*.

Emmy had known that it would be Veronica: but she was not prepared for the near-hysterical outburst that scorched along the telephone wires and exploded in her ear.

"Aunty Emmy! Oh, gosh, I'm glad I got you! Something awful has happened! Really awful! Uncle Henry's here and everyone is going mad and it's *horrible* but terribly exciting and they've only just taken her away . . . "

"What *are* you talking about, Ronnie?"

"Haven't you seen? It's in the Standard already, and there are policemen and reporters everywhere and Uncle's having a fit . . . "

"Henry is having a fit?"

"I didn't say he was. I said Uncle."

"Veronica, do try to make sense. Where are you speaking from?"

"From *Style*, of course. I mean, not actually. Actually from a phone box round the corner. Uncle Henry said I could go and . . . "

"Henry? What on earth is Henry doing at *Style*?"

"Well, of course he's here. Naturally."

"Why naturally?"

"Because she's been killed."

"Who's been killed?"

"Well, I don't actually know . . . "

"Ronnie!"

"I was going to say, I don't actually know her myself. I mean, I didn't. Miss Pankhurst. She was second-in-command to Miss French, the editor. They say she was poisoned, and I think Uncle knows something that he won't tell Uncle Henry . . . of course, he doesn't know he's Uncle Henry."

"I think," said Emmy, "that you'd better get into a taxi and come round here at once. This conversation is beginning to undermine my reason."

"You think *I'm* being unreasonable?" said Veronica. "Gosh you haven't seen *anything*. I'll be along in ten minutes."

Chief Inspector Henry Tibbett arrived at the *Style* offices soon after nine. Outside in the street, a small crowd had already collected, and several pleasant, patient young constables were doing their best to get it to move along. Otherwise, the place seemed calm enough. Henry went into the eighteenth-century hallway, which was guarded by a solid-looking sergeant.

"Glad to see you, sir," said this worthy, as if he meant it. "We're in for trouble here, and no mistake."

"How do you mean?"

"Women," said the sergeant, pessimistically. "Hysterics. Models and the like."

"I don't see any," said Henry. "Where have you put them?"

"They've not arrived yet, thank God," said the sergeant. "Just got a batch of charwomen and the doorman who found the body, so far."

"Then what makes you so sure?"

"You know what this place is, don't you, sir?" The sergeant was plunged in gloom. "Fashion magazine. Ruddy hen-house."

"What time do the staff arrive?" Henry asked.

"Half past nine, in theory," said the sergeant. "But according to the doorman, there's a lot may be late this morning."

"Why's that?"

"Some sort of late-night working session last night, as far as I . . . " There was a commotion at the outer door, and Henry turned to see a hefty constable wrestling with a young man in a leather jacket. The sergeant sighed. "You see?" he said to Henry. And then, to the young man, "I've told you ten times to *go away!*"

"My envelope!" shouted the young man. "You don't understand! I must have my envelope! It's Paris!"

"What's Paris?"

"The envelope, of course. We were supposed to go to bed at eight!"

"Mad," said the sergeant phlegmatically. "And that's only the first of them."

"Wait a minute," said Henry. He addressed the young man. "Do I understand that you're waiting for some reports from Paris which should have been with the printers by eight o'clock?"

The young man seemed to find a gleam of hope. "Can you get them for me, sir? It's bloody urgent, really it is."

"There's been a serious accident, you know," said Henry. "Someone has died. You'd better ring your printers and tell them there's bound to be a delay, and then wait down here. I'll do my best for you."

"Thank you, sir. You can't miss the envelope. It'll be in Editorial, and marked 'Pictorial Printers—to be called for.' And if you *can* get it soon, sir . . . "

His pleas were still echoing round the hall as Henry and the sergeant got into the lift.

"Now," said Henry, "put me in the picture." He looked small and insignificant beside the big sergeant—an unremarkable, sandy haired man in his forties, with gentle blue eyes, a diffident manner and a quiet voice—but his air of mild vagueness was as deceptively simple as any of Monnier's little black dresses. The sergeant knew very well that he must give a concise and complete report, and chose his words carefully.

"I was called," he said, "by P.C. Hutchins, the man on this beat, at seven fifty-six. It seems our friend with the Paris envelope came running out of the house and nearly knocked him over. Hutchins had spoken to him earlier—about a quarter past seven —when the lad was trying to wake up the building to get hold of his precious envelope. It's clear that the lady who should have given it to him was lying there dead all the time. He even went and telephoned, while Hutchins waited outside the door here and watched his motor bike, but of course there was no reply.

"Anyhow, it seems that the doorman, Alfred Samson, arrived as usual at ten to eight, and went up to see what was going on. He found the lady dead. Cyanide poisoning, no doubt about that. The doctor's with her now, but I remember that case last year—this is cyanide, all right. Very unpleasant."

"Who is—or was—she?"

The sergeant consulted his notebook. "Miss Helen Pankhurst, assistant editor," he said. "That's about as far as I got with Samson before the chars started to arrive. I didn't let them go up, of course. I've got them all cooped up in a sort of reception room if you want to see them."

"Good. What else did you do?"

"I telephoned the editor," said the sergeant. "A Miss Margery French. The doorman gave me her number. She's coming round right away. I thought it was best."

"Very sensible," said Henry. "Any line on the next of kin?"

"Not so far. Miss French will probably know. I thought it best not to touch the handbag or anything like that until you arrived."

The lift slid to a smooth stop at the fourth floor. Henry stepped out and looked around him.

The eighteenth-century dwelling which now housed *Style* had made a determined effort to retain its identity, in the face of stiff odds. On the ground floor, the pretty, period hallway held its own between the modern plate-glass entrance doors and the neon-lit dreariness of the Accounts' Department at the back. Here, in the main editorial section on the fourth floor, the façade was maintained at the front, in that part of the building that overlooked Earl Street and The Orangery.

Henry found himself standing on a dark lilac carpet in a corridor charmingly paneled in honey-coloured waxed wood. Two doors, with cornices and pilasters matching the paneling, stood facing him, each discreetly labeled with an engraved visiting card framed in gilt. The left-hand one read, *Miss Helen Pankhurst, Assistant Editor*; the other, *Miss Teresa Manners, Fashion Editor*. At the end of the corridor, where it turned at right angles and ran towards the back of the building, was a similar door marked *Miss Margery French, Editor,* while its opposite number, to Henry's right, was designated more simply and boldly by a projecting wooden plaque with the one word FASHION.

Even from the lift, Henry could see that the lilac carpet ended abruptly at these limits, and gave way to plain concrete corridors and whitewashed walls. Beyond the editor's office, a functional notice with a large black arrow proclaimed STUDIO THIS WAY; underneath it, another sheet of cardboard bore the sinister injunction, "ART DEPARTMENT. Absolutely NO ADMITTANCE on ANY pretext whatsoever." On the door marked FASHION, two further announcements were attached with celluloid tape. One said cryptically, "Messengers and models for fitting in here"; and the other, "WALK STRAIGHT IN. If you knock, nobody will hear."

The sergeant cleared his throat, a little apologetically. "She's in there, sir. In her own office."

"Tell me a little," said Henry, "about this late-night working session. I presume she was part of it."

"I couldn't find out much," said the sergeant. "You'll have to ask Miss French. All the doorman knew was that people were going to work late because of some special number on the Paris fashions. He doesn't know exactly who was here, but he says it's always what he calls 'the top brass.' Apparently, this poor lady did the actual writing, so she always stayed all night on these occasions, and handed the stuff over to our young friend downstairs at seven. The others would have gone home earlier. That's all I can tell you."

"Oh well," said Henry, "let's have a look at her." He opened the door of Helen's office and walked in.

There are few objects more compelling to the attention than a dead body in the centre of a small room. Nevertheless, when Henry first entered the office, his immediate impression was not of Helen herself: it was, simply, an impression of overwhelming confusion. The desks were bad enough. There were two of them, one for Helen and the other, presumably, for her secretary. Both had disappeared under a deluge of papers, as though some maniac had been rifling the green filing cabinet in the corner, and had scattered its contents like falling blossoms round the room. Even worse, however, and less expected was the state of the floor behind Helen's desk, for it was littered with a selection of pink and white feminine underwear, festooned with nylon stockings, and scattered with shirts and sweaters and beads and hairbrushes; all of which had presumably erupted from the open, empty suitcase which stood in the centre of the chaos. A box of face powder had flown open, cascading its pink dust over the room, and there was a reek of heavy, cloying scent emanating from a broken bottle with a Paris label, which lay on the floor. The combined effect of central heating and the still-burning electric fire had intensified the pungency of the perfume to the point of suffocation. Henry felt slightly sick.

In the midst of the disorder, Helen Pankhurst lay sprawled across her desk, her contorted face resting against the uncovered typewriter. The victims of cyanide poisoning are notoriously unattractive to look at, but even so Henry could see that this had been a striking woman, if not a strictly beautiful one. Her dark hair was set by a master coiffeur, and her slim figure, dressed in the simplest of grey skirts and a fluffy white polo-necked sweater, had even in death the mysterious mark of elegance which *Style* confers in some degree on all its employees. Her shoes were made of dark grey suede as soft as glove leather, and had ridiculously fragile heels; one of them had been kicked off, and lay under the desk, next to a matching grey handbag. On the desk was a pair of spectacles in rhinestone-studded frames, with one lens smashed. Helen's left hand still rested on the keys of the typewriter; in her right hand, she still clutched the base of a shattered blue and white pottery mug, from which a dried-up stream of tea had dribbled onto the mauve whipcord carpet, making a dark stain. A shabby red Thermos stood with an air of spurious innocence on the far side of the desk.

"Stinks in here, doesn't it?" said the sergeant. "I daresay the Doc was glad to get out of it. He'll be waiting next door to see you, I wouldn't be surprised."

Henry nodded absently. He was looking at the dead woman's hands. They seemed to be in contrast to the rest of her appearance. They were well shaped but sturdy, with cropped nails devoid of varnish. The hands of a worker. Henry noticed that she wore no rings on her left hand, but that on the fourth finger of the right hand was a little gold ring sentimentally embellished with intertwined hearts; the sort of trinket which could be bought for a few shillings in Queen Victoria's day, and now commands an inflated price in antique shops.

Henry turned his attention to the typewriter. Its keys were veiled in a film of pinkish powder, and there was a sheet of paper in it, on which was typed "Ink-blue roses scattered sparsely over chalk-white mousseline de soie give drama to . . . " Here the writing stopped. It was clear that the young man downstairs was going to have a long wait for his Paris copy. Very delicately, Henry removed the cork from the Thermos flask, first wrapping it in a clean handkerchief, in spite of the fact that it bore clear traces of fingerprinting powder. He sniffed the contents of the flask, and was not surprised that the still-warm tea smelt strongly of bitter almonds.

"Well," he said, "there's not much doubt about what happened—cyanide in the Thermos flask. The tea will have to be analysed, of course, but I can smell it from here." He put the cork back into the flask. "Have the photographers and fingerprint chaps got all they want?"

"Yes, sir."

"Then you can have the poor girl taken away, but be very careful nothing else is touched. I'll see the doctor now."

"He's in there, sir—in the editor's office." The sergeant indicated the communicating door.

"Right. Meanwhile, when the staff begin to arrive, keep them all downstairs for the moment. I don't suppose we can disrupt the working of the office indefinitely, but we can't have them up here until we've taken a good look round. And you'd better tell that unfortunate young man that he'll be lucky if he gets his Paris envelope today."

"I'll do that, sir," said the sergeant, with a certain satisfaction.

Henry went into the adjoining office. This was a sharp contrast to the room he had just left. It was considerably larger and beautifully uncluttered, with its deep violet carpet and freshly distempered lemon-yellow walls. The furniture consisted of one enormous leather-topped desk, one smaller wooden one (on which stood a shrouded typewriter), and several chairs. The inevitable filing cabinets were there, but they were unobtrusive. What took the eye were the early Picasso lithographs above the desk, the framed costume sketch by Bérard (on which the artist had scribbled "A ma chère amie, Margery"), the Forain caricature. Everything was spotless and tidily efficient, down to the newly sharpened pencils on the desk and the neat row of ball point pens in various colours. This room was everything that an editor's office should be, with a pleasant air of femininity thrown in.

The police doctor was sitting at the big desk. He was a large, sad man with the face of a baffled bloodhound.

"Oh, it's you," he said lugubriously, as though Henry were the last person he expected to see. "Good. I'd like to get off soon. Work to do."

"What's the verdict?"

"Cyanide poisoning, of course. Should have thought even you could see that. Probably administered in her tea."

"Almost certainly. I wonder why she didn't notice the smell before she drank it. It almost tempts me to think it might have been suicide."

The doctor shook his big head, slowly. "Suicide or not, that's

33

your business," he said, "but I can tell you that she had a stifling cold when she died. I very much doubt whether she could smell or taste anything, and I imagine she had a fever. Can't think why else she'd have switched that fire on."

"What about the time of death?"

"I haven't had a chance to do a P.M. yet, you know. I can only guess. Somewhere between three and six o'clock this morning, I'd say. Can I take her away now?"

"The sergeant's already arranging it."

"Good. See you later."

The doctor gave the twitch of his melancholy countenance which passed for a smile, got up and went to the door. Before he could open it, however, somebody knocked smartly on the other side of it. The doctor glanced interrogatively at Henry, who nodded. He opened the door, to reveal the sergeant.

"Sorry to disturb you, sir," he said, "but Miss Margery French is here."

"Must be off. See you . . . " mumbled the doctor, and disappeared with surprising agility.

"I'll talk to her straight away," said Henry. "Ask her to come up."

3

Henry had had no very clear idea of what he expected the editor of *Style* to look like, but the moment that Margery French walked in he realized that she filled the role to perfection. Everything was right—the beautifully cut suit, the big mushroom of a felt hat, the blue-rinsed hair, the impeccable make-up, the fine, sensitive hands embellished with one outsize topaz ring on the wedding finger. It was hard to believe that this woman, who must be nearer sixty than fifty, had been working late into the night, and still more difficult to remember that she had just been woken from her well-earned rest with news of shocking disaster. Certainly, the sergeant's forebodings about hysterical women were unfounded in this instance.

"Good morning, Inspector Tibbett," said Margery briskly. "This is a terrible and tragic business. Please tell me all about it, and let me know how I can help you. Your sergeant gave me very few details, but the fact that you are here at all makes it obvious that poor Helen's death was not natural."

She sat down at the big desk, and opened a tooled leather cigarette box. "Do you smoke? Please take one, and do sit down."

"Thank you," said Henry, fighting off the growing feeling that it was he who was being interviewed. He pulled up a chair and took a good look at Margery French. She was lighting her cigarette, and her hands trembled very slightly. He could also see, now, the dark circles under her eyes, nearly but not quite disguised by make-up. Perhaps she was playing her part a shade too well.

Henry said, "I'm afraid Miss Pankhurst was murdered, Miss French."

"Are you sure?" Margery was quite calm. "Have you ruled out the possibility of suicide?"

"You think that she might have had some reason to . . . ?"

"I am not a gossip," said Margery slowly, "and I never pry into the private lives of my staff. However, one can't help but be aware of certain things, and I think it is my duty to tell you that I have been very worried about Helen recently." Margery paused. Henry had the impression that she found it extremely distasteful to talk in this way, and that she was, quite literally, performing an unpleasant duty. She went on, choosing her words carefully. "Any organization which employs both men and women must face the fact that sentimental attachments will form from time to time between members of the staff. We are no exception. In fact, things are perhaps even more complicated here, because our employees are rather exceptional people. The men—the photographers and art editors—are artistic, volatile characters. The girls tend to be above average beautiful. And the world of fashion, for some reason, always seems to attract people of emotional temperament."

Henry longed to say, "Then how do you come to be in it?" but he remained silent.

"Normally," Margery went on, "I would never break a confidence, but the circumstances are unusual. The fact of the matter is that Helen had been having a somewhat tempestuous love affair with one of our photographers. A man named Michael Healy."

"Why should that drive her to suicide?"

"Because, apparently, things were going wrong. Very wrong. I am afraid that Michael is something of a philanderer, and I can't believe that he ever intended anything more serious than a passing flirtation. In fact, I was extremely surprised when the rumour of their affair started leaking out—they were certainly an ill-matched couple. Helen was a passionate and intense person, and several years older than Michael. Lately, she really began to go to pieces. She was obviously in a state of nerves and worried to distraction, and—once again according to rumour—it was because Michael was attempting to disentangle himself from a situation which had gotten out of hand. In fact, between ourselves, I was planning to send Michael to America for a few months, until things calmed down. Not, of course, that that would have cured the atmosphere in the office, but . . . "

"What do you mean by that, Miss French?"

Margery was silent for a moment. She took a long pull on her cigarette, and then said slowly, "Michael Healy, I should explain, is married to my fashion editor, Teresa Manners."

"Is he indeed?" said Henry. "So there was no love lost between Miss Manners and Miss Pankhurst?"

"On the contrary. They were very good friends."

"That seems rather unusual, in the circumstances," said Henry.

"Not at all," said Margery sharply.

"Then why were you expecting the unpleasantness in the office to go on, even after Mr. Healy went away?"

Margery studied her scarlet-painted fingernails with some concentration. Henry had the feeling that she was aware of having made a slip, and was intent on correcting it. At last she said, "I must have expressed myself badly. I meant that Helen would naturally have taken some time to get over her infatuation. In fact, for the first few weeks she would probably have been worse than ever."

"Well," said Henry, "this is all most interesting, but I'm still inclined to rule out suicide, for several reasons."

"How," Margery asked steadily, "did Helen die?"

"She was poisoned," said Henry. "Somebody put cyanide in her tea."

"I see." Margery did not appear shocked. Just thoughtful. "Poor Helen. But could she not have put it there herself?"

"She could," said Henry, "but I don't think she did. For several reasons. First, there was no note of any sort. Second, it would seem an extraordinary time and place to choose—right in the middle of a working session. Third, her office appears to have been rifled—not only her papers but her personal possessions . . ."

"Her personal possessions?" Margery looked up. "What on earth do you mean, Inspector?"

"Perhaps you would come and take a look next door. You

might be able to throw some light on . . . "

"Certainly." Margery stood up and walked over to the door which led to Helen's office. "Is she still there?"

"No," said Henry. He noticed that she had not shown any signs of alarm or distress at the thought of seeing Helen's body. She had merely asked a question.

Margery opened the door, and stood for a moment quite still, looking at the scene of confusion. Then she turned to Henry, with a slight smile. "I think I can throw some light," she said. "For a start, I'm inclined to agree with you that Helen was murdered."

"Why do you say that?"

"Because of all this." Margery swept out a hand to indicate the confusion. "Because she had not finished her work. Helen would never have left the Paris copy half done. If I had found a tidy office, all the captions and layouts neatly in their envelope and a list of carefully typed instructions to the printers, I should have been inclined to think she had killed herself. It would have been typical." Margery paused, and looked at the paper in the typewriter. "Incidentally, Inspector, I shall have to finish this captioning myself and get everything sorted out and down to the printers as soon as it's humanly possible. You must realize that this is our most important issue of the year, and our deadline is stretched to the limit already."

"I know that," said Henry. "I'm being as quick as I can. Please go on. What other light can you shed?"

"Well, I can tell you that the office wasn't rifled. The state of the papers is quite normal. Helen always worked surrounded by chaos, especially when she was under pressure, and then tidied everything up most meticulously afterwards. Perhaps you don't realize that this—" Margery gestured towards the drifts of paper on the desk—"this represents a whole sixteen-page form, with all the merchandizing details and . . . "

"How do you explain the suitcase then?"

"That isn't Helen's suitcase," said Margery. "It belongs to my secretary, Miss Field. She was in Paris yesterday, and came straight from the airport to the office. She must have left her case in here owing to a somewhat exaggerated idea of the sanctity of my office."

"Why didn't she take it home with her?"

"Because of Mr. Goring," said Margery.

"Mr. Goring?"

"May we go back into my office?" Something in Margery's voice made Henry look up sharply. He saw that she had gone very pale, and had put one hand on the desk for support. "I'm so sorry, Inspector. It's just the heat in here."

"Of course. Let's go back," said Henry.

Margery walked quite steadily through the doorway and back into her own office. She seemed to have recovered completely.

"Mr. Goring," she said, "is our managing director. I should tell you that he will be here soon. Naturally, I telephoned him as soon as I heard the news."

"I'll look forward to meeting him," said Henry. "Meanwhile, how is he connected with your secretary's suitcase?"

Quickly and accurately, Margery described Godfrey Goring's arrival at the office in the early hours, his invitation, and the reason why the luggage had been left behind.

"Miss Pankhurst was not included in the invitation?" said Henry.

"Of course not. She was staying here to work."

"What happened then? You all went back to Mr. Goring's house . . . "

"Yes. Two other friends of his were there also—Nicholas Knight, the dress designer, and Horace Barry, the manufacturer. We had a glass or two of champagne, and then Mr. Goring's chauffeur drove us all home."

"All of you?"

"All except for Nicholas Knight and Mr. Barry. Mr. Knight had his own car. Oh—and he gave a lift to Miss Field, as he was going in her direction. The three of them left a little before the rest of us. Barker, the chauffeur, dropped Teresa and Michael in Chelsea first, and then took me on to Sloane Street. After that, he was to take Mr. Walsh to Islington."

"What time was this, do you remember?"

"Ten to three," Margery answered promptly. "I noticed the time as I went into my flat."

Henry considered for a moment. Then he said, "I'm afraid there are still a great many questions I must ask you, Miss French. First of all, can you give me some idea of Miss Pankhurst's background—her family, where she lived, and so on? We haven't yet been able to inform—"

"She had no family, that I know of," said Margery. She lit another cigarette. "Her parents were dead. I believe she had a married sister in Australia. She shared a flat in Kensington with Olwen Piper, my features editor. Helen was with *Style* for ten years. She came to us as a secretary, and worked her way up to her present post. She was an excellent worker, and rather more . . . more businesslike than some of the others."

"Did she have any enemies on the staff?"

"Certainly not. The secretaries were frightened of her—she could be very ferocious at times." Margery smiled. "I must confess I found it useful. She relieved me of the necessity to be a martinet myself. She wrote well, but she had no fashion flair. Of course, that wouldn't interest you."

"Apart from her affair with Michael Healy, what do you know of her private life?"

"Helen had no private life," said Margery, quickly and decisively. "She was entirely absorbed by her work here—by the office and the people in it." She stopped for a moment. "I do realize what I'm saying, Inspector. If she was killed, it was certainly one of us who did it. Who—or why—I cannot imagine."

"Let's talk about *how*," said Henry. "Where would anybody in this office be able to get hold of cyanide?"

"I'm afraid that's very simple. There is a supply of cyanide in the darkroom. It is used for reducing prints. Michael can tell you all about it."

"Doesn't that point, then, to somebody who worked in the darkroom?"

"Not necessarily. All of us here are in and out of the studio and the darkroom all the time, and it's a matter of routine that every new employee, however humble, is warned about the cyanide and shown where it's kept and how to recognize the bottle, just in case of accidents."

"Isn't it kept locked up?"

"Normally, yes," said Margery, "but there are occasions when the rules go by the board, I'm afraid, and Collections night is one of them. Michael was making his own prints, and I can remember that the store cupboard was open. I may as well tell you, too, that the cupboard is in the room where the tea is made, and that we were all popping in and out of the darkroom all the evening. All except Miss Field, that is, and Helen herself. I don't think either of them left their offices. But any of the rest of us could easily have poured poison into the Thermos."

"Thank you, Miss French," said Henry. He was fascinated by the precision and alertness of this woman's mind. She had run ahead of him, forestalled him at every turn. She could be an invaluable ally, or a formidable opponent. He wondered which.

As if in answer to his thought, Margery said, "I want to help you in every way, Inspector. I will put an office at your disposal. I presume you'll want to interview everybody who was here last night."

"Yes." Henry glanced at the notebook which he held in his hand. "Perhaps you'd just go through them with me. I have yourself, Teresa Manners, Michael Healy, and Patrick Walsh. Oh, and your secretary, Miss Field. Now, was there anybody else?"

"Donald MacKay was here—Patrick's assistant in the art department. He left shortly before the rest of us. And Ernie was here until about midnight—that's Ernest Jenkins, the darkroom boy. Oh—and Olwen. I was forgetting."

"That would be Miss Piper? The girl Miss Pankhurst shared her flat with?"

"Yes. She came along to write her copy after the theatre."

"Do you know what time she left?"

"I've no idea," said Margery shortly. "I saw her in her office soon after half past twelve, and I told her to go home, but heaven knows how long she stayed." She paused. "That's everybody."

"Except Mr. Goring."

"Godfrey? But you can't really . . . "

"I suppose there was nothing to stop him from going into the darkroom before coming into your office?"

"No . . . but . . . "

It was at that moment that pandemonium broke loose in the corridor outside. Henry could hear sounds of a scuffle, and the stentorian voice of the sergeant shouting, "Sir, I forbid you to . . . " but this was drowned by a vast, bass, Irish bellow.

"Get out of me way, you miserable little man! By God, something's going on here, and nobody's going to keep me out of me own office!"

"Sir, the Chief Inspector has given orders . . . "

41

"The Chief Inspector be damned to hell! If you don't get out of me way, I'll break every bone in your wretched body, God's truth I will!"

Margery French, with a smile, said quietly, "Patrick has arrived."

"So I hear," said Henry, returning the smile. "I think I'd better go and investigate. The sergeant seems to be in need of reinforcements."

The corridor seemed to be entirely filled with flailing arms, encased in rough tweed. The sergeant was pinioned, as though crucified, against the door which was marked "Absolutely NO ADMITTANCE on ANY pretext whatsoever." This statement was clearly being challenged by the huge man in tweed, who was making bull-like assaults against the door, shouting as he did so. Fortunately for the sergeant's arms, Henry's arrival diverted him for a moment. He wheeled to counter this attack from the flank, and demanded, "Who th'hell are you?"

"Chief Inspector Tibbett," said Henry. "I presume that you are Patrick Walsh."

"You damn well presume rightly," said Patrick. "Now, will you kindly tell this whippersnapper of yours to get out of me way and let me go into me own office?"

"No," said Henry, "I won't." There was an electric pause. "There has been a murder. Will you come into Miss French's office and talk reasonably for a moment?"

"Murder?" All the fury went out of Patrick, and he stood quite still, with his great arms swinging by his sides. "Why did nobody tell me? Who is it?"

"Helen Pankhurst," said Henry, "was poisoned last night. She died here after you had all left."

Embarrassingly, without warning, Patrick began to cry. He leant against the wall and moaned with Celtic abandon. "Helen, me darlin'. Helen, me beautiful. It's not true . . . Helen . . . "

"Patrick." Margery French's voice was sharp as a razor. Patrick stopped moaning. Then Margery said gently, "Pull yourself together, Patrick, my dear. Come into my office."

Docile as a lamb, Patrick followed her. The sergeant mopped his brow. "Couldn't stop him, sir," he said, ruefully. "Came roaring up them stairs like a bulldozer. Shook off two constables easy as swatting flies. I'm sorry, sir."

"Never mind," said Henry. "I'll deal with him."

"You're welcome," said the sergeant, and added meaningly, "I told you so, didn't I?"

Margery French came out of her office, and said, "I'll be in Mr. Goring's room on the floor above if you need me, Inspector." Then she disappeared up the stairs, leaving a faint smell of expensive scent behind her. Henry went into the office and closed the door.

Patrick Walsh had pulled himself together. His face was even redder than usual, but the emotional outburst was over. He stood with his back to the door, looking out of the window and down into the wet street below. He did not move nor look around when Henry came in.

Henry cleared his throat. "Mr. Walsh," he said formally, "I am afraid I shall have to ask you to make a statement."

Slowly, Patrick turned away from the window and came over to the desk. He slumped into the chair facing Henry's, passed a huge hand over his face, and said, "I'm sorry."

"It's very understandable," said Henry. "This must have been a shock to you."

"Shock. Yes."

"Will you tell me what happened here last night?"

"Last night?" Patrick seemed to come to life a little. "There were some fine fights," he said.

"Fights?"

"Teresa wanted to use the Monnier chiffon, and crop Michael's Dior picture into a big close-up of the hat, and Margery . . . "

"You said there were fights . . . "

"That was one of them. Then there was the Balmain spread. Margery thought we ought to show at least three dresses, but I wasn't going to have . . . "

Henry sighed. "You mean, what you call fights were purely professional discussions about what pictures were to be used?"

"Of course." Patrick looked surprised. "What else would there be to fight about?"

"When did you last see Miss Pankhurst yourself?"

"I didn't. Didn't clap eyes on her all evening. Last time I saw her was at lunchtime. I took her out for a meal. She needed it, poor kid."

"Why do you say that?"

"Why do I say what?" Patrick was growing belligerent again. "I say what I damn well please, and nobody's going to go round being bitchy about Helen now the poor girl's dead."

"Who was being bitchy about her?"

Patrick looked surly and suspicious. "Nobody," he said. "Not a living soul."

"You liked Helen personally?"

"I loved her," said Patrick, simply.

"Do you know of anyone who disliked her?"

There was a long pause. Then abruptly, Patrick said, "No."

"Are you sure, Mr. Walsh?"

"Sure? Of course I'm sure! Sure as the devil! Everybody loved her."

"Including Michael Healy and Teresa Manners?" Henry asked mildly.

Patrick jumped to his feet. "What have people been saying?" he shouted. "What filthy lying bastards have been putting ideas into your head? I know. I can guess. It's not true, d'you hear me? Not a bloodstained word of it, and may I drop dead if I'm not telling God's truth!"

"I haven't the faintest idea what you're talking about," said Henry, not quite truthfully. "I simply asked you if Michael Healy and Teresa Manners liked Helen, that's all."

"That's not all, and well you know it," yelled Patrick. "I'm not saying another word, and you can't make me!"

"Very well," said Henry. "Let's talk about something else. Like cyanide, for example. I suppose you know where it's kept."

"I know where the darkroom store cupboard is."

"Will you show me?"

"A pleasure."

Patrick led the way out of Margery's office by the communicating door into his own art department—a big, light room furnished with drawing boards and liberally decorated with layouts and cropped portions of letterpress and photostat pictures.

"All these rooms intercommunicate," explained Patrick, "from the studio to the darkroom, through the art department and into Margery's office on the corner of the building. From there, into Helen's office, through editorial into Teresa's den and the fashion room. We've all got our own doors out into the corridor, of course, but this way we can lock ourselves away from the general run of pests and still keep in touch with the people who matter."

He opened a door on the far side of the art department. "The darkroom," he said.

A whiff of chemicals greeted Henry as he stepped into the gloomy, unlit anteroom that led to the photographic section. Patrick switched on a dim light, and Henry saw that they were in a small room lined with cupboards. It had three doors—the one from the art department through which they had just come, another on their left leading into the passage, and a third, heavily curtained, ahead of them, which presumably led to the darkroom proper. Against the fourth wall was a sink, where some prints were still washing, and on the floor beneath it stood an electric kettle.

Patrick waved a vague hand. "This is the storeroom," he said. "Everything's kept in here—paper, chemicals, the lot. Don't ask me where the cyanide actually is, because I haven't the faintest idea."

It did not take Henry long to locate it. All the cupboards, he found, were unlocked, and most of them contained ranks of shiny yellow boxes of photographic paper. One, however, was stacked with dark brown bottles and bulging paper bags. Very prominent was a bottle marked in red on its label, *Cyanide. POISON*. It was empty.

"I'll have to take this for fingerprinting," he said.

Patrick shrugged. "Since it's empty, I can't see any objection," he said. "I suppose there's more somewhere."

Henry looked down at the two suitcases in the corner of the small room. "Whose are those?" he asked.

"Teresa's and Michael's," said Patrick. "They came back from Paris last night." He seemed to have lost interest in the conversation. Suddenly he said irritably, "Well, we can't hang about here all day. I have a lot to do. When can we start work?"

"Very soon," said Henry. "Come back into Miss French's office for a minute, will you?"

Patrick did not reply, but led the way silently back through the art department and into the editor's office.

Henry said, "Did you know Miss Pankhurst's Thermos flask by sight?"

"Of course. Everybody did. It was a sort of tradition—a terrible, battered old thing that Helen would never be parted from on

45

Collections night."

"Did you notice it standing around unattended at any time?"

"It was there in the storeroom the whole evening," replied Patrick promptly. "I suppose Ernie had made Helen some fresh tea, and then forgotten to take it along to her." He grinned ruefully at Henry. "We're all suspect," he said. "We were all in and out of there, and any of us could have slipped cyanide into it." He paused. "And please don't insult me by saying, 'And how did you know she was poisoned by cyanide in her tea, Mr. Walsh?' You've as good as told me."

"I agree," said Henry. "Now, tell me about the party at Mr. Goring's house last night."

Patrick snorted. "What is there to tell? Damn silly idea, if you ask me. I'd have got out of it if I'd been able. Not my idea of fun—sipping genteel champagne with pansies and vulgar bloody upstarts."

"What—or whom—do you mean by that?"

"Nicholas Knight and Horace Barry," said Patrick, with infinite contempt. "I don't know which I despise more. Godfrey may have to be civil to them, in the name of the great god advertizing, but I don't see why we should be subjected to—"

"Just tell me what happened."

"I've already told you. Nothing. We had a glass of champagne, and made hideous small talk, carefully avoiding tricky subjects. Then I got fed up and so did Michael, and we began being fairly damn rude to Knight and Barry, in a subtle way. You'd be surprised how rude I can be, Inspector."

"I wouldn't."

"Anyhow, they soon had enough of it, and went off, taking Rachel Field with them. The rest of us . . . "

"What did you mean by tricky subjects?"

"Nothing that would interest you."

"Most things interest me."

"Not this sort of thing."

"I wish you'd tell me."

Without warning, Patrick became angry again. "I'm damned if I'll tell you, you bloody nosey-parker," he shouted. "Why can't you concentrate on finding out who killed the darling girl, instead of grubbing round, meddling in people's private affairs . . . "

Henry sighed. "I'll talk to you later on," he said, "when you're in a more reasonable frame of mind."

"Reasonable!" thundered Patrick. "Of all the people in this madhouse, I'm the one reasonable—"

"Please go away now," said Henry very distinctly. He was beginning to sympathize with the sergeant.

"You're damned right I'm going," said Patrick. He stalked into the art department and slammed the door behind him.

Henry watched him go with mixed emotions. Then he climbed the stairs to the fifth floor.

This was clearly the part of the building dedicated to the business—as opposed to the editorial—side of *Style*. It, too, was carpeted, but in sombre navy blue. The door which faced Henry, corresponding to Helen's office on the floor below, was marked *Managing Director*. The door of the office above Margery's had a small stenciled sign on it saying NO ADMITTANCE, and Henry surmised that this was, in fact, Goring's office. Other doors were labeled *Advertizing Manager, Chief Accountant,* and *Staff Director*. The atmosphere was masculine, and redolent of big business. Henry contrasted it with the floor below, and began to respect Margery French more than ever. She, obviously, was at home in both worlds. Henry walked boldly up to the door marked NO ADMITTANCE, knocked, and walked in without waiting for an answer.

Godfrey Goring and Margery French were standing by the window with their backs to the door. Their faces, as they wheeled abruptly to look at Henry, bore the expressions of people who have been interrupted in the middle of an important and private conversation, and who are worrying about how much has been overheard. He also thought that Margery French looked considerably shattered about something.

This was, however, a fleeting impression. Both of them recovered their composure in a split second, and Margery said, "Godfrey, this is Chief Inspector Tibbett. Inspector—Mr. Goring, our managing director."

Goring advanced, hand outstretched. "My dear Inspector . . ." he said. He looked, not unnaturally, very worried indeed, but at the same time he exuded the confidence-inspiring air of a man of affairs who has weathered worse crises in his time. "Margery has told me the terrible story. I realize that we shall have to—"

he checked himself—"that you will have to have an absolutely free hand to pursue your enquiries, and you must think of us as here to help you in any way we can. I would ask, though, that you arrange for the normal working of the office to go ahead again as soon as possible. We are all busy people, you know."

"I know," said Henry. "That's one of the things I wanted to talk to you about. I'm afraid Miss Pankhurst's office will have to be put out of bounds for the time being, but if Miss French will come down there with me, she can sort out the papers she needs for her Paris edition, and take them. I shall also have to seal off the storage compartment of the darkroom for the moment. Once that is done, your staff can come up and start work. Miss French has kindly promised me an office where I can hold interviews."

Goring nodded. "I am delighted that we have such a business-like person to deal with," he said, with a rather strained smile.

"You'll be here for the next hour or so, will you, Mr. Goring?" said Henry. "I'd very much like a word with you later."

"Don't worry, Inspector. I won't run away." There was neither animosity nor humour in Goring's voice.

"Good," said Henry cheerfully. "I'll see you later, then. Shall we go down, Miss French?"

Helen's office was as stifling and depressing as ever, but this time Margery showed no signs of weakness. She sorted quickly and expertly through the piles of paper, and eventually said, "Right. I have everything I need here."

"Splendid," said Henry. "Now, where may I establish my HQ?"

"There's an empty office beyond the fashion room," said Margery. "I'll show you."

The room to which she escorted Henry was small and bleak, with a linoleum-covered floor and a small window overlooking a dingy area.

"Sordid but private," said Margery shortly. "You can telephone for anybody you want to see. There's a list of internal phone numbers on the desk. I'll be in my office if you need me." She smiled quickly, and went before Henry could thank her.

Henry sat down at the desk, and studied what he had written so far in his notebook. Then he telephoned down to the sergeant, confirmed that the staff could be released from durance, and asked that Ernest Jenkins should be sent to his office.

"I don't think he's arrived yet," said the sergeant. "I'll check up. You say I can let the others out?"

"That's right."

"Blimey," said the sergeant, with deep depression. "You don't know, sir. You just don't know."

It was about a minute later that Henry heard the tide of voices surging up towards him. A shrill, excited tide, pitched in a high feminine register, squealing and squeaking and giggling and exclaiming and rapidly increasing in volume as it reached the landing and began flowing towards the various offices. The main concentration seemed to come from the fashion room next door, and since there was no sign of Ernest Jenkins, Henry decided to go out into the corridor and take a look.

The first person he saw was his wife's niece, Veronica Spence. She was going into the fashion room in the company of a very tiny and exquisitely pretty girl in a grey flannel suit, which (had Henry known it) was an excellent copy of a Balenciaga. Both were chattering excitedly. Veronica was saying over and over again, "Gosh! *Really*, Beth? It can't be true, can it? *Really?* Gosh!"

"Veronica," said Henry loudly.

Veronica wheeled around. "Uncle Henry!" she cried. "Gosh, Beth, it must be true. I mean Uncle Henry wouldn't be here if it wasn't. Would you, poppet?" she added, and flung her arms round Henry's neck. "Gosh, it was awful being shut up downstairs. Gosh, I am glad to see you!"

Firmly, Henry removed Veronica's clinging arms from his neck. The corridor was by now full of a crowd of the most elegant young women that he had ever seen—outside, as he reflected, the pages of *Style*. Voices were raised in glorious confusion.

"I don't care what Uncle says. Those layouts are . . . "

"Helen, of all people! I always thought . . . "

"We're all going to be third-degreed by divine policemen . . . "

"I suppose the pink and white cotton is *just* usable . . . "

"What does one wear for being grilled? I think the well-dressed suspect should concentrate on . . . "

"All I'm asking for is a purple Jaguar and two wolfhounds at Ham House this afternoon . . . "

"Nancy in the white with masses of jade beads, and Ronnie in . . . "

"Who's going to do the copy, anyhow? Helen and I were supposed . . . "

"Oh, well, if Teresa takes that attitude I suppose I'll just have to start tramping up Poland Street again. How she thinks I can . . . "

"Darling, I'm sorry, but I am *not* going to kill the mink. I've *told* Uncle . . . "

"*Helen!* Now if it had been . . . "

Breathlessly, Veronica said, "Beth, darling, this is my uncle. Henry Tibbett."

More brusquely than he had intended, Henry said, "What are you doing here, Ronnie?"

"A job, of course," said Veronica. "A retake with Miss Manners, and then Young Style cotton dresses with Beth. This is Beth Connolly, the Young Style editor."

"How do you do, Mr. Tibbett," said Beth Connolly, wrinkling her miniscule nose and looking up at Henry like a baby doll. "I'm afraid you've caught us on a bad day. Even more of a shambles than usual."

She smiled enchantingly, and Henry's heart sank. Clearly, it was going to be extremely difficult to conduct a serious enquiry among these scatterbrained children, charming though they might be. Even as this thought crossed his mind, Beth Connolly turned away and said crisply to a tall, blonde girl, "Marilyn, I want you to telephone Barrimodes at once and cancel the white lace. Send a messenger to Gardell's to pick up the blue silk, number eight-seventy-two, and then get me lots of gold bracelets and some river pearls. Mr. Howard of Mayfair Jewels knows about it—I've spoken to him. And we'll need the blue glacé kid pumps from Fairfeet in Veronica's size. Then tell the studio that we won't be starting till noon, and make sure that Michael is free after lunch. If he's not, book him for as soon as you can, and get the models lined up." She turned back to Henry. "I'm terribly sorry," she said. "I just had to speak to my secretary. My whole sitting is being reorganized because of Paris."

Henry felt ashamed of his earlier assessment. This girl, young as she was, was an expert in her own field, and very far from being a scatterbrained child. He said, "May I borrow Veronica for a few minutes?"

"Of course. I shan't need her until noon."

"Thank you."

Beth smiled again, and went into the fashion room.

Henry and his niece faced each other across the desk in the bleak office.

"You're the last person I expected to find here," said Henry.

"Why? I do a lot of work for *Style* now. Uncle Henry—is it really true—that she's dead, I mean?"

"I'm afraid it is."

"Murdered?" Veronica's eyes were as large as saucers.

"We don't know for sure yet," Henry answered diplomatically. "As a matter of fact, Ronnie, you can probably help me quite a bit."

"Can I?"

"You know the people here personally."

"Not all of them. I never met Miss Pankhurst—everyone says she was an awful dragon. But then they said that about Miss Field, and she turned out to be sweet in the end. I really only know Beth and Miss Manners and Michael."

"Michael Healy, the photographer?"

"That's right. We were all in Paris together till yesterday. Oh, and of course I know Uncle vaguely—everyone does."

"Who's Uncle?"

"Patrick Walsh, the art editor. He's a poppet. Everyone calls him Uncle, but not to his face. He *roars* at people," Veronica added.

"I know he does," said Henry feelingly. He consulted his notes. "Do you know his assistant, Donald MacKay?"

Veronica, to Henry's surprise, blushed. "Yes," she said, and studied the sharp toes of her shoes with unnecessary concentration.

"And what about . . . ?"

The telephone rang. Henry picked it up. "Ernest Jenkins is here," said the sergeant. He sounded exhausted.

"Good," said Henry. "Send him straight up." He rang off and said to Veronica, "I want to see this boy straight away. You'd better be off. I'll see you again later on."

"Can I go out?"

"Of course. But you have to be back at twelve, don't you, for your sitting?"

"Oh, before that. Half past eleven. I have to make up."

"You've got quite enough make-up on already," said Henry, rather primly.

Veronica smiled pityingly. "All the girls in Paris," she said, "had dead white faces and sooty eyes and brown lips outlined in black. I've brought some of the new lipstick back with me."

"It sounds repellent."

"It's marvellous. You wait and see."

"If you think it's going to make you more attractive to . . . " Henry began, committed now to pomposity and uncledom, and regretting it. He got no further, however, for at that moment bedlam broke loose in the corridor outside.

It was heralded by a sharp knock on the door. Before Henry had time to say "Come in," Patrick's voice bellowed from somewhere down the passage, "Olwen! What in hell do you think you're doing?"

"That's Uncle," said Veronica.

"I know," said Henry gloomily.

A girl's voice, deep and with a Welsh lilt to it, said, "I'm going to see the Inspector and tell him . . . "

"You're bloody well not!"

"Come in!" Henry called loudly.

The door opened slightly, and was immediately slammed again from the outside, to the accompaniment of scuffling sounds.

"Let go of me, you great brute!" The girl's voice was rising now, and she sounded near to tears. "Let go of me! I'm going in there!"

"You don't know what you're doing, idiot!"

"Oh yes, I do. It's you . . . "

"Will you listen to me, imbecile child!"

"You're hurting me!"

The door started to open again, and again was slammed. By this time, not unnaturally, other doors had opened, and the corridor was full of voices—angry, hysterical, conciliatory.

"I think," said Henry to Veronica, "that I had better see what's going on. You wait here."

He took hold of the door handle, turned it, and pulled as hard as he could. Henry's weight, combined with pressure from outside, evidently turned the scales and defeated even Patrick's strength. The door flew open, and Olwen Piper literally fell at Henry's feet. Behind her, still grasping her arm, Patrick loomed, enormous and cross. Behind him again was a blur of faces and a babble of voices, amongst which Henry could pick out a high, aristocratic female bray which kept repeating, "I can't stand it! Stop her, Uncle! I can't stand it!" The only other distinguishable voice was young, masculine, and cockney, and kept on saying, "The sergeant said for me to come up. 'E said for me to come up. I tell you, 'e said . . . "

"Now, now," said Henry, in his best policeman's voice, "what's all this?"

"I'm trying to save this lunatic girl from making a bloody idiot of herself, that's all," said Patrick.

"I wish you'd stop interfering," said Henry. He helped Olwen to her feet. "You must be Miss Piper, the features editor."

"Yes, I am," said Olwen defiantly, as if she expected the statement to be challenged.

Henry looked at her. He saw the same earnest young face, the same spectacles knocked slightly awry in the fray, the same dumpy figure and lack of chic which had caused Margery French such a painful moment of truth the previous night. He also saw that Olwen had been crying, and would almost certainly do so again soon.

She gripped his arm. "You must let me speak to you, Inspector," she said.

"Of course you can speak to me."

"Olwen," said Patrick. "I'm warning you. If you tell—"

"Mr. Walsh," said Henry, "what makes you think you know what Miss Piper wishes to say to me?"

"I can guess."

"Well, what is it?"

"A bunch of damned lies!"

"It's not!" cried Olwen. "It's not!"

"You don't understand . . . "

"I shall see Miss Piper now," said Henry firmly. "Mr. Walsh, if you don't go away I shall have to call up my men and have you removed by force. Is Ernest Jenkins there?"

"I'm 'ere," piped the cockney voice. "The sergeant said for me to . . . "

"I know he did," said Henry. "I'm sorry, I'll have to see you later. Wait in the darkroom until I call you. Now, everybody else—*Go Away!*"

For a moment, Patrick stood facing Henry, his big head lowered dangerously. Henry seriously thought that Patrick might attack him. The moment passed, however. Patrick raised his head, and said, "Well, don't say I didn't warn you." And with that he turned on his heel and strode away down the passage. The rest of the crowd, subdued and silent now, drifted back to their own rooms.

Henry turned back into the office.

"Ronnie . . . " he said. But his niece had gone.

4

Olwen Piper sat down in the chair opposite Henry, and burst into tears. Henry, feeling very sorry for her, proffered his handkerchief. She shook her dark head vigorously in refusal, and brought out her own from a rather shabby handbag. Then she blew her nose loudly, and said, "I'm terribly sorry."

"That's quite all right," said Henry. "Do you feel strong enough to talk now?"

"Yes," said Olwen, rather uncertainly. There was a pause.

"All this must have been a terrible shock to you," Henry went on. "You shared a flat with Helen Pankhurst, didn't you?"

Olwen nodded mutely.

"You got on well, the two of you?"

"Oh, yes. Well, that is . . . mostly . . . "

"Not all the time?"

"Not since Michael . . . " said Olwen, and began to cry again.

"Why did you want to come and see me so urgently? What did you want to tell me?"

Getting no reply to this apart from sniffs and sobs, Henry said firmly, "Look here, Miss Piper. I may as well tell you that I know all about Helen's affair with Michael Healy."

Sheer surprise seemed to take Olwen completely aback. She stopped crying and looked at Henry, wide-eyed. "All about it? How do you know?"

"Never mind. The point is that I know. What I don't know is whether or not it has any bearing on her death. Can you help me?"

"Of course it has." The words came out with a rush. "He killed her! He killed her just as much as if he'd actually murdered her!"

"What do you mean by that?"

"I mean that he was a cad and a swine, and that Helen was absolutely desperate. That's why she did it. I heard her saying she'd kill herself . . . "

"Miss Piper," said Henry, "your friend Helen almost certainly didn't kill herself. She was murdered."

"Murdered?" Olwen faltered. "Oh, no. No, that can't be true. Who on earth would murder Helen?"

"That's exactly what I want to know," said Henry. "Now, please tell me all you know about Helen and Michael Healy."

"It started about six months ago. Helen began going out in the evenings without saying anything to me; she'd never done that before. Of course, I'm out at the theatre a lot, because of my job, so at first I hardly noticed. But then it got worse and worse. I . . . I was very upset. You see, I admired Helen more than anyone in the world, and we'd always been such friends . . . "

"She was quite a bit older than you, wasn't she?"

"Oh, yes, more than ten years . . . but it didn't seem to matter. She was the most marvellous person . . . until all this started."

"When did she first meet Michael Healy?"

"That's the funny thing," said Olwen. "She'd known Michael and Teresa for ages—long before she knew me. When I first started asking Helen where she went in the evenings, she just said she was dining with the Healys, and although I was a bit cross and felt lonely and miserable, I never suspected anything. I just felt mad at them for monopolizing her. Then, one evening, when she was supposed to be having dinner there, I went to the theatre and saw Teresa there with a party of people. So I knew at once that Helen must be somewhere alone with Michael." Olwen sniffed. "When she got home that night, I said something quite casually about Teresa, asking how she'd been, and Helen said, 'Oh, she's fine. She cooked us a wonderful dinner.' I asked her what they had done, and she said, 'Oh, nothing. Just dined

and talked, the three of us.' It was horrible! She did it so naturally . . . and I realized then that she'd been lying to me for
months!"

"Did Mrs. Healy—Miss Manners—know what was going on?"

"I . . . I don't know. Sometimes I think she must, and then
at other times I'd see them being so friendly in the office, and I
couldn't believe that she'd . . . " Olwen stopped, and blew her
nose again. "You don't realize how splendid Helen was, Inspector. If she didn't leave a note, it must have been because she
she didn't want to upset Teresa."

"I have a feeling, Miss Piper," said Henry, not unkindly, "that
all the rumours about Helen and Michael which have been going
round the office may have originated with you."

Olwen did not attempt to deny this. "Why shouldn't I?" she
said. "I thought Teresa ought to know, and put a stop to it.
But I suppose for some reason the story never got to her. I
couldn't very well go and tell her straight out. Anyhow, none of
that matters now. You don't know what hell it's been . . . "

"What has?"

"Seeing Helen so desperate and unhappy as she was the last
month or so. Michael was getting tired of her. I know that's
what it was. And then, in the end . . . well, I knew this would
happen."

Henry noticed that Olwen seemed to have dismissed his suggestion of murder as completely unimportant. He found himself
wondering if it could possibly have been suicide after all. Margery French did not think so. And apart from that, there was
other evidence. Even if in the end it turned out to have been
suicide, it was by no means the simple case that it appeared. He
became aware that Olwen was speaking again.

"I still haven't told you the worst," she said, "but of course the
doctor will find out. You probably know by now, anyway."

"You mean," said Henry, "that Helen was pregnant?"

Olwen nodded miserably.

"Does anybody else know about this?"

"Yes. Somebody."

"Who?"

"I don't know. Not Michael. I mean, she must have told him,
obviously, but she told someone else as well. And she never told
me!" It was a cry of hurt misery. "Why didn't she tell me?"

"How do you know about it, then?"

"Yesterday," said Olwen, "Helen left the office early—just after lunch—because she was going to work all night. I got home to change for the theatre about half past six, and she was talking to somebody on the telephone when I arrived. I heard her say, 'The doctor says it's quite definite. I don't know what I'm going to do. He'll never leave her, you know that as well as I do. I honestly wish I were dead.' Then she heard me, and she said, 'I can't talk now. Goodbye,' and she rang off. When I went in, I tried to say . . . I mean, I asked her if she was all right, and she simply smiled and said, 'Fine, apart from my wretched cold.' Then she went off to the office, and the next thing I heard . . . "

Anxious to prevent another storm of tears, which was clearly in the offing, Henry said, "Was that the last time you saw her? I believe you came to the office yourself to do some work later on, didn't you?"

"Yes. I did just catch a glimpse of Helen. I said goodnight to her on my way to the lift. Her door was open, you see. I didn't disturb her. Nobody ever dared disturb her when she was working."

"What time was this?"

"I honestly don't know. Late. After three, I think. Everyone else had gone."

"So she was alive and well after three o'clock. Did you notice the Thermos in her office?"

"I didn't see it. I remember wondering where it was—she always had it on her desk when she worked at night."

"How did you get home at that hour?"

"I walked."

"All the way to Kensington, in the rain?"

"I was so miserable," said Olwen simply. "I wanted to think. I'd had such an exciting evening at the theatre that I'd almost forgotten about Helen. Then, seeing her brought it all back. I wanted to decide what to do . . . how I could help her . . . "

"Miss Piper," said Henry, "how did you get into the offices here after the theatre? Wasn't the front door locked?"

"Oh, I have my own key." Olwen fumbled in her handbag, and produced a jumbo-size Yale-type silver key. "There it is. I often work late."

"Who else has keys?"

Olwen considered. "Miss French, of course. And Teresa and Patrick and Miss Field. And Helen had one."

"Nobody else?"

"I don't think so."

"Well," said Henry, "thank you for telling me all this. You were quite right to do so. For the moment, keep it to yourself."

"Of course I will."

Henry smiled encouragingly. "I can imagine how distressing all this must be for you," he said.

"I'll be all right," said Olwen. "I've got plenty of work to do."

She stood up, and Henry had an impression of mingled youth, vulnerability and toughness. Olwen Piper had all the intensity and quick emotionalism of her race, but she also had strength.

"Good girl," he said, smiling. Then he added, "Later on, this evening, probably, I'd like to take a look at your flat, if I may."

"Of course, Inspector. What time?"

"It's difficult to say exactly. May I telephone you?"

"Very well. I'll be at home from about five o'clock until I go out to the theatre."

Olwen wrote down her telephone number in strong, neat handwriting, and went out of the office, leaving Henry to the job of questioning Ernest Jenkins.

The latter was a tall, thin youth, white-faced, with sharp, humorous features. He agreed cheerfully that he was one of *Style*'s darkroom assistants, and that he had been on duty the previous evening, helping Michael Healy.

"Not that I 'ad much to do," he admitted. "Mr. 'Ealy, 'e likes to make 'is own prints, if it's anything important. Won't even let you in the darkroom while 'e's working."

He agreed that he had made a fresh Thermos of tea for Helen at about half past eleven, but had not taken it to her office. Michael Healy, he explained, had been angry because he had abandoned a print he was reducing in order to make the tea, and had called him back to work. The word "reducing" rang a bell in Henry's mind.

"Isn't that what you use the cyanide for?"

"That's right."

"What does 'reducing' mean, exactly?"

"Makin' the print lighter," said Ernie. "If the neg's very contrasty, like, you can't get the light part to print without the

59

dark's too dark. So you reduce it."

"How?"

"By rubbin' the dark part with cyanide."

"How much was in the bottle when you used it?"

"More'n half full," replied Ernie without hesitation.

"What's the procedure for getting cyanide from the cupboard?"

"Ordinary like," said Ernie, "Fred 'as the key—that's the chief printer—and we ask him for what we want an' sign for it. But last night was Collections, see."

"So who had the key?"

"Mr. 'Ealy. That's to say, the cupboards was all open, and I just took wot I wanted."

"And he didn't lock them up again when he left?"

"I dunno when 'e left. 'E sent me 'ome about midnight."

"How did you get out of the building? Did you have a key?"

"Me? Blimey, no. It's easy enough to get out, though—one of them locks you can always open from the inside, and then slam, like a sort of super-Yale."

"I see," said Henry. "Thank you, Ernie. That'll be all for now. I may need to see you again later on."

"I'll be in the darkroom, guv, worse luck," Ernie said cheerfully, and withdrew.

Left alone, Henry assembled his somewhat scattered thoughts. In the heightened atmosphere of explosive temperaments, he realized, he had allowed his investigations to get out of sequence. He telephoned to the sergeant, and asked him to bring the dead girl's handbag to the office. It had, the sergeant assured him, been tested carefully for fingerprints, but, like the Thermos flask, bore no evidence of having been handled by anybody other than Helen herself. The cyanide bottle, the sergeant added, bore no fingerprints of any sort.

The contents of Helen's handbag were not very rewarding. There was a gilt powder compact and an expensive lipstick, two large dirty handkerchiefs and two clean ones, a comb, a fountain pen, and a key ring containing three keys, one of which Henry recognized as a twin to Olwen's. The pigskin wallet-purse contained eight pounds and some small change, together with the stubs of several theatre tickets, a receipt for a pair of shoes, some visiting cards, and the unused half of a day return from London to Hindhurst, in Surrey. A small ivory card case was filled with Helen's professional engraved visiting cards, replicas of the one on her office door. There was also a small diary, and Henry turned to this with hope, only to be disappointed, for the entries were no more than brief records of business appointments. Two items, however, caught his attention—one dated a month previously and the other on the last day of Helen's life. In each case the entry consisted of a single word—"Doctor." Henry looked again at the railway ticket. The date of its issue coincided with the date of the first doctor's appointment—a Saturday. Here was something to be followed up, but in view of what Olwen Piper had said, the explanation seemed sadly obvious. Henry sighed, returned Helen's possessions to her bag, and sent for Teresa Manners.

Teresa walked composedly into the office, and as soon as she said, "Good morning, Inspector," Henry recognized the high-pitched, aristocratic voice which he had heard earlier in the corridor.

Even Henry realized at once that Teresa possessed what Margery French had described as "fashion flair." It was only on very close inspection that he registered the fact that she was not a very beautiful woman, for her impact was shattering. She was very tall, with the figure of a model, and she wore a straight dress made of scarlet jersey, which gave the impression of being the most artless of garments, but which was, in fact, most intricately cut and seamed. Round her neck were hung about ten long golden chains of varying calibre, and one slim wrist was circled with as many gold bangles. Her bleached hair was exquisitely set, her make-up smooth and flawless. The fact that her face was slightly too round and plump, her eyes too close-set and her forehead too low, simply did not register. She sat down and crossed her elegant legs.

"May I smoke, Inspector?"

"Of course."

Teresa brought out a gold case from her enormous crocodile handbag, selected a cigarette and lit it from a matching gold lighter. She reminded Henry of a thoroughbred racehorse, with her brittle wrists and ankles, her unmistakably "county" air, and her slightly jerky, nervous movements. She was obviously making a great effort to keep herself under control. Pursuing his analogy, Henry decided that she might, under stress, take the bit between her teeth and bolt.

Henry took her gently over the first fences. She confirmed what he had already been told about the previous evening—the working session at the office, Goring's arrival and invitation, the brief champagne party, the drive home. She agreed, shying slightly, that she had been into the darkroom several times during the night to speak to Michael, and that she had noticed the Thermos flask standing in the storeroom.

"By the way, Inspector," she added, "can Michael and I take our cases home today? It's most inconvenient without them. Michael did bring a toothbrush home in his brief case last night, but all my make-up things and so forth are . . . "

"I quite understand," said Henry. "Yes, you can take them."

"Thank you."

Henry then took a deep breath, and approached the tricky part of the interview. It was surprisingly easy.

"I believe that you were very friendly with Miss Pankhurst?"

"Yes, I was."

"Both you and your husband?"

"Yes. Both of us." There was no hesitation at all. Then, rather surprisingly, Teresa added, "Especially Michael, of course."

Henry was intrigued. "Why do you say that?"

Teresa considered for a moment. "I don't know what Olwen Piper has been saying to you . . . "

Henry said nothing. Teresa went on, speaking very fast. "All sorts of silly rumours were going round about Helen and Michael. Some of them may have reached you. They weren't true. At least, only half-true. Helen was brilliant, and I'm a half-wit, as anyone will tell you. She and Michael had a lot in common. They used to dine together. Go to the theatre and concerts. Things like that. Perhaps there was even some sort of a mild flirtation. I didn't know and I didn't care. If there was, it couldn't have mattered less to any of us. Things get exaggerated in a small world like this, you know. My marriage is perfectly happy and always has been. Helen was my friend." She spoke in short, cropped sentences, with pauses like exclamation marks between them.

"Since you knew her so well," said Henry, "can you tell me anything about her private life and her friends—outside of you and your husband?"

Teresa looked a little startled. "No," she said. "Helen didn't have friends outside the office, as far as I know. Uncle—I mean, Mr. Walsh—has adored her for years, in his funny way. And of course Olwen had a sort of schoolgirl crush on her."

"They seem to have been a strangely assorted pair to share a flat."

"Yes, they were. It only happened because Helen was too good-natured. Olwen arrived a year ago, fresh from university, as assistant to our features editor. She had nowhere to live and knew nobody in London, and Helen's sister, with whom she used to live, had married and gone to Australia. So Helen took pity on Olwen and fished her out of some ghastly hostel and gave her a room in the flat. It was only intended to be the most temporary arrangement, until Olwen found somewhere else to live—in any case, it would have been far too expensive for her. But then the features editor left suddenly, and Olwen was promoted and took over, and with her extra salary she found she could pay her fair share of the expenses. She begged Helen to let her stay on, and Helen was soft-hearted . . . and anyway she'd been finding it a bit of a financial load, running that flat all alone. So . . . there they were."

"Has it occurred to you, Miss Manners," Henry asked suddenly, "that Helen might have killed herself?"

There was a dead silence. The question had obviously taken Teresa completely by surprise, and she could not make up her mind how to answer it. Henry had a strong suspicion that her hesitation was caused not by any doubts about coming to a truthful conclusion, but by speculation as to which of several replies would be most politic.

At length she said, "Frankly, I hadn't considered it. Everyone seemed so sure . . . " She checked herself. "Now that you mention it, I suppose it is possible . . . "

"Why do you say that?"

"Oh, no reason. I mean, people do commit suicide for the oddest reasons, don't they? If you say she did . . . "

"I said nothing of the sort. I asked for your opinion."

Teresa raised her hands and dropped them again in a gesture of bewilderment. "How could I possibly know?" she said.

"You were a great friend of hers."

"She certainly didn't say anything to me that could have . . . "

"I've been told," said Henry, "by several people that she had been nervous and unhappy lately. Didn't you notice that?"

Teresa looked profoundly nervous and unhappy herself. "Well . . . that is . . . I thought she was a bit tired, yes."

"You don't think," Henry pursued, "that her friendship with your husband may have gone deeper than you guessed? That she may have been deeply distressed by her conflicting loyalty to you and affection for him . . . "

"Yes, that's quite possible." Teresa spoke firmly, and with a sort of relief. She seemed to have come to a decision. "Yes, the more I think about it, the more feasible it seems. Of course, it wasn't Michael's fault. How could he have known? Helen wasn't the kind of person to wear her heart on her sleeve, but she felt things very deeply, and she *had* been worried and upset. Yes, now that you explain it, I'm sure that's what must have happened."

Henry looked at her with considerable scepticism. Not for the first time that morning, he had the feeling that some sort of disorganized conspiracy was at work to conceal some inconvenient fact from his knowledge. Patrick, with typical ham-fistedness, had made it obvious; Margery French had handled it adroitly; Teresa Manners had done her best, but had neither the intellect nor the wit to improvise when taken unawares. The question now was to decide which of the three could most easily be persuaded to tell the truth, and the best method of making them do so. For the moment, Henry decided not to rush things. After all, he still had to speak to Michael Healy.

Emmy looked at her beautiful niece with some concern. "I don't like the idea of you being mixed up in all this, Ronnie," she said.

"Uncle Henry said I could help him!"

"He had no right to," said Emmy severely. "You must keep well out of it. Murder may be Henry's business, but it's not yours."

"But don't you see, Aunt Emmy—everybody knows who Uncle Henry is, and if someone's got something to hide, they'll never give themselves away to him. I'm such a nit, nobody will think of being careful of what they say in front of me. I shall be able to find out masses of things that he can't."

"Everybody must know by now that you're Henry's niece."

"No. Only Beth, and she's promised not to say a word. Beth's an angel."

"Angel or not, she'll tell everyone just the same," said Emmy with relief. "So you see, you won't be able to do any good. In any case, I won't have you playing at being a detective. Murder isn't glamorous, you know. It's a nasty, sordid, dangerous business. I don't know what your mother will say."

"She'll pretend to be horrified, but she'll be all agog for the latest juicy bits of news," said Veronica, with brutal candor. She looked at her watch. "Heavens, I must go. My sitting's at twelve. I'll come along this evening and tell Uncle Henry what I've found out."

"Of course, we'd love to see you this evening, dear, but . . . "

"Can't you just see the headlines?" said Veronica gleefully. " Model girl solves murder mystery. 'We were baffled,' admits Chief Inspector Tibbett of Scotland Yard . . . "

"Ronnie!" Emmy was genuinely shocked. "Don't you dare!"

"Must go now. See you this evening."

"Ronnie . . . "

Veronica blew her aunt a kiss. "You'll see," she said ominously. And with that she was gone.

By the time that Henry had concluded a routine but unproductive interview with Alf Samson, which merely confirmed what he already knew, the office clock stood at ten minutes past twelve. Henry dialed the number of the studio, and was told tartly by Ernie that Mr. Healy was in the middle of a sitting and could not be disturbed.

"Very well," said Henry amicably, "I'll come along to the studio."

"No visitors allowed," said Ernie positively.

"I am not a visitor," said Henry. "If either you or Mr. Healy want to argue the point, talk to Mr. Goring about it."

The mention of the great man's name had an immediate effect. "Oh well," said Ernie, resignedly, adding, "Mr. 'Ealy won't like it, I can tell you."

"Too bad," said Henry. He rang off, and went along the corridor to the studio.

The studio was a huge, high-ceilinged barn of a room. Clearly this part of the old house had been completely gutted and reconstructed to accommodate it. Lamps and screens, electric flex, and junction boxes made it something of an obstacle race to get in at all; inside, there was a hushed and cathedral-like atmosphere which it would have taken a brave man to shatter.

The whole place was dark, except for a brilliantly lit area at one end, where a girl whom Henry recognized with difficulty as his niece Veronica stood in a circle of blazing white light, against a background screen of crumpled silver paper. Her honey-coloured face had been plastered with thick, pale make-up, and her eyes darkly and boldly outlined in deep brown. True to her threat, she had also used the same dark brown to outline her sepia mouth. She was wearing a long, slinky black dress and an extravagance of diamonds, and she looked a good ten years older than her age. The most startling thing of all, however, was the fact that she held in her right hand a thin chain which was attached to the collar of a large and dangerous-looking cheetah, which was engaged in sniffing and pawing the ground with obvious ill-humour.

Facing her, a tall, slim man in shirt-sleeves stood with his head bent in dedicated concentration over a small camera on a tripod. In the dim background, Henry could make out two other female figures—Beth Connolly and Teresa Manners.

Without looking up, the thin man said, "What's the reading, Ernie?"

Ernie darted out from the shadows, holding a small light meter in his hand. He approached Veronica and the cheetah with reluctance, and shoved the meter to within an inch of Veronica's nose.

"A hundredth at five-six," he said.

"And the reading on the cheetah?"

Tentatively, Ernie extended his arm and brushed the cheetah's nose with the light meter. This clearly displeased the animal, which sat back on its haunches and let out a ferocious growl. Ernie jumped back like a frog into the shadows, and Teresa let out a little squeal. Veronica remained motionless, apparently unconcerned. The photographer looked up, annoyed, and saw Henry.

"There you are at last," he said irritably. "For God's sake, do something with that animal of yours!"

"But . . . "

"Make it stand up and prowl towards the camera."

"I'm not . . . "

"Ernie!" bellowed Michael. "Make the bloody thing get up and walk towards the camera!"

"Mr. 'Ealy, I don't like to . . . " came a thin wail from the shadows.

"Go on, poppet. Walkies," said Veronica sweetly. Without altering her pose, she prodded the cheetah gently in the backside with the sharp toe of her satin slipper. The cheetah rolled over on its back and began to purr.

"Marvellous!" cried Michael. "Hold that! A little smile, Veronica! Head a bit to the left . . . that's it! Wonderful! Terrific! Now kick the beast again!" The camera was clicking like a ticker-tape machine.

Once again, Veronica extended her foot and prodded in an exploratory manner. This time the cheetah, becoming bored and doubtless feeling the effects of the hot lights, merely went to sleep.

"It's gone to sleep," said Veronica helpfully.

"Never mind," said Michael. "Leave it alone for the moment. At least it's quiet, and I've got to reload. Ernie! Reload! There should be some beauties there." He turned again to Henry. "For the next reel," he said, "I must have it standing up. Can it rear on its hind legs?"

Henry was spared the embarrassment of answering this question by the sudden and breathless arrival of a small, red-faced man in corduroys and a dirty green sweater. He carried an ancient canvas rucksack.

"My goodness," he exclaimed, "I've been looking everywhere! Did you know there was a policeman downstairs? How's my Beauty, then?" He fell on his knees beside the cheetah, which snored loudly. "I hope she's been a good girl. She's been a little fractious lately . . . constipated and off her food, you know." He produced an unattractive-looking bone from his rucksack. "Eat up then, Beauty. Who wants a bone, then?" The cheetah's nose twitched. Then the animal stretched langorously, sat up and began to gnaw the bone noisily. "There!" said the little man proudly. "Yes, a policeman, if you'll believe it. Apparently they let Beauty in at the back entrance with no trouble, but when I came in by the front door, they stopped me. I couldn't make the bobby understand the simple fact that I was looking for my cheetah which was having its photograph taken . . . "

Henry, picturing the sergeant, could not suppress a grin. He was interested, however, in the mention of the back door, and made a mental note to investigate it.

"She's been as good as gold," said Veronica. "Haven't you, poppet?" She bent down and tickled the cheetah's ears.

"I'm so relieved," said Beauty's owner. "Oh, I wouldn't do that, Miss. She doesn't usually bite, mind you, but sometimes people make her nervous."

"Not me," said Veronica serenely. "We're friends." She bent to stroke the cheetah again, and winked surreptitiously at Henry. Ernie came back with the recharged camera.

"Right," said Michael. "Let's get on. Veronica, darling, move over to the right a bit."

"You'll probably have to carry me," said Veronica cheerfully. She began to hobble inch by inch across the studio, and Henry saw, with a pang of disillusionment, that the smooth, skin-tight lines of the black dress had been achieved by pinning it in at the back with huge paper clips, so tightly as to make movement virtually impossible.

"That'll do," said Michael. "Now, I want the cheetah up on its hind legs, like a heraldic beast, looking out left."

"Here, I say," protested the green-sweatered man, "that's asking a bit much."

"I always ask a bit much," Michael said charmingly, "and I usually get it."

"Well, I suppose I can try," said green-sweater dubiously. "Perhaps if I stood on a ladder and held the bone up in the air . . . "

"I don't give a damn what you do so long as you're not in the picture." Michael swept a hand through his hair. "And I want the train of the dress sweeping out of the frame on the right, as if it were being blown. Teresa, put a thread in it, and hold it up, and shake it when I tell you. Ernie, I need a reflector here, to catch her face . . . "

"We'll have to get the bone away from her first, of course," said green-sweater without enthusiasm. "They can be touchy about that. We don't want any unpleasantness, do we?"

They managed it in the end. The cheetah was patiently tempted by succulent morsels from the rucksack until she surrendered the bone. Henry held the wobbling stepladder, while green-sweater, perched precariously on the top step, dangled the bone invitingly above Beauty's head. Teresa held the train of the dress on the end of a thread, and twitched it at Michael's bidding. Ernie stood on a chair brandishing a board covered in silver paper, so that it reflected extra light on to Veronica's pale face. Beth hovered in the background among the electric wires and lamps, adjusting the paper clips on Veronica's back. It was a bizarre, if not ludicrous scene, but all that the camera saw and registered was the splendid, rearing beast, the proud pale girl, the moulded dress swirling into a wind-blown train behind her, and the faintly glimmering background that might have been moonlight reflected on a restless sea. It was one of the photographs of the year.

When it was all over, and Veronica, with Beth and Teresa, had gone to the dressing room to change, Henry went up to the tall photographer and said, "Can you spare me a moment, Mr. Healy?"

"If it's about the cheetah," said Michael, "ask Miss Field. She booked it." He wiped his brow with his handkerchief.

"It's not about the cheetah. I've never seen the creature before."

"Oh, I suppose you're from Nicholas Knight about the dress. Well, that's Miss Manners' business. Don't bother me." Michael sat down on the stepladder and lit a cigarette. He looked very tired.

"I'm not from Nicholas Knight. I'm from Scotland Yard."

"Good God," said Michael, but he did not sound surprised. "About Helen, I suppose."

"Yes."

"Well, we can't possibly talk now. I'm in the middle of a sitting."

"We've got at least five minutes," said Henry, "and this is urgent. I want to know the truth about your relationship with Miss Pankhurst."

Michael studied the tip of his cigarette. "Is this an official interview?" he said at last.

"It's official," said Henry, "in that I'm here in an official capacity, and anything you tell me I shall use as I think fit. It's unofficial in that there's nobody with a notebook taking down everything you say to put into a signed statement."

"Well, what do you want to know?"

"I've told you."

"Helen," said Michael slowly, "was a rather frightening person. She gave the impression of being very strong-minded and caring for nothing and nobody. In fact, she was as vulnerable as a schoolgirl emotionally, and she felt things desperately. It was easy to hurt her without meaning to. She'd never scream and shout and throw things, like Teresa. Everything was bottled up inside her, until it exploded.

"I expect you've heard stories about her and me. I can only tell you that they are exaggerated. We were good friends—nothing more. I wasn't to know what was going on under that enameled intellectual shell."

"You must have known, of course," said Henry quietly, "that she was pregnant."

There was no mistaking the shock effect that this remark had on Michael Healy. He dropped his cigarette and stood up with a jerk.

"It's not possible!" he said. "It's a lie. She can't have been!"

"She was," said Henry.

"My God," said Michael. He had gone very white indeed. "I can't believe . . . and yet . . . I suppose it was possible. I never thought of that. Christ, how awful."

"So you see," Henry said, "you can't ask me to believe that things hadn't gone very far between you."

Michael seemed not to have heard. He had sat down again, and was shaking his head slowly from side to side, as if still trying to assimilate what he had heard.

"I gather she hadn't told you," Henry went on.

"Me? No, of course not. I mean . . . no. It's too bloody for words. Poor darling Helen."

"You're not going to persist in your denial that you and she were lovers?"

Michael produced a faint, painful grin. "There doesn't seem to be much point in denying it, does there?" he said.

"Good," said Henry. "We're getting somewhere. Now, is it true that recently you had been tiring of her, and trying to disentangle yourself from . . . "

"There was nothing to get disentangled from."

"Please, Mr. Healy. After what you've just admitted . . . "

Michael said, a little helplessly, "I suppose she must have taken it more seriously than I did."

"You didn't consider it important in your life?"

"Well . . . no."

Henry did not comment on this, but said, "Now tell me about the cyanide and the keys of the darkroom store cupboards."

"What about them?"

"They were in your charge last night."

"They were in my pocket," said Michael. "They still are."

"And you went home leaving the cupboards unlocked?"

"Guilty, Inspector."

"That was a pretty careless thing to do, wasn't it?"

"My dear Inspector," said Michael, with light irony, "if you had ever had to put a Paris edition to bed immediately after a solid week of Paris Collections . . . In any case, one hardly expects violent death to occur among one's colleagues in a place like this."

Henry let this pass. "When did you last notice the bottle of cyanide?" he asked.

"I told Ernie to reduce a print around midnight. He must have used it then."

"But when did you actually see it?"

"I didn't. Not consciously. It's always there. I didn't use it myself."

"You've no idea how full it was?"

"Not the faintest."

Michael threw down his cigarette and stood up. "Back to work," he said. He sounded relieved.

Henry turned to see that Veronica had come out of the dressing room. The change in her was remarkable. The sophisticated white make-up had disappeared, and she was once again the girl next door—simple, ingenuous, and young. Her golden hair had been released from its coiled chignon, and bobbed disarmingly about her brown cheeks. She wore a pink and white striped cotton dress and flat sandals. She was followed by Beth Connolly, who carried a huge wicker basket full of fresh flowers.

As Veronica passed Henry, she nudged him and whispered, "See you this evening." She took her place under the lights.

"Why did it bloody well have to rain today?" Michael complained. "This needs open air and a duckpond."

"I know," said Beth. "I've done my best for you. You've no idea what it's like getting spring flowers in January."

Michael looked critically from Veronica to the flowers and back. Finally, he said, "Can you get a young calf and a five-barred gate?"

Gently but firmly, Beth said, "No, Michael dear. I can't."

"Well, I must have a young animal. What about a kitten?"

Beth sighed. "It'll take half-an-hour by taxi from Knightsbridge."

"Never mind. Send off for one. Very young and fluffy, and grey if possible. Then we'll have the flowers all over the floor, with Veronica lying on her back among them, holding up the kitten. How's that?"

Henry left his niece lying on a sheet of white paper on the studio floor, surrounded by blossoms like a dying Ophelia. He went back to his own office.

As he came into the room, the telephone rang. He picked it up.

"Inspector Tibbett? This is Godfrey Goring. How are things going?"

"Slow but sure," said Henry.

"Good. Good. I was wondering if you'd care to lunch with me. I generally go to The Orangery about one. It's just over the road. We could talk quietly there."

"Thank you," said Henry. "I'd enjoy that."

"I'll see you there in ten minutes," said Goring, and rang off.

At once, the phone shrilled again. This time, it was the lugubrious doctor from police headquarters. "I've got a bit more news for you, Tibbett," he said, gloomily.

"I know you have," said Henry.

"Definitely cyanide poisoning, definitely administered in the tea. Time of death, between four and five thirty A.M. Body aged about thirty-three, well-nourished and . . . "

"Don't prolong the agony," said Henry. "I already know."

"You already know what?"

"That she was pregnant."

"Pregnant?" For once, the doctor was shaken out of his sad monotone. "What in hell do you mean, pregnant?"

Henry felt at a loss. "Well . . . wasn't she?" he said, feebly.

The doctor, probably for the first time in many months, laughed. "Not only was she not pregnant, my dear Tibbett," he said, "but she was a virgin. Put *that* in your meerschaum and smoke it." He chuckled again and rang off, leaving Henry contemplating the telephone receiver in his hand with very mixed emotions.

5

The Orangery is, of course, one of the plushiest restaurants in London, with a world-famous cuisine and cellar, and prices virtually inaccessible to those without expense accounts. Henry felt consciously and conspicuously out of place as he stood in the vestibule, surveying the décor of dark tangerine and gold, the swathed velvet curtains caught back by gilded claws, and the shiny leaves of the small orange trees, so miraculously burdened with fruit in the middle of an English winter. Only later did he realize that each golden orange was carefully tied onto its branch by a thin wire. There was a lingering aura of expensive scent and cigar smoke, and the voices which greeted Henry's ear spoke in the bland, rich tones of financial success.

As usual at lunchtime, the bulk of the clientele was masculine, middle-aged, smoothly tailored, affable, and sure of itself. Here, behind the façade of eating, drinking, and telling jokes, important business deals were grimly negotiated. Actors and agents bargained over contracts and percentages, property mergers were delicately mooted, indefatigable public relations men insinuated the excellence of their wares into the cynical ears of journalists, sharp-witted advertizing agents skilfully persuaded their manufacturer clients of the profitability of costly campaigns. The actual—and considerable—amount of money which The Orangery spirited, so discreetly, out of the pockets of the diners was as nothing compared to the sums which effectually changed hands there daily, between the magic hours of twelve thirty and three.

A dark, impeccable *maitre d'hotel* stepped up to Henry.

"You have reserved a table, sir?" he asked. His manner was faultless, yet Henry sensed at once the slight coldness accorded to one who was not a regular customer, whose suit had not been made in Savile Row, and whose financial status was therefore a matter for conjecture.

"I am lunching with Mr. Goring," said Henry.

Immediately, subtly, the manner changed. "But of course, sir. Mr. Goring is already here. You know his usual table?"

"No."

"Ah, I will show you. This way, sir . . . "

Henry followed the *maitre d'hotel* into the restaurant proper, which was lit by darkly shaded lanterns, and garnished with splendid displays of hothouse flowers, smoked salmon, and exotic fruit. It was impossible to imagine that daylight had ever penetrated into this temple of gastronomy.

Godfrey Goring was sitting at a secluded corner table, reading the *Times*. He looked up with a smile when he saw Henry approaching.

"My dear Tibbett, this is a great pleasure," he said. "Come and sit down. What will you drink?"

Henry sat down and declined an aperitif. "Quite right," said Goring, approvingly. "Never touch them myself. But you'll take some wine with your meal, I trust?"

Henry said that he would be delighted to do so. There followed an earnest discussion of the menu and the wine list, on both of which Goring spoke with the authority of a connoisseur. Henry was surprised to see that, when the meal arrived, Goring—who had murmured to the waiter "Just the usual for me"—contented himself with a frugal meal of cold chicken and plain salad, accompanied by a bottle of Vichy water, while Henry regaled himself on *pâté maison* and *canard à l'orange,* together with an excellent Burgundy.

He knew enough of the protocol of business luncheons, however, not to be surprised by the fact that Goring studiously avoided any reference to the matter in hand until the coffee arrived. Until then, the managing director of Style Publications talked fluently and amusingly on the rival merits of French and Italian cooking, the current trends in the London and Paris theatres, the advisability of taking a southern holiday in the sun in January, and the continental influence on British motor-car design. Henry had a feeling that these preliminaries were not so much rehearsed as automatic—a ritual which inevitably preceded the real business of the day.

At last, however, when the waiter had poured coffee and departed, Goring said, "Now, you must tell me how I can help you over this shocking business of Helen Pankhurst."

"What I am trying to do at the moment," said Henry, "is to fill in the background for myself. When one is called in on a case of this sort, one is hampered by having no personal knowledge of the dead person. I am hoping, by talking to her friends and colleagues, to build up a picture of Miss Pankhurst—her character and her interests and her way of life. That must be my starting point."

Goring nodded. "Very sensible," he said. "I would tackle the job in the same way myself." It was clear that this was the highest praise he could bestow. "Helen was an employee of mine. Naturally, I can only give you a professional assessment of her."

"You did not know her personally . . . socially . . . ?" Henry asked.

"Any good employer," said Goring, "makes it his business to be interested in the lives of his senior staff. But in Helen's case, I can only say that she was a girl who was completely wrapped up in her work. As such, she is a terrible loss to the company. I don't know how we shall replace her."

"Tell me about her from your point of view."

"Helen came to us as a secretary nearly ten years ago," said Goring slowly. "It was Margery French who, two years later, first proposed to me that Helen should be promoted to the executive staff. She was convinced, and rightly, that the girl had exceptional qualities. I interviewed her myself then, and was immensely struck by her. She had intelligence and ability, combined with—how shall I put it?—the *savoir faire* and . . . I can only call it breeding . . . which is essential in my senior staff. She was made an editorial assistant, then subeditor, and eventually promoted to assistant editor. I can tell you in confidence that, had she lived, she would almost certainly have become editor. Now, it is likely that Teresa Manners will get the job when Margery retires. Don't think that I have anything against Teresa—on the contrary, she and her family are personal friends of mine. All the same, whatever Margery may say, I don't think she is the right person to edit a magazine. However . . . " He broke off. "I must apologize for talking shop."

"Not at all," said Henry. "It's all most interesting. Will Miss French be retiring soon, then?"

There was a little pause, and then Goring said, "I am telling you this in the strictest confidence, Tibbett. Margery is a very sick woman. She doesn't like to admit it, but she is. In fact, her doctors have ordered her to give up work within the next couple of months. As you can imagine, the question of her successor has been the biggest problem on my mind for some time. A magazine like ours stands or falls by its editor. Margery was the ideal. I don't consider it practical to bring in anybody from outside, so the choice lay between Helen and Teresa. I haven't attempted to conceal from you that I favoured Helen. In fact, from that point of view, her death is a great . . . " he hesitated " . . . a great personal tragedy to me."

"I have been told," said Henry, choosing his words carefully, "that she was involved in some sort of emotional entanglement with another member of the staff."

Goring's face hardened. "That had nothing to do with it," he said. "I was concerned only with Helen's work."

"All the same, when you are contemplating giving somebody such an important job . . . "

"Margery mentioned it to me," said Goring. Clearly, the subject was distasteful to him. "She wished Teresa to be editor, of course, and . . . no, that is less than fair. She was right to bring to my attention anything which might conceivably disrupt the smooth running of the office. However, I think I convinced her that it was something which could be ironed out, if handled rightly. Alas, it seems that I was wrong. However . . . "

At this point, the conversation was interrupted by the arrival of a newcomer—a short, slim young man, who wore clothes that were just too well-cut, and hair that was just too long. He came hurrying across the restaurant with a strange, almost skipping step, crying in a high-pitched voice, "Godfrey, my dear! Whatever *is* all this? I've just . . . " He stopped abruptly when he saw Henry.

"Hello, Nicholas," said Goring. He sounded displeased.

"My dear, I've just bought the *Standard*, and I'm shattered. Utterly shattered. I positively can't believe—"

"Inspector," said Goring, with quiet emphasis, "may I introduce Mr. Knight? Nicholas, this is Chief Inspector Tibbett of Scotland Yard."

The young man sat down suddenly. He had turned even paler than before. "Oh," he said. "Oh, yes. Delighted to meet you."

"Mr. Knight," said Goring, "is one of our most brilliant young dress designers."

"I've heard all about you, Mr. Knight," said Henry.

"About . . . about me? You couldn't . . . I mean . . . have you? Nice things, I hope," he added, with a painfully nervous smile.

"You were at Mr. Goring's house last night, weren't you?" said Henry.

"Was I? I mean . . . yes, of course. Lovely, lovely party, Godfrey. Terrible to think that . . . well . . . I must go. Nose to the grindstone, you know. Goodbye, Inspector."

Knight jumped up and began to make his way back between the tables.

"Mr. Knight," said Henry loudly. Knight stopped with a jerk, and turned round reluctantly. "I'd like to have a chat with you some time. Perhaps you could come to the *Style* offices this afternoon?"

The young man was as nervous as a rabbit. He glanced over his shoulder, as though fearful of being overheard, and then said, almost in a whisper, "No. Come to my *salon*. Terribly busy, you understand. This building. First floor. Anyone will tell you." He disappeared gracefully between the velvet curtains at the back of the restaurant.

"A most talented young man," said Goring, when he had gone. "Don't be put off by his . . . his somewhat fantastic manner. People in his business tend to adopt extravagant attitudes. He is, in fact, a very shrewd businessman, but he takes pains to conceal the fact."

Remembering Patrick Walsh's remarks earlier in the day, Henry decided to make a stab in the dark, and said, "All the same, hasn't he been involved in some sort of a scandal lately?"

Goring looked sharply at Henry. "Knight?" he said. "Not that I know of. Certainly not."

"Oh, well," said Henry, "I must have been confusing him with somebody else. I know very little about the fashion world, I'm afraid."

There was a silence. Henry waited, patiently, for Goring to make the next move. He felt convinced that the real purpose of the luncheon had not yet been touched upon. At length, Goring said, "The fashion world. And what a strange world it is, Inspector. You may have some surprises before this case is over. We're . . . well, we're rather unusual people, I'm afraid."

It struck Henry, not for the first time, that nearly every member of *Style*'s staff had gone out of their way to emphasize what a curious crowd they all were. And yet, so far, apart from Patrick's histrionics, he had found them to be very much like other people. Was it, he wondered, a sort of quirky, misguided conceit which made them imagine that they were so different from the ordinary run of mortals? Or did their apparent normality disguise deeper eccentricities? He supposed he would find out soon enough.

Goring went on, "I always have particular difficulty in finding the right men for my staff. I don't mean for the purely business side—I'm talking about the artistic angle. My art directors and photographers have to be very exceptional characters. First of all, they must have real talent and originality; then, they must be prepared to work in what is largely a woman's world, under feminine leadership—but without ever losing their masculinity, which is a tremendously important force in our work. I refuse," Goring added belligerently, "to employ homosexuals, however brilliant they may be. This is not a question of morals. It's simply that there are few enough men on the creative side of the magazine, and each one must contribute one hundred percent masculinity, as a balancing factor against the predominantly female element. Do you follow me?"

"In principle," said Henry, cautiously.

"Ideally," Goring continued, "the men should be rocks of common sense in this ephemeral world, free from temperament and emotionally stable, as well as creatively adventurous. Unfortunately, paragons such as I have described are rare. I cannot pretend that all my male staff measure up to these standards."

79

Thinking of Patrick, Henry smiled and said, "I can appreciate your difficulties."

"The one man whom I always felt to be a perfect example of what I want was Michael Healy," Goring went on. "It was his character as much as his talent which decided me to take him on when he left *Woman's Way*. In doing so, I broke one of my most rigid rules, for he was already married to Teresa Manners—she was my assistant fashion editor then—and I had always been adamant that I would never employ two staff members married to each other. I am well aware that most people thought I had relaxed the rule because of my personal friendship with Teresa and Michael. This is not true. It was done purely on the basis of talent and character, and for some years I felt that my confidence had been entirely justified. Just recently, however, things have started to worry me, and to make me wonder whether I was wrong, after all."

Henry thought, "Now we're getting down to it at last." Goring paused and lit a cigar, while the waiter poured more coffee.

"I am glad, in a way, Inspector," he went on, "that you brought up the unfortunate episode of Helen and Michael, for I would have been loath to mention it, and yet I feel that it is my duty to warn you. Michael is not—has not been for some months—the balanced and sensible individual that he appears to be on the surface. His work, while even more brilliant than ever, is becoming steadily more outré, more frenetic. And his personality seems to be indulging in the same tendency to fantasy. A few years ago, an affair between Helen and Michael would have been unthinkable. Now, he seems to have lost all sense of responsibility. It may be that his marriage is going through a difficult phase. It may be merely his development as an artist. I don't know. I can only tell you—and warn you—that these days he tends to do and say things which are . . . how shall I put it? . . . divorced from reality."

"You mean," said Henry bluntly, "that I shouldn't believe a word he says."

"I certainly would not say that," said Goring hastily. "I merely meant . . . treat his statements with caution. I really believe that he is capable of convincing himself that something is actually true, if it seems to him desirable or artistically satisfying. He will embroider a pyramid of fantasy onto a shred of fact.

Please don't think I'm accusing him of lying. I'm just advising you to be careful."

"You may be right," said Henry. He was thinking of the discrepancy between Michael's admissions and the doctor's findings.

Goring sat back and stirred his coffee. "Now Helen," he said, "didn't realize that this change was taking place in Michael. All she knew was that an old and steady friendship had suddenly and dazzlingly become a romantic love affair. I'm afraid it's a matter of feminine psychology that no woman—not even Helen —would attribute such a metamorphosis to growing lack of mental balance. On the contrary, she decided that any change in Michael was the result of his love for her, instead of *vice versa*. When it became apparent that she was wrong, and that his professed devotion was as ephemeral as his other fancies, she was desperately upset. She was in despair. I blame myself now, when it is too late. I feel sure that if Michael had been sent away, and Helen given the editorship, her love of work and the challenge of the new job would have prevented her from . . . you see what I am leading up to, Inspector?"

"You are trying to persuade me that Helen committed suicide," said Henry.

"I am giving you my considered opinion that she did," said Goring. "No other explanation is feasible. She had no enemies. There was not a soul in the world who would want to kill her."

"Except possibly Michael Healy—or his wife."

"No, no. My dear Inspector, I never meant to imply any such thing. It's out of the question."

"Even in Michael's present state of mind?"

"Out of the question," said Goring again. He was obviously shocked and distressed at the suggestion. "I only mentioned all this because . . . "

Once again, they were interrupted. Goring, who was sitting facing the restaurant, broke off suddenly and jumped to his feet. Henry turned to see a very lovely woman of about forty making her way across the room to their table. She was bareheaded, her long red hair trailing over the collar of a magnificent mink coat. Henry was immediately struck by the contrast between this woman and the girls from *Style*. Where the latter were conscientiously groomed, living tributes to their own journalistic advice, this creature was simply beautiful and rich, careless and probably something of a slattern. She wore her fur as if it were an old mackintosh: her hair looked uncombed and her purple lipstick clashed with her scarlet dress. *Style* would certainly have condemned as vulgar and ostentatious the simultaneous display of three ropes of pearls and two large diamond brooches. Worst of all, she wore no stockings, and the heels of her crocodile shoes were slightly scuffed. Nevertheless, she was wonderfully and vividly alive, and Henry was certain that he had seen her somewhere before.

"Lorna," said Goring, "what on earth are you doing here?"

"Oh, darling, I had to come." The woman's voice was husky and exciting. "I heard . . . "

"My dear," said Goring, "this is Inspector Tibbett of Scotland Yard. Inspector, my wife."

While Henry murmured greetings, Goring said, "Well, you'd better sit down. Have you eaten?"

"Of course not. I simply leapt into the car as soon as I heard."

"You shouldn't have." Goring sounded annoyed. "What am I going to do with you all day?"

"You're very ungracious, darling, I must say," said Lorna Goring. "You're surely not going to send me back to Surrey without any food, are you?" Without waiting for an answer to this rhetorical question, she turned to the waiter, who was hovering at her side, smiled brilliantly, and said, "I'll have some smoked salmon and chicken suprème, Pierre, with some Chablis —you know the one I like." Then, to Goring, she said, "Now darling, you must tell me *all* about it, every single tiny thing, and then I'll be as good as gold and get out of your way. I'll go along to the Lyric and see Madge. She has a matinée this afternoon."

At the mention of the theatre, Henry remembered. This was Lorna Vincent, the actress who had made such a resounding success about fifteen years before, had amassed a sizable fortune, and then had married and announced that she would retire and devote herself to domesticity. What was surprising was the fact that she had, in fact, done so. No more had been heard of Lorna Vincent, apart from the odd photograph in a gossip column. It simply had not occurred to Henry that Godfrey Goring was the man she had married. Her husband, as he recalled, had been described by the newspapers as "a businessman"; a colourless figure beside the flaming personality of Lorna Vincent.

"Who was she?" Lorna went on, avidly. "One of the walking sticks?" She turned to Henry. "I always say the *Style* girls look exactly like walking sticks. Straight stocking seams, straight black suits, straight black hats, ramrod backbones, and lacquered hair. I can't tell one from the other. If you see several of them walking down the street together, it's like the parade of the wooden soldiers."

Henry, while he considered Lorna's remarks unfair, was compelled to smile at the grain of truth they contained. Goring, however, looked furious.

"Helen Pankhurst is dead," he said, in an even, angry voice. "And there is no need to insult my staff."

"He's terribly proud of his girls, aren't you, darling?" said Lorna without malice. "Helen Who? Do you mean the dark one with the big nose?"

"Yes," Goring replied shortly.

"But what happened? It's fearfully exciting. Was she murdered? The papers said—"

"Lorna," said Goring, "for God's sake, eat your lunch and go to your matinée. Inspector Tibbett and I have to get back to work now. Are you going to stay in town tonight?"

"It seems the sensible thing to do."

"Very well. I'll see you at home this evening."

"I'll come and pick you up at the office."

"No," said Goring. "No outsiders are allowed. There is a police investigation going on." He stood up, and then suddenly bent and kissed his wife. "Don't be an idiot, darling. I'll tell you all about it later."

As they left the restaurant, Goring said quietly to Henry, "If my wife should come to the office this afternoon . . . visitors aren't allowed, are they? Perhaps you could give your men instructions . . . "

"If your wife wishes to come in, Mr. Goring, I'm sure that . . . "

"No, no." For once, Goring seemed at a loss for words. "I'd rather she . . . people might think . . . in fact, I'd rather she was not allowed in."

"Very well," said Henry, "I'll tell the sergeant."

They went back to the offices of *Style*.

Henry re-established himself in his poky domain, and dialed the number of the editor's office. Immediately, a crisp, efficient voice answered.

"Miss French's office. Good afternoon."

"Is this Miss Field?"

"It is. Can I help you?"

"This is Inspector Tibbett. I was hoping to have a word with you."

"Certainly, Inspector."

"Right away now?"

"Of course."

"I'm in the small office next to the fashion room," said Henry.

"Oh, yes?"

There was a silence fraught with misunderstanding. Then Rachel Field said, "Well? What do you want to ask me?"

"I'm afraid I can't do it over the phone, Miss Field. Can you come along here?"

"Oh, no, I'm afraid not," Rachel replied promptly. "Miss French isn't in the office at the moment. I can't possibly leave it."

"I can reassure you," said Henry. "Police investigations have absolute priority."

"I'm afraid I can't . . . "

"If you don't believe me," said Henry, "you can ask Mr. Goring."

Once again, Goring's name worked its magic. "Oh, well . . . in that case . . . I'll come along right away, Inspector."

Like most people encountering Rachel Field for the first time, Henry was both impressed and intimidated by her efficiency. She had not, in fact, brought her shorthand notebook with her, but as she sat facing Henry across the desk, her legs crossed primly and her hands folded in her lap, it was difficult to believe that she was not waiting respectfully to take a letter. She wore a neat, sensible suit made of navy blue flannel, complete with those "touches of white" so dear to the hearts of women's magazines of more popular appeal than *Style*. Her shoes, too, were sensible and highly polished, her nails clipped short and painted in colourless varnish, and her hair set with more precision than fashion sense. One quality, and one only, she shared with Lorna Goring. Both existed within the periphery of *Style*, but on neither had that arbiter of elegance made the faintest impression.

Rachel turned out to be an excellent and concise witness, as Henry had guessed she would. She described her return from Paris the previous day in company with Michael, Teresa, and Veronica, the late night working session, and Goring's party.

"Did you enjoy the party?" Henry asked suddenly. It had occurred to him that Rachel must have cut an incongruous figure among the splendours of Brompton Square.

"It was very kind of Mr. Goring to invite me," said Rachel primly. "In fact, I didn't really want to go," she added, in a burst of confidence, "but he insisted, so I couldn't very well refuse."

"I understand that afterwards Mr. Knight drove you home in his car?"

"Yes. He was going in my direction."

"Where do you live, Miss Field?"

"I have a flat just off Holland Road."

Henry raised his eyebrows slightly. "Mr. Knight lives here, in Earl Street," he said. "To go to Holland Road must have taken him in absolutely the wrong direction."

"He was dropping Mr. Barry in Kensington in any case," said Rachel shortly.

"I see," said Henry. "Now, if you don't mind, I'd like to talk about your suitcase."

"My suitcase? What about it? I'd like to have it back, if I may."

"You left it in Miss Pankhurst's office last night, didn't you?"

"Yes. I couldn't have Miss French's room cluttered up."

"What was in the case, Miss Field?"

Rachel looked surprised. "Don't you know?" she said. "I should have thought you'd have searched it by now. There were just my things from Paris—clothes and so on." She looked steadily at Henry. "I wasn't smuggling, Inspector, I assure you. We have no time for shopping sprees when the Collections are on."

"I'm sure you don't," said Henry. "So there was nothing in the case except your personal possessions."

Rachel looked a little embarrassed. "I did bring a bottle of perfume back as a present for a friend," she said.

Henry smiled. "That's reasonable enough," he said. "Now, can you think of any reason why someone should want to ransack your case?"

Rachel gave a little gasp. "Ransack? What do you mean?"

"I'd like you to come and take a look for yourself," said Henry.

He got up and led the way to Helen's office, where a policeman stood guard over the door. Rachel hesitated. "Is she . . . ?" she asked tentatively. She had gone very pale.

"It's all right," said Henry reassuringly. "There's nothing in there, except . . . well, you'll see."

He opened the door, and they went in. Rachel's eyes widened as she saw the chaos, and a look of unmistakable anger came into her face.

"My things," she said. "How dared he . . . ?"

"Why do you say 'he'?" Henry asked quickly.

Rachel looked taken aback. "Well," she said, "it must have been a man, mustn't it? I mean . . . "

"It may not have been a man," said Henry. "What I want you to do is to check up and see if there's anything missing—anything at all."

At once, Rachel became businesslike. She went down on her knees and began to sort through the disorderly piles of clothes. Once she looked up and said, "What about fingerprints?"

"That's all right," said Henry. "It's already been attended to."

"I see. Good." She went systematically through the scattered contents of the case, and then said, "Everything seems to be here."

Henry looked thoughtful. "So," he said, "either somebody was looking for something which wasn't there, or . . . " He paused. "Miss Field, would anyone else have had an opportunity of putting something into your case in Paris, without you knowing it?"

Rachel said, with no hesitation, "Oh, yes. On these trips we use our hotel rooms virtually as offices. I try to keep other people out of mine, so that I can work in peace . . . but of course they come wandering in with queries and so on. In fact, Veronica Spence was there nearly all the time I was packing."

"Was she?" Henry asked slowly. He did not like the way his niece was involved in the case, but in spite of himself the thought crossed his mind that she could indeed be a useful source of information. For a fleeting moment he felt a stab of fear that she might be mixed up in the affair in a more sinister way, but he put the thought firmly aside. It was unthinkable. To Rachel, he said, "Well, I suppose we shall find out eventually what it was that somebody hoped to find. Meanwhile, you can repack your case and take it away now, if you like."

"Thank you," said Rachel.

She repacked hurriedly, and Henry saw that her hands were not quite steady. For such a meticulous person, she seemed to be cramming things in higgledy-piggledy; shoes and lingerie and dresses were pushed carelessly one on top of the other. Still, it was understandable that even such an imperturbable character as Rachel Field should be rattled at such a moment.

When the case was shut again, Henry thanked her for her help, told her to leave her address with the sergeant, and sent her back to her own office. Left alone, he took another long look around him. Somewhere in this room, he felt sure, lay the basic clue to the mystery, but he could not see it. He considered the evidence he had heard so far. Several of the witnesses were concealing something; that much was clear. But what? Something to do with Helen's private life, he guessed—a private life which was inextricably mixed up with her work. Perhaps a visit to Hind-hurst might provide the answer. Henry sighed, and went off to have a look at the back door of the *Style* building.

There was nothing remarkable about it. The door was served by a battered lift at the rear of the house—a lift which was used, according to Alf, for bringing up heavy goods such as furniture to the studio for photographing. The door led out into a grubby mews, and was secured by a Yale lock. Alf assured Henry that the two keys to this lock were in his possession. One he carried always on his key ring. The other was kept hanging on a hook in his cubbyhole, in case of emergencies. Anybody with goods to deliver at the back door would ring a bell which sounded in Alf's cubicle in the front hall, and he would detail one of the messengers to go and let them in. He admitted somewhat shame-facedly that he had sanctioned the admission of the cheetah that morning, seeing no harm in it.

"I knew it was expected for Mr. Healy's sitting," he explained. "I didn't like to leave a dangerous beast like that out in the mews."

"You should have asked the sergeant's permission," said Henry, "but never mind."

He left Alf in the middle of a spate of self-justification, and went across the road to have a talk with Nicholas Knight.

6

Beside the entrance to The Orangery, Henry found a door with a smart black plaque on it, on which was written in white lettering, *Nicholas Knight—Haute Couture—First floor."* He climbed a narrow staircase, and found himself facing a pair of swing doors which bore another plaque, similarly inscribed. He pushed them open, and went in. The blast of warm, scented air which greeted him was suddenly and disquietingly reminiscent of the room in which Helen had died.

The long *salon* covered the entire floor of the building. It was close-carpeted in white, with black satin curtains held back by thick ropes of white braid, and a huge vase of white lilies and red roses stood in the empty fireplace. There were small gilt chairs along one wall, and an enormous mirror occupied most of another. Just inside the door was an antique walnut table, at which sat an impossibly blonde girl, painting her fingernails silver. She got up when Henry came in, and swayed langorously towards him.

"Cain Ay help yew?" she enquired, in an accent so affected as to be almost incomprehensible. She looked at Henry's elderly raincoat as a keen gardener might look at a slug.

"I'd like to see Mr. Knight, please," said Henry, and gave the girl his card.

"Just tayk a seat," said the blonde. "Ay'll see if he's free."

She teetered off down the room on her stiltlike heels, leaving Henry perched uncomfortably on the edge of a gilt chair. A minute later she was back.

"Mr. Knayte will see yew rayt away," she said. There was more respect in her voice now. "Would yew come up?"

Henry followed her through the draped black curtains at the far end of the room, and up a small, twisting staircase. Here, as in the offices of *Style*, he noticed an abrupt change of décor once across the borderline between the public façade and the working quarters. The staircase was shabby, its dingy white paint peeling, and worn brown linoleum had replaced the plushy white carpet of the *salon*.

At the head of the stairs, Henry became aware of the sound of chattering female voices, which appeared to be coming from behind a half-open door on his left. On the right was a door marked "Private."

"He's in the aytelier," said the blonde. "Won't yew go in?"

She pushed open the left-hand door, and stood back to let Henry pass.

Once inside, Henry's first instinct was to bolt straight out again. He found himself in a huge, fantastically untidy room, full of people. Bales of fabric, bobbins of thread, pins, discarded scraps of material, tape measures, fashion sketches, feathers, lengths of veiling, artificial flowers, dressmakers' dummies, and ropes of beads were just some of the things that contributed to the heady confusion. From the far end of the room came a perpetual whirring of sewing machines, as half a dozen pale girls in brown overalls pedaled and wheeled and guided the precious cloth under the needles with deft hands.

None of this, however, caused Henry any alarm; what did from his startled nose, were—as far as he could make out—about a hundred and twenty exquisitely lovely girls, dressed only in the briefest of panties and bras. It was only when he caught sight of an infinite series of Nicholas Knights diminishing down apparently endless corridors into the distance that Henry realized that the effect had been caused by the placing of two huge mirrors in such a way as to reflect each other. There were, in fact, only three scantily clad girls, but that was quite enough.

Nicholas Knight was engaged in draping a swathe of green satin round the slim hips of a fourth model—a brunette with a head like Nefertiti, who stood like a resigned statue, regarding her purple fingernails with more interest than pleasure. She, too, was naked from the waist up, except for a scrap of white bra.

"Do come in," said Knight indistinctly, through a mouthful of pins.

"Perhaps I'd better . . . " began Henry nervously, preparing to retreat.

"Shan't be a moment. Get Mr. Tibbett a chair, somebody."

One of the unclothed beauties moved a roll of deep blue velvet to reveal a wooden stool underneath it. Another nymph pulled out the stool, dusted it perfunctorily with a piece of gold lamé, and planted it down conveniently for Henry. He thanked her and sat down, feeling more at ease. He was fascinated by the fact that the girls showed absolutely no self-consciousness at the arrival of a strange man. A moment later, a messenger boy arrived with a bale of cloth, which he carried down the room and slung neatly onto a high shelf with the ease of long practice. The girls greeted him cheerfully, and he replied with equal good humour. There was no squealing or rushing for wraps; no sniggers or suggestive remarks. Henry felt positively ashamed of his earlier reticence. Smut, he decided, was in the eye of the beholder, and did not exist here.

Knight took a swathe of green satin, draped it across the model's bosom, and secured it with a pin.

"Turn round slowly, Rene, there's a love," he said.

With no change of expression, the girl began to revolve gracefully. Knight watched her critically. "Go on. More. A bit more. Stop!" He made an adjustment. "Right. Go on, darling. Now walk away from me." Rene swayed elegantly towards the sewing machines, her hips undulating. Knight watched her through half-closed eyes. "Yes. All right. Stop. That'll do, love. Martha!"

"Yes, Nicholas?" A plump, middle-aged woman dressed in black had materialized at Knight's elbow.

"Get that off Rene and to the cutters," he said. "Use the *toile* of number 18 for the underskirt, and these drapes. It's urgent. Lady Prendergast."

A Chinese girl sauntered up, wearing one of the strangest garments Henry had ever seen. It was, in shape, a full-skirted evening dress, but it was made entirely of tough, cream-coloured cotton crash, liberally ornamented with pencil marks.

"I have wearing the *toile* of number 24, like as you said, Mr. Knight," said the wearer, in a delightfully tinged accent.

"Oh, *dear.*" Knight sounded petulant. "I'd forgotten *all* about that. Well, it will just have to wait. I'm busy."

"Miss Martha say . . . " began the girl.

Knight stamped his smartly shod right foot. "Martha can say what she *likes,*" he exclaimed crossly. "I have an appointment. Go away."

The girl shrugged slightly, intimating that it was none of her business, and sauntered off. Knight turned to Henry.

"I'm most terribly sorry to have kept you waiting, Inspector," he said. "This is the *busiest* time for us poor dressmakers. My summer show next week, and all the big winter parties in full swing, and not a woman in London who doesn't decide to have a new dress, but at the *last* minute, positively the *last.* I don't know *what* they think I am. I've worked my fingers to the bone since before Christmas. *Literally* to the bone."

While doubting this, Henry had already noticed that the young man did look tired and strained. Considering the atmosphere of nervous tension coupled with lack of organization in which he worked, this was not surprising.

"Come into my office," Knight was saying. "Perhaps there we can get a *little* peace."

He led the way out onto the landing, and in through the door marked "Private." Nicholas Knight's office was, if anything, more chaotic than his atelier, because it was smaller. The desk and walls were covered with ink-and-wash sketches of dresses, boldly and competently drawn. Most of them had several scraps of fabric pinned to them. The rest of the room seemed to have disappeared under a ~~~~~~~~~~~~~~ and photographs among which Henry caught sight of one of Veronica apparently about to leap off the Eiffel Tower.

Knight swept an armful of papers off a chair, and indicated that Henry should sit on it. Then he himself sat down in the leather swivel chair on the far side of the desk, offered Henry a black cigarette from a gold case, took one himself, and said, *"There.* Now we can talk."

Henry began almost diffidently. "I don't suppose you can tell me very much, Mr. Knight," he said, "but I have a feeling that your opinions as what I might call an interested outsider may be very valuable."

Nicholas beamed. "Anything I can do . . . " he said, with an expansive gesture. He seemed to have recovered from the nervousness which he had shown in the restaurant.

"For a start, then, did you know Helen Pankhurst?"

"No. That's to say, hardly at all. I knew *of* her, of course, but her job was mainly in the office. I know the fashion staff of *Style* intimately, of course, Teresa and Beth and the others."

"What I'm trying to get at," said Henry, "is a true picture of the relationships between various people."

Knight's smile faded abruptly, and for some reason he looked terrified. "What *do* you mean, Inspector?"

"I mean," said Henry, "Miss Pankhurst's relationships with other people in the office."

"Oh." Knight looked relieved. "I'll tell you all I can." He paused, as if choosing his words carefully. "Of course, you realize that this world of fashion is a *curious* one."

"So people keep telling me," said Henry.

"It isn't that people are not what they seem," Nicholas went on. "On the contrary, they tend to *exaggerate* what they are to the point of absurdity."

Henry nodded. "I have noticed that," he said.

"Take Uncle," said Nicholas. "I presume you've met Uncle by now."

"I have," said Henry, feelingly.

"Well," said Knight, maliciously, "he's an utter fraud, and a nasty one at that. All he is really is an ordinary, pig-headed Irishman. *Very* ordinary," he added, with what sounded like regret. "But he's been practically *forced* to turn himself into a character. The great thing about Helen Pankhurst was that she didn't play that particular game—she remained herself, no more and no less. Or so they tell me."

"So who tells you?"

"Oh, it's common knowledge," said Nicholas, waving a well-cared for hand. "Then take Teresa and Michael. What sort of a marriage is *that,* I ask you?"

"Well, what sort is it?" Henry asked.

"My dear, it's a *farce.*" Nicholas laughed. "When they got married, Teresa was already assistant fashion editor of *Style,* but

Michael had only just started his own studio—one sordid room in Charlotte Street. He was photographing embroidered tea cosies at three guineas a go. Oh, yes, one can see why he married her. For *many* reasons."

"What do you mean?"

"You know who Teresa is, don't you?" Knight asked.

"No."

"Lord Clandon's second daughter," said Nicholas. *"Rolling.* Positively rolling. Teresa took a job simply to amuse herself, and then turned out to have this fantastic flair. Michael was smart enough to jump on the bandwagon. He'd never have got *anywhere* without Teresa. I believe the Clandons were *livid* when she married him. Of course, the *ironic* thing is that the boot's on the other foot now."

"How do you mean?"

"My *dear*," cried Knight, "Michael is *comme il faut*. If he didn't happen to be their son-in-law, the Clandons would never be lucky enough to get *him* at their dinner table. Oh, no."

Privately, Henry doubted this, but he did not say so. He merely remarked, "All that doesn't necessarily mean that their marriage is a farce."

"I don't want to sound bitchy," said Nicholas primly, "but Teresa is *solid bone* above the neck. Solid. A wonderful fashion sense, and nothing else. And Michael has *always* had *all sorts* of other interests." The way in which he said these words was chilling in its venom. Henry wondered exactly what Knight meant, and asked him as much.

At once, the designer became cagey. "Oh, this and that," he said. "One hears rumours, you know."

"Did any of these rumours concern Helen Pankhurst?" Henry asked.

Knight looked genuinely surprised. "Th h ..." "No no.." "Th not Helen ... that is ... " he hesitated, and then went on, with blatant untruthfulness, "I'm not a gossip, Inspector. It's perfectly possible that there *have* been rumours about Michael and Helen. I just don't happen to have heard them, that's all." He sounded faintly aggrieved by the fact.

"What are the rumours you *have* heard?" Henry persisted. But he could not persuade Knight to be more definite. Michael had artistic and intellectual interests, he said. He and Teresa had nothing in common—never had had. Michael moved in a different world. Michael was really more interested in the theatre and ballet these days than in fashion. Henry gave up, and—resolving to return to the matter on another occasion—asked about the events of the previous evening.

"I'd been working late up here," said Knight. "It must have been about midnight when I decided to go down to the pub underneath for a nightcap."

"By 'the pub underneath,' you mean The Orangery?"

"Yes. Terrible place, isn't it? Really sordid. But useful, if one lives here."

Henry glanced out of the window, and saw that he was looking across Earl Street, and directly at the *Style* building.

"Did you notice the lights on over the road?" he asked.

"I didn't exactly *notice* them," said Nicholas. "I knew they'd all be there late, because of the Collections. I'd probably have noticed if the lights *hadn't* been on, if you follow me."

"So," said Henry, "you went down to The Orangery, where you met Mr. Goring and Mr. Barry."

"That's right. They were just finishing dinner. Both in crashingly good form, I regret to say. Horace told *endless* stories, *so* true it wasn't unfunny. Godfrey was putting on his hearty, one-of-the-boys act, which must have been hell to do on tonic water. I can only presume he'd done some sort of a deal with Horace, and the dinner was to clinch it. I was exhausted—but *exhausted*. I don't know *how* I stood it."

"Then why," said Henry, "did you accept Mr. Goring's invitation to go to his house afterwards?"

Nicholas looked a little uncomfortable. "I've *always* said," he replied, "that I *refuse* to kowtow to people I don't like, just because they're important. Nevertheless, one can't get away from it—it wouldn't *do* for me to be bad friends with *Style*. It simply wouldn't. You do see that, don't you?"

"Yes, I see it," said Henry. "So you and Mr. Barry drove on to Brompton Square, while Mr. Goring picked up the others from the office. By the way, was Mrs. Goring there?"

"Lorna? No, she wasn't. She was in the country. They've got a place in Surrey, you know, as well as the town house. There's another clever fellow who married money."

"Tell me, did any of the *Style* people strike you as being unusually upset or nervous, or different from their normal selves?"

"Normal?" Nicholas gave a little shriek of laughter. "None of them are particularly *normal* at the best of times. Uncle was as rude as ever—thoroughly *offensive,* in fact. Michael was teasing the pants off poor old Horace, which I must say I rather *enjoyed.* Teresa was a bit quiet, I thought, and Margery looked positively ill once or twice."

"And what about Miss Field?"

"Miss Field? Who's she?"

"Miss French's secretary. You gave her a lift home."

"Oh, the siren of Surbiton. Well, what about her?"

"Did she appear to be just as usual?"

"I've no idea," said Nicholas. "I'd never met her before. She could hardly have been *more* usual, poor dear, if you follow me."

"So you dropped Miss Field and Mr. Barry home, and then came back here?"

"That's right. I live in the attic, in elegant squalor. Do you want to see my little nest?"

"No, thank you," said Henry firmly. "Did you notice what time you got in?"

"It was round about three," said Knight. "I can't tell you exactly. I know I left Brompton Square at half past two."

"And when you got back here," Henry went on, "did you notice anything out of the way? Any comings or goings?"

"I *did* notice one thing. When I went to pull the curtains in my bedroom, I saw a girl coming out of the *Style* building. A most *odd*-looking creature in a terrible orange dress and a white stole and spectacles. *That's* not one of the fashion staff, I said to myself."

Henry nodded. "That must have been Miss Piper, the features editor," he said. "What did she do?"

"Walked off down the street."

"And you didn't see anybody else?"

"I caught a glimpse of Helen, as a matter of fact. She was typing away. She was certainly alive then. After that I pulled the curtains and went to bed and simply *died.*"

"I see," said Henry. "Thank you very much." He consulted his notebook. "I suppose I should have a word with Mr. Barry some time," he said. "Can you tell me where to contact him? You know him well, I believe."

"I work for him," said Nicholas shortly.

"Work for him?" Henry was surprised. "But I thought that
. . . I mean, you operate on a very high level, and he . . . "

"He makes mass-produced little garments to sell in Wigan.
That's what you mean, isn't it?" Nicholas sounded amused.

"Well . . ." said Henry, embarrassed.

"You're quite right, Inspector," said Knight, "and yet you are
abysmally wrong. You don't seem to have understood the revo-
lution in popular taste. What's wrong with Wigan? Wigan may
not lead the world in fashion—Paris does that. But Wigan is as
bright as a button and literally treading on the *heels* of Paris.
And the working girls have a mint of money to spend." Knight
leant forward. Launched on his own subject, he had lost much
of his affectation, and Henry remembered Goring's remarks
about the young man's business ability. "People like me are an
anachronism," Nicholas went on. "The money is in ready-made
clothes these days, and that's where the good designers should
be working. And indeed they are. Every great name in couture
has some sort of a wholesale outlet nowadays. It's plain common
sense. Five thousand dresses at ten guineas bring in more profit
than one dress at a hundred guineas. The point of a *salon* like
mine is to get one's name and designs *known*—that's worth any
sacrifice. Any sacrifice at all."

He paused, looking a little embarrassed. "I was lucky. My . . .
a friend provided enough money for me to start up here. Now
I'm known. I really knew I'd arrived when Barry approached
me six months ago and asked me to design for his wholesale
collection. You see, I have a certain . . . flair, if you like . . .
for translating Paris designs for my customers. I did about a
quarter of the last Barrimode collection, and next time I'm
going to have a special line all to myself. Barry himself is vulgar
and boring, but he knows the business inside out."

"Where do I find him?" Henry asked.

"Two-eighty-six Pope Street. Just off Poland Street. That's
where most of the wholesalers cluster, God help them," said
Knight.

As he was leaving, something struck Henry. "By the way," he
said, his hand on the door handle, "were you in Paris last week?"

To his surprise, Knight turned very white, and when he answered, his voice had a high note of hysteria in it. "I was *not!*"

he cried. "Certainly not! I *never* go to Paris. *Everyone* knows that. I was here the *entire* week. *Anyone* will tell you!"

"There's no need to get so excited," said Henry, considerably intrigued. "It just occurred to me that you might have been, since you told me that you translated Paris designs."

"I have an *eye*," squeaked Nicholas. "I look at the photographs and I can *see* the cut. I can *see* the seaming. I don't *need* a *toile*." He stopped abruptly.

"What's a *toile*?" Henry asked.

Knight became calmer. "You remember the Chinese girl in the atelier, in the dress made of cotton?" he said. "That was a *toile*. One of my own, naturally. It's the model made and cut exactly as the original, but in cheap cotton. Manufacturers buy them from Paris—and very dear they are, too. Hundreds of pounds, a good *toile* will cost you. But once a wholesaler has bought the *toile*, he can adapt and copy it as he likes."

"I see," said Henry. "Thank you. I'm learning a lot. So you make Paris copies without buying *toiles*."

"There's no law against it," said Knight defensively. "I told you, I don't go near the Collections. I work from photographs, by eye."

"That must save you a lot of money," said Henry guilelessly. He opened the door and went out. On the landing, he paused for a second—long enough to hear Knight picking up the telephone and saying, "Get me Barrimodes."

At that moment, the woman called Martha came out of the atelier, and Henry was forced, regretfully, to abandon his eaves-dropping. He walked slowly down the stairs, for he had plenty to think about.

In the street, he looked at his watch. It was half past four. He had only one more interview to conduct at *Style*—an inter-view which he did not expect to reveal a great deal. This was with Donald MacKay, the assistant art editor, in whom Veronica seemed so interested. It did not seem to Henry that he would have much to contribute. However, as so often happens, he found his talk with Donald unexpectedly rewarding.

As far as the events of the previous evening were concerned, Donald had nothing new to add. He had noticed the Thermos flask standing in the darkroom, and confirmed that it was still there when he went home at half past one. He had been working flat out, he said, preparing sample layouts for Patrick, and had not noticed the bottle of cyanide at all. Like everybody else, however, he knew it was there, and he knew where it was kept. He told Henry about his meeting in the street with Goring, and added that he had, after much searching, finally found a taxi to take him to Battersea.

When Henry broached the subject of Helen and Michael, Donald was relaxed, and in a mood to talk. "Oh, that," he said. "Yes, of course I'd heard about it. Olwen made sure of that. But I'll tell you one thing—there was something phony about it. Don't ask me what. I'm only a junior employee here. The magazine is run by a tight little clique—Margery, Teresa, Uncle, and Helen." He paused. "I suppose you realize that any one of them, except possibly Uncle, could make a fortune by going into public relations?"

"What exactly do you mean by that?" Henry asked.

"Just what I say," said Donald. "I also mean to imply that they are adept at making people believe what they want them to believe." He leant forward. "You're not dealing with amateurs, Inspector. You're dealing with professionals. Correct me if I'm wrong," he added earnestly, "but I imagine that in your job you generally come up against people who are pretty overawed by your official status, and who'll tell you the strict truth unless they have something really guilty to hide. That simply doesn't apply here." He paused. "I don't really have the faintest idea what I'm talking about, except that there's something *wrong* with this whole setup of Michael and Helen."

"You mean," said Henry, "that this story may be a smoke screen to hide something else?"

"Yes," said Donald. "I do. Just that."

"The same thought had occurred to me," said Henry, "but what?"

"I have no idea," said Donald.

"Mr. Walsh," said Henry, "was very fond of Helen, wasn't he?"

"He certainly was," replied Donald promptly. "We all . . . that is, everybody liked her. Except Miss Field."

"Was that important?" Henry asked. "I mean, Miss Field is only a secretary, isn't she?"

Donald grinned. "A bit more than that," he said. "She's a very influential person, in her own way. When Margery retires—which she's bound to do soon—it will make a big difference to Miss Field who becomes editor. She disliked Helen, because Helen was too much like her. As editor, Helen would have wanted to keep her finger on everything, even the filing system. She wasn't a person who could delegate responsibility. Miss Field despises Teresa as a person, but she knows that if Teresa were editor she'd leave all the administration to her secretary, and Miss Field would become more powerful than ever. Do you see what I mean?"

"Yes," said Henry, thoughtfully. "Yes, I do see."

7

Henry arrived home at half past six. He was tired, and it was raining. He had a dismal journey in a Number 19 bus, capped by a damp walk through small, dripping streets, and as he put his key into the front door of the flat, he was absorbed by visions of a large Scotch and soda, slippers, a quiet supper, and a hot bath.

Consequently, he was annoyed to hear, as he came into the hall, the sound of feminine voices raised in laughter. He was, in fact, prepared to be very grumpy indeed, until he reached the living-room door and was able to identify the voices as those of Emmy, his wife, and Veronica, his niece. Since these were his two favourite women, he was prepared to forgive them a great deal. Nevertheless, it was with the firm intention of sending Veronica home as soon as possible that he entered the living room. His resolution was somewhat damped by the fact that neither of them even noticed him come in.

Emmy was on her knees on the floor, cutting out—with the aid of a paper pattern—what appeared to be sections of a parachute in nubbly blue tweed. Veronica was lying on the sofa with her legs hooked over the back of it, revealing a large amount of shapely leg encased in bright woollen tartan tights.

"And there was the wretched Duchess," Veronica was saying, "in the *identical* dress—but absolutely the same, Aunt Emmy—and you should have seen the drama that went on. You see, she'd been to Monnier and bought the model for heaven knows how much, and to be confronted by Felicity Fraser in positively the *same* . . . "

Henry shut the door behind him with a certain amount of noise. Emmy jumped up guiltily. "Darling! Home already! Goodness, how the time goes. I wasn't expecting you for hours. Would you like a drink?"

"Yes, please," said Henry, with a touch of pique. "What are you doing?"

"Making a skirt," said Emmy. "Ronnie says this nubbly tweed it the latest craze in Paris. *And* it doesn't crease. Feel it."

"Do you mind if I just have my drink?" said Henry. "I'm very tired."

"Poor Uncle Henry." Veronica smiled at him upside down. "He's been wonderful. Everyone's tremendously impressed."

"I dare say," said Henry. "Meanwhile, if nobody minds . . . "

"Uncle Henry, I've been doing masses of detecting for you. You've no idea."

"My dear Veronica," said Henry, "I'm sure that Scotland Yard will be suitably grateful. But for the moment, all I'm interested in is food and drink and a bath and bed."

"But, Uncle Henry, you *said* . . . "

"Darling Ronnie," said Henry, "I'm sure you'll be tremendously useful to us—but please, not now."

"Pig," said Veronica. "I was just telling Aunt Emmy about the time when the Duchess of Basingstoke turned up at a ball in exactly the same dress as . . . "

"So I heard," said Henry.

"Here's your drink, darling," said Emmy. "Has it been an awful day?"

"Pretty vile," said Henry, feeling considerably better. He sank into his favourite armchair and kicked off his shoes.

"And Uncle Henry, the funny thing is that . . . "

"Ronnie," said Emmy, warningly.

"Oh, well," said Veronica, in a slightly hurt voice, "if you don't want to hear what I've found out, it's your loss. I've got to go anyhow. Donald is calling for me at eight."

"Donald MacKay?" Henry asked, from the comfortable depths of his chair.

"Yes, of course." Veronica swung her legs off the back of the sofa and stood up.

"Do you know him, Henry?" Emmy asked, with a trace of anxiety in her voice.

"I've met him," said Henry.

"What's he like?"

"I'd say he was a very astute young man," said Henry.

"He's an angel-poppet," said Veronica. She kissed Henry on the nose, and disappeared in a flash of tartan stockings.

Emmy started to clear her dressmaking off the floor. "Ronnie was telling me . . . " she began, but Henry stopped her.

"I'm dead beat, Emmy love," he said. "Please, can we just eat and go to bed?" Thus, he gave himself a lot more work than he need have had, together with considerable worry. One never can tell about such things.

The next day, after a short session in his office at Scotland Yard, Henry telephoned Barrimodes and made an appointment to see Mr. Horace Barry. He took a taxi to Pope Street, and was glad he had done so, for he doubted whether he would ever have found it on foot. Although it lay just off Oxford Street, this was a part of London with which Henry had had little previous contact. He was fascinated by the maze of small, bustling streets, whose every house seemed to be the headquarters of one or more wholesale businesses connected with the clothing trade. Where there were shop windows, they were full of wax models and tailors' dummies, or devoted to "display materials"—wicker hat stands, white wire shoe racks, and those faintly indecent severed legs made of transparent plastic and designed to exhibit stockings. There were small shops which sold nothing except the shapeless felt "hoods" which would eventually be steamed and seamed into smart hats, and others dealing in buckram interlining, buttons of every conceivable size, shape and colour, and all the braids, veilings, ribbons, and trimmings which are the garnish of fashion.

The little streets were full of urgent messenger boys carrying bales of fabric, and outside many doorways stood vans labeled with famous names. A glimpse into the interior of one of these showed Henry that it was, in fact, a huge mobile wardrobe, in which rows of dresses hung tidily on racks, waiting to be delivered to shops and stores all over the country. It was an area which proclaimed its particular commercial interest as unambiguously as Billingsgate or Covent Garden.

Two-eighty-six Pope Street was a tall, dingy house with a series of plaques on the wall of the bleak entrance hall. These informed Henry that all enquiries for Barrimodes should be addressed to the first floor, that the fourth floor housed Marcelle Millinery Ltd., and the fifth, Beadcraft and Simon's Belts. He also learned that No Hawkers or Circulars were welcome. Henry climbed the concrete staircase to the first floor.

Barrimodes' showroom was a replica of a hundred others in the neighbourhood. A large room with a beige carpet, it covered most of the first floor, and was equipped with long racks on which hung specimens of Horace Barry's latest collection. Two smart, middle-aged women with shrewd faces were sitting in armchairs sipping coffee and making notes, while a series of tired-looking mannequins pirouetted and postured for their benefit. Occasionally one of them would lean forward and catch hold of the skirt of a dress, rubbing the fabric knowledgeably between her fingers. A very smart young man with a carnation in his buttonhole hovered between them, plying them with cigarettes, coffee, and pleasantries, and enlarging on the merits of the Collection. Henry guessed, rightly, that they were buyers from provincial stores. They were obviously valued customers, and accustomed to being pampered. In fact, they received the young man's blandishments with a spine-chilling lack of interest, which, Henry supposed, must be a necessary defence mechanism on the part of people whose profession called for hard-headed judgment in the face of continual flattery and persuasion.

A girl in a dark blue suit came forward to greet Henry. "Oh, yes," she said, glancing at his card. "Mr. Barry is expecting you. Will you come up?"

She escorted Henry out of the showroom, and up to the floor above. This was virtually a warehouse, stacked with row upon row of garments. The girl led the way through the aisles of coat racks, and knocked on a door marked "Private."

"Come in," called a rich, fruity voice with a markedly mid-European accent.

The girl opened the door. "Chief Inspector Tibbett, Mr. Barry," she said, and stood aside to let Henry pass.

Horace Barry was a small, stout man, with sparse grey hair

and thick horn-rimmed spectacles. He looked more like a banker or a stockholder than a leader of fashion, and his un-English origin was pronounced as he said, "Ah, Inspector. Come in. To sit down, if you please. This is a terrible affair, no? You come about the murder at *Style*, no?"

"Yes," said Henry. "I'm sorry to have to trouble you . . . "

"No trouble, Inspector. No trouble in the smallest. I fear I shall not be able to give you a great help, but anything I can do . . . "

Henry sat down on the other side of the big, shiny desk, and said, "You have evidently heard what happened."

"I have read the papers." As Barry gesticulated, his stubby fingers reminded Henry of those of a musician; they had great strength combined with artistic sensitivity.

"Miss Pankhurst was poisoned," said Henry. "I have come to see you because you dined with Mr. Goring on Tuesday evening, and went to his house afterwards. I thought you might be able to give me your impressions of the people who were there."

"I can indeed . . . you would care for a cup of coffee or a drink, Inspector?"

"No, thank you," said Henry. "Just tell me about Tuesday evening."

"Well, for a start I dined with Goring, and we finalized my plans for colour advertizement in the May issue. Then Nicholas joined us—Nicholas Knight. You know him?"

"I have spoken to him," said Henry.

"A brilliant boy. Brilliant. He has flair. He captures the essence of Paris."

"He tells me he is working for you."

"That is correct. He designed a part of my autumn collection, and I have big plans for him in the summer. My new advertizing campaign will be built round his name. I am bringing out a new range of higher-priced garments with a label quite different, very high-class and discreet. Imagine . . . black satin with white lettering . . . 'A Nicholas Knight design for Barrimodes.' Dignified. Simple. My agents wanted me to use a cheap slogan . . . 'Paris-Plus by Barrimodes' . . . some such nonsense. I refused. I chase now the customers with class. 'A Nicholas Knight design'—no more. But I am boring you?"

"Not at all," said Henry, "but I'd like to get back to Tuesday night. You know the staff of *Style* fairly well, I presume?"

"Some of them." Barry smiled expansively. "Miss Connolly, she who does the Young Style, she comes often to me for garments to photograph, for I make good clothes in her price range. Ah, what a girl!" Barry kissed his fingertips. "What talent! What brains! The first time she is here, is two years ago. She look my Collection, she say, 'Mr. Barry, you make this dress plain white, remove the pockets and cut the sleeves short—so—and I will give it a whole page.' I was wild in anger. 'So a child should tell me my business?' I think. But *Style* is *Style*, so I do as she say and I sell two thousand copies. I never forget that, all my life. I never again not listen what she say."

"But Miss Connolly wasn't there on Tuesday evening," said Henry, patiently. "What about the others?"

"Miss French—great lady. Great power. She does me honour to come twice a year to my big Collections. Ah . . . there is authority. Nobody like her. Miss Manners, too—she knows fashion. But not always do we agree. 'Your taste is too good, my dear Miss Manners,' I tell her. 'Your taste is for the reader of *Style*. Very good. But me, I have to sell also to those whose taste is other.' Ah, but wait till she see my new Nicholas Knight range . . . "

"Going back to Tuesday," said Henry doggedly. "You all went back to Brompton Square. What happened there?"

Mr. Barry's normally cheerful face assumed an angry frown, as if at some unpleasant memory. "Patrick Walsh and Michael Healy," he said, darkly. "Such rudeness. This I do not tolerate. There was another lady there, whom I had not met before . . . Miss French's secretary, I believe. A Miss Field. I feel sad for her, for she is . . . how shall I say . . . out of her *ambiance*. I speak to her about cats, of which we are both fond. Michael Healy is talking of art, as usual. That young man should stick to his camera. With it, he is a genius. I am not denying. Does that give him the right to be insulting?" Barry sounded really angry. "I tell him. 'Mr. Healy,' I say, 'I may not be competent to judge the plays of Ionesco, as you remark. I may not appreciate what you call the line of Nureyev, but I know my own line. I make money and I pay you well to photograph for me. If I did not mind my business, there would be no pay for you, remember. So I mind my business, you mind yours.' Oh, yes, he is good photographer, but is not the only one. He needn't think I will go on using him if he insults me so."

"Did anyone mention Miss Pankhurst during the evening?" Henry asked.

"I do not remember that they did. We did not stay there long, at Brompton Square. I tell you frankly, Inspector, I was not enjoy myself, with Walsh and Healy both taking pleasures to be rude to me. So—they call me vulgar. So—I put good money in their pockets? What for they complain? So I go and speak of cats to this poor Miss Field, who has spoken to nobody all the time. I was happy when Nicholas came up and said we should leave. He say he also take Miss Field, for she live in the same direction as I. She too is glad to leave, I can tell. And if you believe it, Inspector, while she go collect her things . . . that man Walsh . . . " He broke off. "Now that I think, Miss Pankhurst *was* mention. The man Walsh come up and start insulting Nicholas, as always."

"How did he insult him?"

Barry looked uncomfortable. "He make bad innuendo about . . . morals," he said unhappily. "Then he say, 'You think you got the support of *Style,* don't you, you little—' He use bad word. 'Well,' he say, 'I can tell you, some of us don't like your particular carry-on. Me for one and Helen for another. We know about you, and we're after you. You *and* your friend.' "

"What was Knight's reaction?" Henry asked.

"Poor boy. He was without words. Such an attack . . . and such untruth. Anyhow, before he could reply, Miss Field returns and we go. Nicholas is worried and upset, I can see that. He say little in the car. He drop me home soon before three. There, I have told you all."

"Thank you," said Henry. "Did you know the dead girl at all?"

"By name only. I never met her."

"By the way," said Henry, "were you in Paris last week?"

"But of course." Barry beamed again, all his good humour restored. "Is expensive, but one cannot afford not to go. I buy some *toiles* for my Collection, sure, but mostly I pay my entrance fee just for to look and remember the line."

"You mean that you have to pay to get in to a Paris Collection?" Henry asked, intrigued.

"Of course . . . a wholesaler must always pay. It is only the press and private customers who go in free. How else could couture exist?"

"Did you come across any of the *Style* team while you were there?"

"No, no. Press shows, buyers' shows, they are quite separate. No, I did not see any of them."

"I see," said Henry. He was feeling depressed. He could not make up his mind whether the smoothly unrevealing statements which he was accumulating in his notebook were as innocent as they seemed, or whether—as Donald MacKay had hinted—he was up against a very professional conspiracy to deceive him.

"How well do you know Mr. Goring?" Henry asked.

"How well? I know him for business. I lunch with him. I dine with him. I play golf with him. We respect each other."

"Do you know his wife?"

"Ah, the beautiful Lorna. I meet her when I spend week end for playing golf in Surrey, at their country house."

"At Hindhurst, isn't it?" said Henry.

Barry looked puzzled. "Hindhurst?" he said. "This name I do not know. No, no. Goring's house is near Virginia Water. Convenient for Sunningdale."

"Of course," said Henry. "Stupid of me. I was mixing him up with somebody else. Mrs. Goring is a very striking woman, isn't she?"

"A spitfire," said Barry. "A personality too large for her life. She should not have left the stage. Oh, but she leads him a dance. I wouldn't be in his shoes, I can tell you. But there—he is crazy for her, and he is happy. Perhaps it is good for a man who is like a god in his business to be treat like a puppydog in his own house," he added, shrewdly. "I remember many years ago I was in Prague with my brother and his wife. She was like Lorna Goring—the same red hair and no fashion sense. And while we were there . . . "

Mercifully, the reminiscence was cut short by the ringing of the telephone. "Excuse," said Barry, picking up the receiver. "One moment only . . . "

"I really must go," said Henry. "Thank you very much, Mr. Barry. Goodbye."

He walked quickly out of the room, leaving Barry engaged in

a lively discussion with Manchester on the delivery date of Shantung shirtwaist dresses.

Back in his office at Scotland Yard, Henry wrote a long and thoughtful report on the progress of the case. Several times he put a large query in the margin, indicating an inconsistency of evidence which required investigation. Then he called his sergeant.

"If anyone wants me this afternoon," he said, "I'm not available. I've had enough of London for the moment. I'm going to get some country air. Order me a car, will you? I'll drive myself."

"Very good, sir," said the sergeant, giving a passable imitation of the incomparable Jeeves. "Where would you be going to, then, sir?"

"First, Virginia Water and then Hindhurst. They're at opposite ends of Surrey, but I should have time to do both. I want you to find out for me the address of Mr. Godfrey Goring's country house near Virginia Water. Then get onto the Hindhurst police, and get them cracking on enquiring among the local doctors to find out if Miss Pankhurst consulted any of them. I'll be with them about five o'clock, and I shall need a photograph of the dead woman to take with me."

As the sergeant was leaving the room, Henry added, "Don't get on to *Style* about Mr. Goring's address. Look it up in the local phone book."

Henry had already put on his overcoat and scarf, preparatory to going out for a bite of lunch at his favourite pub, when his telephone rang, and Veronica's breathless voice cooed over the line. "Uncle Henry, where *have* you been?"

"What do you mean, where have I been?"

"I mean, you haven't been at *Style*. There's nobody there but that poker-faced sergeant."

"I've been doing other things, if you must know," said Henry.

"You haven't been taken off the case, or anything, have you?" Veronica asked anxiously.

"No, of course not."

"Oh, *good*. Because in that case you can take me out to lunch, because I've got something *terribly thrilling* to tell you."

"Oh, very well," said Henry. He was experiencing the sense of satisfaction that always followed the tabulation of a report, however inconclusive, and he was looking forward to his afternoon in the country. "It'll have to be a quick snack, though. I haven't much time. Where are you now?"

"I'm in the phone booth at the back of *Style*. I thought we might go to The Orangery."

"Oh, did you? Well, you can think again. I'm not made of money, even if you are. I'll meet you outside the Coventry Street Corner House in ten minutes."

"O.K. Can we have roast beef and baked potatoes and ice cream?"

"We can have anything you like," said Henry, "but don't be late."

She was, of course. Ten minutes. She arrived wind-blown and breathless and lighting up the raw, grey January day like Persephone escaped from Hades, as she ran across Leicester Square with her fair hair flying and her scarlet coat swirling behind her.

"I couldn't get a taxi anywhere," she announced, shaking her hair out of her eyes. "I had to *walk!*"

Henry, who did not enjoy being the center of attention, took her arm and led her firmly into the restaurant. When one went out with Veronica, one had to face the fact that she did not go unnoticed, and already people were turning to stare.

Veronica was not old enough to respect Godfrey Goring's conventions when it came to business lunches. She was bursting with information, and had begun to impart it even before she and Henry were settled at their corner table.

"I'm sure it's terribly important, Uncle Henry. I found out quite by accident, you see. I wonder if she'll tell you herself . . . "

"We'd better order, Ronnie," said Henry, aware of the waiter at his elbow.

"Roast beef and baked potato," said Veronica briefly. "You see, it was because Beth wanted to borrow one, and Miss Field seemed to be the best person, and I was with Beth because of my sitting, and . . . "

"Two roast beef and baked potatoes," said Henry to the waiter. To Veronica, he added, "Keep your voice down a bit, Ronnie. What did Beth want to borrow from Miss Field?"

"Her key." Veronica's big eyes were wide with excitement. "Beth has a lot of extra work to do, you see, because of the murder holding everything up and the Paris stuff being late. And then Teresa came in when we'd almost finished the sitting and said that Beth had to do her whole feature again for April, which I think is absolutely . . . "

"Keep to the point," said Henry. "Beth Connolly thought she'd have to work late, so she asked Miss Field to lend her the key to the front door. Is that right?"

"Yes," said Veronica. "And Miss Field went and looked in her bag, and then . . . " She paused for effect " . . . then she came back and said she'd lost it!"

"The key?" asked Henry sharply.

"Yes. She was terribly upset about it. She swore it had been in her bag on Tuesday, and it had gone. If it had been Miss Manners, or somebody like that, I'd just have thought she'd left it somewhere or dropped it. But Miss Field simply *doesn't* lose things. I'm certain it's been stolen! It must have been! There now, haven't I found out something useful for you?"

"It's very interesting," said Henry. "I'd hardly call it useful. It makes things more complicated. I'd been working on the assumption that only one of the people who had a key could have . . . never mind. I wonder if anyone had the opportunity of getting at Miss Field's handbag on Tuesday evening."

'I suppose everyone did. And yet—I don't know. She generally works with it on the floor beside her desk, and Donald told me that she never left the office the whole evening. Everyone else was milling round the darkroom and everywhere, he said, but Miss Field never budged once."

"Margery French said the same thing," said Henry thoughtfully.

The roast beef arrived, as delicious as always, and for some minutes Veronica concentrated on eating, with the vast appetite of the young and slim. Henry was lost in thought, and was only roused from his speculations by Veronica's voice saying, "Isn't it, Uncle Henry?"

"Isn't what what?" Henry asked indistinctly, through a mouthful of potato.

"You haven't been listening," said Veronica accusingly. "I said, isn't this much more interesting than Nicholas Knight's dresses?"

"Much more," Henry agreed. "Tell me—Donald hasn't got a key of his own, has he?"

"No, he hasn't. But if you're implying that . . . "

"I'm not implying anything," said Henry. "I'm just thinking

aloud. Ernest Jenkins hasn't got a key either, has he?"

"Of course not. Can I have some more butter, please?"

"Here." Henry pushed his butter dish towards her. "Won't all those potatoes make you fat?"

"Nothing makes me fat," said Veronica, smugly and truthfully. "And there's something else I haven't told you."

"What's that?"

"Margery French is going to retire," said Veronica, with the air of a conjuror producing a rabbit from a hat.

"I knew that."

"Oh." Veronica sounded disappointed. "You shouldn't have. It's a deadly secret."

"Then how do you know?"

"I mean—it *was* a deadly secret until today. Today it was announced officially. Miss French retires in March, and Miss Manners is going to be editor. The whole office is buzzing with it. Donald says that Uncle says that Olwen's furious. I don't know why. Am I being useful?"

"Very useful, Ronnie," said Henry seriously, "but . . . " He hesitated. "I think you'd better lay off detecting at *Style.*"

"Uncle Henry! You *said* . . . "

"I don't want to frighten you," said Henry, "but what you seem to regard as a game, is in fact very serious and could be dangerous. We're dealing with a murderer, and I want you to keep out of it."

"You don't mean that somebody might try to kill *me?*" Veronica laughed. "Oh, don't be silly."

"I'm not being silly," said Henry. "Can't you steer clear of the place until all this is cleared up?"

"Steer clear of *Style?* Of course I can't. It's the most important thing in my career. And besides . . . "

"And besides, there's Donald MacKay," said Henry. He did not smile.

Veronica blushed. "That has nothing to do with it."

"Oh, yes, it has," said Henry. "Possibly more than you think." There was a silence. Veronica speared a piece of beef in a markedly stubborn manner.

"Oh, well," said Henry, "I can't dictate to you, I suppose. Your career is your own. But please, Ronnie—no more detecting. I'm very serious. You do your job and let me do mine."

"We'll see about that," said Veronica.

8

Red Field Farm, Downley, near Virginia Water, had not been a working farm for many years. This was immediately clear to Henry as he turned the car into the wrought-iron gateway, flanked by dripping chestnut trees. The pretty, timbered Tudor farmhouse was all that remained of the agricultural past. Now, it stood in an acre of carefully landscaped garden, and its surrounding fields and pastures had been sold off, one by one, as sites for the country residences of prosperous businessmen. These residences, by the look of them, all dated from the present century, and Henry decided that he much preferred those which were unashamedly modern to those which tried, self-consciously, to ape Tudor or Georgian architecture. Among them, like a live lion in a toyshop full of Teddy Bears, Red Field Farm brooded in authentic, if caged, splendour.

The drive widened into a semicircular sweep outside the dark oak hall door. Henry parked the car neatly, walked over to the door, and tugged at the old-fashioned bell-pull. From somewhere inside, a melodious tinkling indicated that his efforts had been successful. He looked up, and caught a glimpse of a face at an upstairs window, watching him with furtive, worried intensity. The face of Lorna Goring.

There was no sign of strain or anxiety, however, when—a moment or so later—the door was flung open with a richly theatrical gesture, and Lorna cried, "Inspector Tibbett! Please, please come in. And excuse my disarray—I had no idea you were coming. Is this an official visit or a friendly one?"

"Both, I hope," said Henry, getting a word in with difficulty.

"Mind your head on that beam—it catches nearly everybody the first time," said Lorna, leading the way into a comfortable, chintzy lounge hall, where two spaniels were sleeping noisily on a sofa in front of a smouldering log fire. "Sit down and have a drink. What would you like? Just chuck the dogs off—they're used to it. Tea, coffee, whisky, champagne . . . "

"I'd love a cup of tea, if it's not too much trouble," said Henry, giving one spaniel a tentative shove. The dog responded by rolling over onto its back and snoring.

"No trouble at all," said Lorna. "Get off, Poopsie, you lazy bitch." She grasped the spaniel's legs firmly and hauled her onto the floor. Poopsie certainly seemed quite accustomed to this treatment, for she immediately went to sleep again.

"Sit down," said Lorna.

Without much enthusiasm, Henry did so. The loose cover of the sofa was filthy and covered with Poopsie's long golden hairs—most of which, Henry reflected gloomily, would certainly transfer themselves to his trousers.

"I'll go and get the tea," said Lorna. "Put another log on the fire, there's an angel." She turned, and as she did so, caught sight of herself in the mirror above the fireplace. "Heavens, I look a fright. I do apologize."

As a matter of fact, Lorna Goring looked very beautiful. She could hardly fail to do so, since Nature had so arranged matters as to give her one of the most classically perfect faces of her generation, and had thrown in a lithe, long-legged figure and magnificent red hair as additional bonuses. Today, however, it was even more obvious than it had been at The Orangery that Lorna considered Nature's bounty to be ample, and in no need of any outside assistance. Her tawny hair was tangled, her only make-up was a splash of carelessly applied lipstick. She wore dark green silk trousers and a pale blue silk shirt. Both were immaculately cut, but the trousers were secured at the waist by a large and eye-catching safety pin, and the shirt was grubby. As she raised her slender hands in a vain effort to tidy her hair, Henry saw that the vivid red varnish on her nails was chipped

and peeling. He thought of Godfrey Goring's smooth impecca-
bility, and of the exquisite, uncrackable façade of *Style* and its
employees, and found it hard to reconcile either with this gorgeous, sluttish creature. He could only suppose that Lorna's
happy-go-lucky flaunting of all *Style*'s precepts made a welcome
change for Goring when his work was done. Welcome or not,
he reflected, it must certainly be a change.

Lorna disappeared into the kitchen, calling to Henry to help
himself to a cigarette. In a few minutes she was back with a tray,
on which stood a teapot shrouded in a pink knitted cosy. This
was so constructed that the woollen hemisphere represented the
skirt of an eighteenth-century beauty, while the lady's upper
portions, made of china, surmounted the pot. The cosy was
stained with tea, and the lady had lost one arm. Two assorted
cups, both chipped, a very beautiful Georgian silver sugar bowl
and a half-pint bottle of milk completed the load.

Lorna evicted the second spaniel, sat down and poured out
the tea. Then she said, "Of course, I'm tremendously pleased and
flattered that you've come to see me, but I don't see how I can
possibly help you. I haven't been to London for months—until
yesterday, when we met in The Orangery."

"I envy you," said Henry. "It must be pleasant for your husband, too, to be able to get down here, away from town."

For a moment, Lorna's face clouded. Then she laughed, rather
too loudly, and said, "Oh, Godfrey hates the country. He lives
in the London house, and only comes down for week ends.
Sometimes. Of course," she added, "he has to be in London because of his work." Henry had the impression that she wished she
had thought of saying this in the first place.

He said, "A lot of people do commute every day from here
to London, don't they?"

"Godfrey doesn't," said Lorna shortly.

Henry did not press the point, but went on, "How well did
you know Helen Pankhurst, Mrs. Goring?"

"I don't know any of them, except to look at," said Lorna.
"Godfrey won't—I mean, he doesn't approve of wives who
meddle in their husbands' business, and neither do I." There
was an unnecessary defiance in her last three words. "I have
to appear occasionally, at the annual office party and so on, but
otherwise I keep my nose out. Between you and me, I think the

Style girls are absolutely grim. The only one of them worth anything is little Olwen, who shared Helen's flat. Of course, the others all despise her. I manage to avoid being intimidated by them by laughing at them, and that makes Godfrey furious." She looked at Henry directly out of her big green eyes, and he found himself thinking that the laughter lines around them did nothing to diminish the loveliness of her face, but merely served to give it character.

"I'm sorry about Helen, of course," Lorna went on, "but there's no use pretending I get on well with any of them, because I don't. I thought I'd better tell you that straightaway, otherwise you'd find out from other people, and maybe get suspicious. I suppose, if I'm to be strictly honest, I'm jealous—not of any particular person, but of the hold that the magazine has on my husband. I can assure you, though, that I didn't murder Helen. I didn't know her nearly well enough for that."

"I never for a moment meant to suggest . . . " Henry began.

She cut him short. "Of course you didn't," she said. "It would be too silly."

Changing the subject, Henry said, "Isn't it lonely for you here during the week?"

"Oh." Lorna shrugged. "I have my dear Mrs. Adams, who comes every morning to help in the house. And I have the dogs."

"And plenty of neighbours, I suppose."

Lorna made a face. "Terrible people," she said. "Rich and respectable. *Style* readers, every one of them. Simple little black dresses and one string of pearls." Suddenly she grinned. "However," she added, "they have their uses, I suppose. It just so happens that on Tuesday evening I had to give a ghastly bridge party here—every so often I have to make a gesture and return hospitality. It dragged on until nearly three in the morning. So there's my alibi, Inspector. I can tell you who was here. There was Mrs. Dankworth and her son, and Lady Wright, and the Petersons . . . "

Conscientiously, Henry wrote down the names in his notebook. Then he said, "Do you know Hindhurst at all, Mrs. Goring?"

Lorna looked bewildered. "Hindhurst?" she said. "No. I've never been there. It's at the other end of the county. Why do you ask me that?"

"I just thought," said Henry, "that you might be able to help me. It seems that Miss Pankhurst consulted a doctor there, and since it's in Surrey, it struck me on the off-chance that it might have been somebody that you or your husband recommended to her. I'm on my way there now, and if I knew which doctor it was, it would save me endless trouble."

"No. I'm afraid I can't help you at all. Our doctor is in Harley Street, and there's a local man here whom I go to occasionally for small things. Was Helen ill then?"

"Apparently not," said Henry. "That's what makes it interesting. Oh, well, it was only a vague hope. I'd better get going now. Thanks for the tea."

"But don't you want to . . . I mean, you haven't asked me many questions."

"I've asked all I want to," said Henry. "You've been very helpful."

"I have? Goodness, I've told you nothing."

"Exactly," said Henry. "You've told me that you hardly knew the dead girl or her associates, and that you haven't been to London for months. So there's really nothing more to be said, is there?"

Lorna laughed. "You're right," she said.

It was when Henry was already on the doorstep that Lorna Goring made a surprising remark. She had been hesitating for some minutes, detaining Henry by small conversational devices, as though debating whether or not to say something. At the last moment, apparently, she made up her mind.

"Well, Inspector," she said, in a very fair imitation of an off-hand manner, "I wish you luck in your search." She paused. "By the way, if you *do* locate that doctor . . . I have a friend who's just moved to Hindhurst, and she rang me only last week, funnily enough, to ask me if I knew a good family doctor in that part of the world. So if it's not a bother, you might let me know the name of Helen's man. If she went to him, he should be reliable."

Henry was careful not to show any surprise. "Certainly," he said, politely. "I'll tell your husband—I'm sure to be seeing him."

"Oh, no, don't do that . . . he's hopeless. He'll never remember to tell me. Ring me here. I'm in the book."

"Very well," said Henry. "I'll do that. Goodbye now, and thank you."

He got into the car and drove away, well pleased with himself. Lorna Goring had told him more than she knew.

It was drizzling steadily when Henry reached Hindhurst. The pretty little town looked sad and drab under the relentless rain, and Henry was glad to reach the comparative cheerfulness and warmth of the police station. Here he was greeted by a beaming sergeant and another cup of tea, but no good news. Helen's name had produced no response at all among the local doctors.

"Of course, sir," the sergeant added, "she may have used a false name, and we hadn't a photograph."

Henry rubbed the back of his neck—a gesture which always indicated that he was abstracted and worried by pieces of a pattern which did not fit.

"She may have been . . . em . . . in the family way," said the sergeant. "That's what occurred to me. Otherwise, why would she go to a doctor so far from home? And if she was, she'd be likely not to give her real name."

"I know," said Henry, "that's the convenient, obvious explanation. But it so happens that she wasn't."

"Oh," said the sergeant bleakly. He was crestfallen that his penetrating analysis should have been dismissed first as obvious and secondly as mistaken.

Henry, feeling sorry for him, said quickly, "We came to the same conclusion ourselves, but the medical evidence proved us wrong."

"Ah," said the sergeant, cheering up.

Henry smiled. "Tell me about the local doctors," he said. "How many are there?"

"Well, now." The sergeant settled back more comfortably in his chair. It was pleasant to display his local knowledge to so distinguished a visitor. "There's old Dr. Herbertson up the hill, with a very well-to-do practice, and Dr. Roberts here in the High Street—most of the tradespeople go to him. Then Dr. Bland and Dr. Tanner share a surgery out along the Guildford road—it's mostly farmers and the like round there. And of course there's young Dr. Vance. I was almost forgetting him. New chap. Came and took over when old Dr. Pearce died. They say he's not doing too well. Most of Dr. Pearce's patients transferred to Dr. Herbertson. People round here are funny like that. Don't like new faces." The sergeant paused. "That's the lot," he said. "And not one of them knew Miss Pankhurst, so they say."

"Her photograph has been in most of the papers," said Henry. "None of them recognized it?"

"Not a hope," said the sergeant. "Mind, those newspaper pictures weren't much good for identification."

"The ones I have aren't much better," Henry said ruefully. "Apparently the girl just never had her picture taken." He pulled an envelope out of his pocket, and gazed at the two small pictures which it contained. One was a snapshot, taken by Olwen Piper on the balcony of the Kensington flat the previous summer, and it showed a slightly out-of-focus Helen watering a begonia in a pot. The other was a passport photograph dating back some seven years. Henry sighed. "Oh, well," he said. "No time like the present. I'll go and call on the doctors now."

It was nine o'clock that night when Henry got back to London. He had been subjected to Dr. Herbertson's interminable and rambling stories of his aristocratic patients ("I said to Lord Wessex, 'All right,' I said, '*go* to Sir James for a second opinion if you like.' He was back next day, very subdued. I knew what was coming, of course. 'What did Sir James say?' I asked him. 'He said, 'My dear Wessex, I wouldn't like to make a diagnosis without my old friend Herbertson in consultation. He knows twice as much about it as I do!' What d'you think of that, eh? I've laughed over that with his Lordship many times since. A remarkable man . . . a great gentleman, and, I think I may say, a friend of mine . . . " And so on). Escaping with difficulty, Henry had next had a brief interview with a busy, worried-looking Dr. Roberts ("Sorry, Inspector. Can't help you. Never seen the girl in my life. Must go. Excuse me"), followed by a sortie into the surgery crowded with ailing rustics where Doctors Bland and Tanner plied their trade cheerfully. Finally, Henry had somehow managed to refuse a pressing invitation to take a drink with young Dr. Vance, who exhibited all the melancholy and persistence of the Ancient Mariner, in spite of his youth. ("God, you could live in this place ten years and still be treated as a stranger—and never forgiven for it, either—that's the thing. Do have some whisky, Inspector. That old fool Herbertson should have retired years ago. Bumbling, incompetent . . . but they all stick to him. Why? Just because he's an old familiar face. How anyone can be expected . . . ") Henry extricated himself firmly, and got into the car. One depressing fact had emerged from the interviews. None of the doctors recognized Helen.

Driving back to town, in steadily increasing rain, Henry turned the problem over in his mind. On that Saturday a month ago, Helen had had an appointment with a doctor. Why? She was apparently perfectly well. She had also traveled to Hindhurst on the same day. That, of course, proved nothing—she might well have consulted a doctor in London before she left. On the other hand, it did indicate that she had friends or acquaintances in the country. More interesting still was the fact that she had not returned by train, for the unused half of the return ticket was still in her bag. That could mean either that she had been driven back by car, or that she had stayed overnight unexpectedly, and thus been obliged to buy a single ticket home the next day, since her day-return was no longer valid. Both possibilties suggested something more personal than an ordinary visit to a doctor.

Henry went on to consider Helen's colleagues. One of them could surely shed light on this matter, if he or she wished to. But which one? Then there was the second appointment with a doctor, the day before she died. She could certainly have traveled to Hindhurst and back between lunchtime and six o'clock, but even so, Henry was fast coming to the conclusion that Hindhurst and the doctor were unconnected. The doctor, he decided, must be in London, and he would start a search for him the next day.

Meanwhile, the Hindhurst visit remained a mystery, which might well have a banal explanation. More intriguing was the phone call which Olwen had overheard. On an impulse, Henry stopped at a telephone booth in Putney, consulted the directory, found Patrick Walsh's name, and dialed his Canonbury number.

The phone rang for some time, unanswered. Then a gruff voice said, "What do you want? I was in me bath."

"This is Inspector Tibbett, Mr. Walsh."

"Well, and it's a hell of a time to telephone, if I may say so. I thought you'd seen enough of me yesterday."

"I've hardly started on you yet," said Henry cheerfully. "May I come and see you?"

"When?"

"Now."

There was a silence, and then Patrick said, "Holy God, what are you at? Why should I have you in my house at this hour?"

"It's only just nine," said Henry, "and I've been busy all day."

"So have I. No, I'm damned if you can come."

"I could insist," said Henry, "but I hope I won't have to. After all, we're both anxious to find out who killed Helen, aren't we? And the trail gets colder every minute we waste."

There was an audible hesitation at the other end of the line. "Oh, all right, come if you must. D'you know the way?"

"I'll find it," said Henry. "I'll be along in about half an hour."

He made a quick call to Emmy to warn her that he would be late, and then continued his drive eastwards.

The Islington address turned out to be a beautiful, decaying Georgian house in a square off Essex Street. The gradual invasion of the area by accommodation-hungry artists and intellectuals had produced an incongruous sprinkling of blue and yellow painted front doors and bright window boxes, but the neighbourhood was still basically shabby, and the house in which Patrick lived was no exception.

The front door was open, and Henry found himself in a drab hallway decorated in flaking chocolate-brown paint, with worn linoleum on the floor. Following Patrick's instructions, he climbed the rickety staircase to the second floor, where he found himself confronted by a door which had recently been repainted in noncommittal black. On it, a white card announced one ink-written word—WALSH. Henry looked for a bell, failed to find one, and raised the brass knocker, which was shaped like a clenched fist. It fell with a brisk thud.

At once, there was a shuffling inside, the door opened, and Patrick Walsh said, "Come in, then, me boy. Come in."

Looking larger and more shambling than ever in red pyjamas, a black toweling dressing-gown and ancient camel's-hair slippers, Patrick led the way into the flat, which consisted in the main of one enormous studio. It was, Henry thought, the epitome of where an artist should live, and he felt suddenly humble. He realized in a flash that his own taste in interior decoration—on which he was inclined to pride himself—was the artificial product of a middle-class mentality abetted by magazines and advertizements. With shame and insight, he recognized that all he and

Emmy had done in their own home was to create a cheap reproduction of the currently fashionable conception of gracious living. Their choice of furniture, curtains, ornaments, and colours had been guided, however subtly, by outside influences. Now, he found himself in an apartment which had been put together by somebody who relied entirely on his own judgment, and damn the consequences. In a bitter moment of self-revelation, Henry acknowledged that if he had done the same thing, the result would have been disastrous. Here, it was triumphant.

The huge room was starkly whitewashed, with the exception of erratic splashes of colour round windows or in alcoves—orange, deep purple, pale blue. It was incredibly untidy, but even the disorder managed to be beautiful. Small Florentine bronzes jostled modern African wood-carvings and Peruvian pottery figures. On a heavy oak farmhouse table, a space had been cleared among books and sketches to accommodate a single golden chrysanthemum in a stone jam jar, and an easel beside the window bore a bold, stylized sketch of the flower in blazing oils. On the stained wooden floor were two deep-red Persian prayer mats, a Norwegian folk-weave rug in black and white, and some strips of plain coconut matting. One window was uncurtained, the other draped with a swathe of orange silk. On the walls were several ink-and-wash drawings of figures, presumably Patrick's own work, a small Byzantine icon glowing in jewel colours, and a particularly effective poster advertizing French railways. The room should have looked a terrible mess, but it didn't. A sure thread of personal taste ran through all the ill-assorted objects, welding them into something valid.

Patrick sat down on a small Victorian tapestry chair, motioned Henry towards a comfortable sofa, poked the open log fire, and said, "Have a drink, then."

"Thank you," said Henry. "I will."

Patrick gave him no choice of beverages, but poured two generous measures of Irish whisky into heavy tumblers. He tossed his own back in one gulp, refilled his glass, and then said, "Well?"

"Helen," said Henry, "telephoned you the evening before she died."

Patrick looked dangerous. "What if she did? Any law against it?"

"Why didn't you tell me?"

"You didn't ask. You asked me if I'd seen her, and I said 'no'."

"All the same," said Henry, "it does make life easier if people occasionally volunteer information. What did she say to you?"

"Nothing in particular. Just a friendly call."

Henry took out his notebook and thumbed through it with unnecessary deliberation. In an unemotional voice, he read, " 'The doctor says it's quite definite. I don't know what I'm going to do. He'll never leave her, you know that. I honestly wish I was dead.' "

The silence that followed was as oppressive as fog. Then Patrick said, "I suppose that damn fool Olwen has been . . . "

"Miss Piper, very properly, told me what she overheard . . . "

"Very properly!" Patrick laughed sardonically. "I don't suppose Olwen-bach has ever done anything in her young life that wasn't very proper. That's her trouble."

Taking no notice, Henry went on, "I don't think she was lying, but one can never be sure. If you would tell me exactly what Miss Pankhurst said to you . . . "

Patrick looked up. His face seemed older, more lined than Henry had remembered. "You tell me Helen was killed," he said. "I doubt it. I think the darling girl took her own life, because she had . . . troubles. If she did, then there's no point in telling you what those troubles were. If somebody *did* kill her, then it can't have had anything to do with that particular situation. In the circumstances, I can see no possible justification for making it public."

"Telling me doesn't make it public," said Henry.

"No?" Patrick looked at him quizzically. "I would doubt that, Mister Inspector. Can't you take my word for it that you're barking up the wrong tree, and leave it at that? You should look in other directions."

"What other directions?"

"I don't know." Patrick sounded genuinely baffled. "If somebody murdered Helen, it was for a reason, obviously. But I know nothing about it. You've come to the wrong place for your information."

"Where do you suggest I should go for it, then?"

"How should I know? That's your job." Patrick was getting angry again.

"Mr. Walsh," said Henry, "can't you understand that I'm

simply trying to get at the truth? I don't enjoy prying into people's private affairs, but so long as you go on making such a mystery about Helen's private life, I have to go on investigating it, in case it has a bearing on her death. If it hasn't, you can be sure anything you tell me will go no further."

In the silence that followed, Patrick refilled both glasses. Then he said, "You've kissed the Blarney, Inspector. If only I could believe you."

"Please do," said Henry.

Patrick brooded, and then seemed to make a decision. "All right," he said, "I'm an old fool, I suppose, but I'll tell you all I know. It's precious little."

Henry waited hopefully. Patrick took a long swig at his glass, and then went on, "Helen was in love. Don't ask me with whom, because she never told me and I didn't ask. She simply told me the situation—without mentioning any names—and a hell of a situation it was for the poor girl. It seems that the man—we'll call him X—had a wife to whom he was tied not only by loyalty but for social and business reasons. Later on, he kept telling Helen, when he was in a position to do so, he'd divorce his wife and marry her. Meanwhile, the whole thing had to be kept quiet. Well, Helen didn't like it, but what could she do? She had to resign herself to things as they were. A few months ago, however, a new and terrible complication arose. Helen began to get seriously worried about X's health; she was a doctor's daughter, and knew a bit about such things. She persuaded him to come with her to a doctor for a checkup, without telling his wife. Afterwards, she spoke privately to the doctor, who of course imagined her to be X's wife, and he agreed that when the results of the various tests came through, he would tell her the worst, but would keep any really bad news away from X.

"Helen knew it would be several weeks before the verdict was in. It was no wonder the darling girl was in a state of nerves. It was the day she died that she heard the news. When she telephoned me, she'd just come back from a private session with the doctor. He'd told her that X was suffering from an incurable cancer, and had at the most a year to live. X himself, of course, didn't know this, and I presume he still doesn't.

"When she rang me and told me, Helen was in despair. Suddenly, all her dreams and hopes of the future were gone. There was only a year left, and she wanted to spend it with him. Divorce didn't matter any longer, if only they could be together. Yet she was determined to spare him from knowing the truth, and she knew that unless she did, he would never leave his wife. Now does it make sense, what Olwen overheard? And do you wonder that Helen killed herself?"

There was a long silence. Then Henry said, "Do you really not know who X is?"

"I don't." Patrick was emphatic.

"Why," Henry asked, "have you been at such pains to prevent me from finding out about Helen and Michael Healy?"

"I haven't," said Patrick. "I . . . " He stopped, and glared at Henry with real dislike. "You're trying to trap me. I knew I shouldn't have trusted you, damn you."

"I'm not trying to trap you," said Henry, patiently, "I'm asking a question. Everyone else has taken a positive delight in telling me all about Helen and Michael. You are the only person . . . "

"Who's been talking?" Patrick was livid. "Olwen, I suppose."

"Not only Olwen," said Henry. "Miss French and Mr. Goring and even Miss Manners—Mrs. Healy—herself. And Mr. Healy didn't deny it."

"Ah, well." Patrick sighed. "Now she's gone, I suppose they feel there's no point . . . "

"You know very well, don't you, that Michael Healy is X?"

"She never told me," said Patrick stubbornly. "Of course, there was talk. That was Olwen's fault. It may have been right, or it may have been wrong. That's all I have to say."

"I see." Henry was thoughtful. He was remembering Michael Healy's haggard face under the harsh studio lights, his frenetic energy, his bitter ironies. He was remembering what Godfrey Goring had said over lunch in The Orangery, and Nicholas Knight's insinuations. It was tragic but not inconceivable that the brilliant photographer, still in his early forties, might be under sentence of death—a sentence of which he was formally ignorant, but which he might well guess in his secret heart. It explained a great deal. Was this, then, the secret which so many of *Style's* staff were concerned to hide? Supposing the fact of Michael's illness were known to others besides Patrick? Helen was dead, but Michael was dearly loved and still alive, and his friends might well fear that Henry's investigation would reveal the truth to him in a brutal manner.

Henry asked himself what he would do in their position. They were intelligent people. They knew that the affair with Michael could not be kept dark, with Olwen only too anxious to broadcast it. Better, then, to mention it at once, to emphasize it—to pass it off as a light-hearted caprice—to hide, at all costs, its tragic aspect. All this made sense—except for certain obstinately puzzling facts. And facts, Henry reminded himself, were his business. Facts, not speculations.

He said, "You have a key to the *Style* building, haven't you, Mr. Walsh?"

"What of it?"

"Nothing. I just wanted to check. Do you often work late?"

Patrick chuckled. "Not me," he said. "I'm too smart and too old for that. Of course, there's the Paris shambles twice a year, but otherwise I make sure of getting away on time. I have my work, you see." He gestured round the room. "D'you imagine I enjoy doing layouts for a fashion magazine when I should be painting?"

"Yes," said Henry, with a grin. "I'm sure you do."

At this, Patrick laughed aloud. "You're right, of course," he said. "Have some whisky. Of course I love it, or I wouldn't do it. But it's not me real work, and I know it. I'm a prostitute, that's what it comes to. A poor bloody tart plying me trade in Earl Street. The only consolation is that my prices are high."

"I'm sure they are," said Henry. "Well, I'll leave you in peace now. Thanks for the whisky, and thanks for being so frank with me."

"I'm regretting it already," said Patrick. "I should never have . . . "

Henry stood up. "There's just one more question," he said. "Why didn't Helen tell you who X was?"

"Why?" Patrick, in the act of rising to his feet, stopped suddenly, startled. Then he straightened, and said, "Now, that's what I call a truly metaphysical question. A question of pure philosophical and psychological speculation. How in hell should I know what went on in the poor girl's mind?"

"Didn't it occur to you to wonder?"

"I suppose she was afraid that if she told anyone his name,

the news of his illness might get back to him . . . "

"She'd been telling you about him long before she knew he was ill—or so I understand."

"I was proud and honoured that she told me anything at all." Patrick drew himself up with an almost Roman dignity, in his toweling dressing gown. "I never asked questions, even in me own mind."

"Are you married yourself, Mr. Walsh?" Henry asked suddenly.

Patrick's face went brick-red. "Certainly not."

"Have you ever been?" There was a long hesitation. Henry added, "I can look it up easily enough, you know, at Somerset House."

Patrick was patently ill-at-ease. At length, in a pleading voice with an exaggerated brogue in it, he said, "Now, Inspector dear, you wouldn't want to make trouble for an innocent man that may have been foolish in his youth, like the rest of us, would you? If I tell you, will you give me your word it'll go no further?"

"That depends on whether it has any bearing on the case."

"None in the world. None in the world."

"That's for me to judge," said Henry. "Well, come on. Tell me."

Patrick bent and threw another log onto the blazing fire. "It was all so long ago," he said. "A runaway affair. I was twenty-one and she nineteen. I was an art student without two pennies to rub together, and she was from a grand family, and reading for a University degree in literature. Of course, it was madness, and anyone could have told us so. Most people did, in fact, but we didn't listen. The first year was fine, while we were both at college still. Then the trouble began. She was ambitious as the devil—always has been. Wanted a great career for herself, and for me, too. I wanted to live in a garret and paint. The rows and the bitterness got worse and worse, and after three years she up and left me. That's all there is to it."

"Did you ever get divorced?"

"Of course not," said Patrick shortly. "We're both Catholics."

"And when did you meet up with her again?"

Patrick turned on him, furious. "What do you mean by that? I never said . . . "

"If you'd really lost touch with her," said Henry, "you'd have made no bones about telling me all about the marriage." There was an angry pause. Henry went on. "Well, if you won't tell me, I'll tell you. I think that your wife is Miss Margery French, the distinguished editor of *Style*."

Patrick gave him a long, appraising look. Then he said, "For God's sake, keep it quiet, will you?"

"Why?" said Henry. "What's the harm in anyone knowing?"

"You wouldn't understand."

"How long has your wife been with *Style*?"

"Thirty-five years. Soon after she left me, she got her first job there, as a secretary."

"And you?"

"I joined the staff three years ago," said Patrick. He carefully refrained from looking directly at Henry.

"You got your job on the strength of your wife's influence, no doubt?"

"No such thing! If you think that Margery would employ anybody for any other reason than that she considered them the right person for the job . . . !"

"And what," said Henry, "did you do during those thirty-two years?"

Patrick scowled. "I painted."

"Successfully?"

"No."

"So you must have been very glad of the job on *Style*," Henry remarked.

Patrick turned on him ferociously. "Get out!" he shouted. "Get out and stay out! And keep your bloody mouth shut or I'll break your neck!"

Henry looked at him with genuine pity. "It's unfortunately part of my job to be inquisitive," he said. "Please believe me, I don't enjoy it, and I am reasonably discreet. Unless, of course, a fact has a bearing on the case in hand. Thanks for the whisky. I'll let myself out."

He clattered down the stairs and out into the misty square. As he drove slowly home, many questions jostled in his mind, and the most pressing of them was just how far could he believe what Patrick had told him? A thought which returned with persistency was that, if one discounted the story of the illness, which could easily be a fabrication, Patrick himself was extremely well-qualified for the role of X.

127

9

The following morning started with the inquest, which Henry was determined to keep as short and noncommittal as possible. He was pleased to see that, although the case had caused some stir in the newspapers, the public was not prepared to turn out on a raw January morning in search of sensation. Apart from Margery French, who had readily agreed to give evidence of identification, and Alf Samson, nobody else was there except for the police witnesses and a handful of crime reporters, most of whom Henry knew and greeted by name.

The proceedings were gratifyingly brief. Margery affirmed that the body was indeed Helen's, and then hurried off to take a taxi to the office. Alf described his finding of the corpse. The doctor gave the medical evidence in a deep, grudging voice. Henry himself took the stand to say that police investigations were in progress, but had reached no satisfactory conclusion, and requested an adjournment. The one constructive piece of business concluded was Henry's agreement that, since there was no possible doubt or dispute about the cause of death, the police were prepared to let the funeral take place. The coroner obligingly signed the burial order and adjourned the proceedings. The whole thing took a bare twenty minutes, and by ten o'clock Henry was in the *Style* building.

On the surface, at least, the magazine seemed to have resumed its normal working rhythm. Models, messengers, and secretaries hurried along the corridors, typewriters clicked busily, and Patrick could be heard bellowing good-humouredly at Donald MacKay. Girls carrying sheafs of photographs, layouts, and proofs bustled in and out of the various offices, narrowly avoiding collision with others who made their uncertain way to or from the fashion room, half-hidden under armfuls of clothes.

Henry did not go into his particular den, but made his way straight to Olwen Piper's office. The features editor was sitting at her desk, which was stacked with review copies of books and decorated with invitations to film shows and art exhibitions.

Olwen was on the telephone when Henry came in. She smiled at him, quickly and a little nervously, and went on with her conversation. "Yes, Mr. Hartley, three o'clock will be fine. . . . Michael Healy will be taking the pictures. . . . Yes, he *is* brilliant, isn't he? I felt he'd be just the person. . . . No, we'll use the stage lighting. I've spoken to Mr. Dean about it. All I want is you in your second act make-up. . . . Yes, *second* act. . . . Really, I'm sure. . . . Well, I know the third act costume is more showy, but . . . no, no, of course I didn't mean that. . . . Of course I know you're only thinking about what will look most effective for us, but you see . . . I have to consider how it will fit in with other pictures on the page. . . . Well, of course, I *hope* it'll be a full page, but I can't promise . . . you know what art editors are like. . . . Oh, Mr. Hartley, I *know* how busy you are. . . . Of *course* I wouldn't want you to waste your time. . . . Don't worry, I think I can definitely promise you a full page . . . yes . . . a big close-up, naturally . . . yes . . . and in the second act make-up? . . . Oh, that *is* kind. I do appreciate it. . . . Until three then . . . Goodbye."

She rang off, looked at Henry, and made a face. "Actors!" she said, with terrible scorn. "They're all the same. Still, I did think John Hartley might be above *that* sort of thing. I'm so bad at dealing with them—I always put my foot in it. I thought for one awful moment he was going to refuse to let us photograph him at all."

"Will he get his full page?" Henry asked.

"Heaven knows. It all depends on Uncle. I'll have to fight for it, that's for sure. And if I don't get it, Hartley will hate me for ever. But what could I do but promise? Oh, *dear*."

"May I sit down for a moment?" Henry asked.

Olwen blushed, and jumped up guiltily. "Oh, I am sorry, Inspector. Of course. Have this chair."

"I'm fine here, thanks," said Henry pulling a straight-backed office chair up to the desk. "I'm sorry to disturb you when you're so busy."

"I'm always busy," said Olwen simply. "I've been here since seven, correcting proofs. And I've got two film shows and an exhibition to fit in before my sitting with Hartley this afternoon." This remark could have been offensive, implying that Henry was a confounded nuisance, but Olwen had spoken quite naturally and without malice, stating facts. Henry could see that she had no intention of being rude; he could also appreciate that her bluntness might antagonize people.

"I'll make it as quick as I can, then," he said. "What I want to know is the name of Helen's doctor."

"Her doctor? Oh, you mean about . . . "

"You were wrong about Helen, Miss Piper," said Henry. "She wasn't pregnant."

"She wasn't?" Olwen looked completely taken aback. "Then . . . what did it mean? What I heard her say?"

"I don't know for sure," said Henry. "That's why I want to see her doctor. He may be able to help me."

"Helen was hardly ever ill," said Olwen. "She and I were both registered with Dr. Markham in Onslow Street, but I don't think she's been to see him for ages. She obviously wouldn't have gone to him about . . . "

"I told you, Miss Piper—Helen was not pregnant."

"But there's no other explanation."

"There is, and I intend to find out what it is," said Henry. He made a note of the doctor's name and address. "Thank you very much. That's all for the moment." He stood up. "I'm glad," he added, "to find you in a more cheerful frame of mind. I felt sure . . . "

"I decided brooding wouldn't do any good," said Olwen briskly. "Helen's dead and nothing will bring her back. I've written to her sister in Australia, and advertized for someone else to share the flat with me. I can't do any more."

"You don't think it might be better to move somewhere else? I mean . . . "

"It's a good flat and the rent is reasonable," said Olwen. "I'd never find anywhere like it for the money." She stood up, a solid, determined little figure, and put on her coat. "Excuse me. I really must go now, or I shall be late."

As he walked back to his own office, Henry considered Olwen Piper. Her violent outburst of emotion two days ago contrasted strangely with her dry-eyed common sense of today. Was it that her calm, deep-rooted country heritage had reasserted itself, or was it heartlessness? Had the tears and near-hysteria been genuine or a calculated effect? He was not sure.

The desk in his office had been dusted and tidied, and fresh white paper inserted in the blotter. On it lay an envelope addressed to him. Inside, a typed note on *Style* notepaper read, "Dear Inspector Tibbett, May I see you as soon as possible on a matter which may be important? Rachel Field." He dialed the number of the editor's office.

"Miss French's office . . . oh, Inspector Tibbett. At last. You were not here yesterday." Miss Field's voice was reproving.

"I'm sorry," said Henry. "I had other things to do."

"I've been trying to contact you since yesterday," said Miss Field accusingly. "I have something very serious to tell you."

"Come along and see me," said Henry.

"Very well, Inspector."

Tempting though it might be to display omniscience by revealing that he already knew what Miss Field had to say, Henry decided against it. He did not intend to have Veronica mixed up in the affair more than was strictly necessary. Consequently, he put up a very good show of surprise when Rachel Field said, "Inspector, my key to the building has been stolen."

"Stolen? You're sure you haven't just mislaid it?"

"Positive. It was definitely in my handbag on Tuesday when I got back from Paris. I keep it on the same ring as my house keys." She produced a neat key ring from her black handbag. "You see? You have to open the ring to get a key off. The others are still there."

"When did you first notice that it was missing?"

"Yesterday morning, when Miss Connolly came and asked me if she could borrow it."

"And you are positive that you had it on Tuesday evening?"

"Quite positive. The front door was already locked when we

arrived here from the airport, and I used my key to open the door."

"Did anybody have the opportunity of stealing it from your bag on Tuesday evening?" Henry asked.

Miss Field looked uncomfortable. "Yes," she said.

"When?"

"I . . . well, I always have my handbag on the floor beside my desk when I'm working . . . "

"Exactly," said Henry. "And I'm told that you didn't leave the office once during the evening. Don't you think the key may have been taken later on . . . at Mr. Goring's house, for instance?"

Rachel Field looked startled. "At Mr. Goring's? Oh, no. Certainly not."

"Just a moment, Miss Field," said Henry. He opened his notebook and began hunting through the previous entries. Rachel watched him with the slight contempt of the quick, efficient worker for the slow, fumbling one.

Looking up, Henry said, "When I spoke to Horace Barry, he said, apropos of his departure from Brompton Square . . . " Henry glanced at his notebook, and then read aloud, "' . . . while Miss Field went to collect her things.' What things, Miss Field?"

"My coat and gloves. They were in the hall."

"Not your handbag?"

"Of course not. I kept that with me."

"I see. But you say that somebody could have tampered with it earlier on."

"Yes." For once, Rachel appeared hesitant. "It's not quite true that I didn't leave the office at all. I was out of the room for about ten minutes, soon after one o'clock."

"Where did you go?"

"I went into the art department first. Mr. Walsh was there on his own. I asked him if he knew where Miss French was, as I had a query about the copy I was typing. He said she was in the darkroom. I then opened the door leading to the storeroom, where the . . . the Thermos flask was, you know." Henry nodded. Rachel went on. "Miss French, Mr. Healy, Miss Manners, and Donald MacKay were all in there, looking at prints as they came out of the wash. I didn't like to disturb them—my query wasn't very important, and I decided it could wait. So I just walked through the darkroom and out of the other door into the corridor, and went to . . . " Rachel stopped, and reddened.

"Where?" prompted Henry gently.

"To the Ladies' Room," said Rachel, embarrassed.

"Very sensible," Henry remarked, "since Miss French was busy and wouldn't be needing you for a while."

"Exactly. Yes," said Rachel gratefully. "After I'd . . . I mean, while I was there, I decided to comb my hair, and that was when I realized that I'd left my handbag in the office. When I got back, Miss French was there, and we started work at once. My bag was in its usual place beside my desk. I can't tell you whether it had been moved or not."

"Tell me," said Henry, "did the people in the darkroom see you when you opened the door?"

"Donald did," Miss Field answered positively. "He was facing the door, and he looked up when I opened it. The others had their backs to me and they were absorbed in looking at the pictures. I don't think they saw me."

"Would Mr. MacKay have recognized you?" said Henry. "I mean—you were coming from the brightly lit art department into the dim darkroom. He'd only have seen a silhouette . . . "

"That would have been quite enough," said Rachel, with a sudden and unexpected twinkle of humour. "My outline, even in silhouette, is markedly different from that of any of the editorial staff, Inspector."

Henry grinned. "We'll take it that he recognized you, then," he said. More gravely, he added, "And Donald MacKay was the only person in the building who did not have his own key to the front door."

"What worries me, Inspector," said Rachel, "is why anybody should want to take my key. I mean, any of us could have put cyanide in the flask. The murderer didn't need a key. It couldn't be, could it, that he's planning something else . . . ?"

"The murderer did need a key, Miss Field," said Henry. "He —or she—may have put poison in the flask during the evening's working session, but somebody—presumably the murderer—came back again later. Much later. After Miss Pankhurst was dead."

"What?" Rachel gave a little gasp.

"The reason that the murderer came back," Henry went on

steadily, "was to look for something . . . something which he expected to find in your suitcase."

"In my . . . " White-faced, Rachel gripped the arms of her chair, and closed her eyes for a moment. Then she opened them, looked at Henry and smiled. "I'm sorry, Inspector. You gave me rather a shock. What could anybody have hoped to find in my suitcase?"

Henry was puzzled by her obvious distress. "You knew the case had been rifled the day before yesterday," he said.

"Yes, but . . . I never realized . . . somebody actually killed her in order to get hold of something in my case . . . "

"It looks like it," said Henry. "And the fact that your key was stolen narrows the field. Now, I want you to think hard. I know I've asked you this before, but I need a more precise answer. Who, of the people in Paris, could have slipped some small article into your case without you knowing it?"

With very little hesitation, Rachel said, "There's only one person, Inspector. Veronica Spence. Now I think of it, neither Miss Manners nor Mr. Healy came into my room at all on the last day, and my case was quite empty when I started packing. But then Veronica was in and out all the time, and I actually left her in my room alone when Miss Manners called me away in the middle of my packing . . . "

Henry suddenly felt very cold. It was ludicrous to connect Veronica with any sort of criminal activity, but he was haunted by the thought that she might have become implicated, unwittingly, in something illegal—something that had led to murder.

"Thank you, Miss Field," he said. "You've been very helpful. I need hardly ask you to keep certain facts to yourself—about the murderer returning later, and so on."

"Of course, Inspector. I appreciate your confidence," said Rachel.

Before the door had closed behind her, Henry's hand was on the telephone. It seemed to him that he should talk to his niece without further delay. He dialed the number of the fashion room, and asked to speak to Beth Connolly.

"Veronica?" Beth sounded slightly harassed. "No, she's not working for us today. . . . Yes, as a matter of fact I can. . . . She's over at Nicholas Knight's for fittings. She's modelling his new Collection next week . . . What? . . . Excuse me a moment." Henry heard a clatter as the receiver was laid down on the table, and then, indistinctly, Beth's voice again saying, "I *told* you to order the pink and not the green, Marilyn. No, it will not do. . . . All right, I don't care whose fault it was . . . Just get the pink and get it fast . . . " The receiver was picked up again. "I'm so sorry, Inspector. Things are a bit chaotic this morning."

"I'm sorry to have bothered you," said Henry. "I'll try to reach Veronica at Nicholas Knight's."

The telephone at Knight's showroom was answered calmly by the super-Mayfair blonde, who was polite but firm. "Ay'm afrayde," she said, "that Ay can't connect yew with the aytelier today. We're rehearsing the show, yew see. Everywan is fraightfully busy. Veronica Spence? One of the models? Oh, no . . . quayte out of the question. Ay'm so sorry."

"Can't you at least tell me when she'll be free, and give her a message?" Henry asked. He had no desire to invoke the magic name of Scotland Yard in order to gate-crash the atelier; he had already seen it on a quiet day. The idea of what it would be like when fraightfully busy was enough to make the strongest man quail.

Reluctantly, the blonde said, "She should be able to get out for lunch about wan, but Ay can't promise, yew know."

"This is her Uncle Henry speaking," said Henry. "Please tell her I shall be lunching at The Orangery, and would like her to join me. I'll be there from half past twelve until half past two."

The mention of The Orangery produced a certain, respectful reaction. "Certainly Ay'll tell her. With pleasure," said the blonde cordially. She obviously envisaged Henry as a plutocratic uncle, and Veronica as a prospective customer. You never knew *who* the model girls were these days. "Ay'm *sure* we can arrange for her to be free. Ay'll speak to Mr. Knayte mayself."

"Thank you," said Henry, and rang off. He was acutely conscious of the fact that he had exactly four pounds ten in his wallet, and would probably have to borrow from Veronica to pay for the lunch. Meanwhile, it was still only half past eleven, and there were things to be done in the *Style* office. Henry picked up his notebook and went along to the art department.

Patrick Walsh was standing with his back to the door, sketching something on a drawing board. As the door opened, he said loudly, without looking round, "Can't you read? Go away. No admission to anyone."

Donald MacKay, who was pasting up layouts by the window, looked up and smiled rather shyly at Henry. "Good morning, Inspector," he said.

"Oh, it's you again, is it?" said Patrick. Still he did not turn round. "What d'you want now? We're busy."

"I want both of you to cast your minds back to Tuesday night, if you will," said Henry. He looked at Donald. "Mr. MacKay, you told me that Rachel Field did not leave Miss French's office once during the evening. If you think for a bit, I imagine you'll realize you were mistaken."

Donald considered. "There was one moment," he said, "when we were all in the darkroom, and the door opened for a couple of seconds and then closed again. I had a feeling that it was Rachel, but she saw we were busy and beat a retreat."

"Her account," said Henry, "is that she crossed the darkroom and went out of the other door, into the corridor, and down to the ladies' cloakroom."

"I'm certain she didn't," said Donald. He sounded nervous.

"What was your impression, Mr. Walsh?" Henry asked.

Without looking up, Patrick replied, "D'you really think I spent Collections night worrying about whether our Rachel had gone to spend a penny or not? Good God, man, I had things to do." After a pause, he added, "She did come in here once. Asked me where Margery was. I told her, in the darkroom."

"What did she do then?" Henry asked.

"She went out again, I presume. I didn't notice."

"By which door?"

"I tell you, I haven't the remotest idea. I went on working, and she just disappeared efficiently, the way she always does."

Henry said, to Donald, "Miss Field is certain that you saw and recognized her."

"Well, I've told you I did. But she simply put her head round the door and then went back to her own office. Heavens, Inspector . . . " Donald sounded at once exasperated and slightly amused. "Why should I lie about it? What does it matter?"

"It matters very much," said Henry. "That is, it mattered to somebody who wanted to get hold of a key to the *Style* building to know that Miss Field's office was empty and her handbag unattended."

Donald went first white and then red, and when he spoke, it was with considerable anger. "If you're implying what I think you are," he said, "it's a monstrous lie."

"As a matter of interest," said Henry, "what did you do next —after Miss Field had put her head round the door?"

Looking uncomfortable, Donald said, "I think I came in here. I can't exactly remember."

"Leaving the others still in the darkroom?"

"Well . . . yes . . . "

"And having come in here, you didn't go on into the editor's office, which you knew would be empty?"

"Certainly not. Did I, Patrick?"

"Don't ask me. I haven't the remotest idea what you did."

"Well," said Henry, pleasantly, "think about it. If you decide to change your story, I'll be in my office."

Quietly, Patrick Walsh said, "Get out and stay out."

"With pleasure," said Henry. He went back to his own room, dialed Miss Field's number, and asked whether Miss French could spare him a few minutes.

"She's extremely busy, Inspector," said Rachel defensively.

"May I speak to her?"

Before Rachel could reply, a crisp voice cut in. "Miss French here. What can I do for you, Inspector?"

"Spare me a little of your precious time, if you can."

"Of course." There was no hesitation. "Just a moment, while I check my engagements." Henry heard a subdued murmuring, in which Miss Field's voice could be distinguished saying sharply, "No, Miss French, you can't put it off. It's very important." Eventually, Margery returned to the phone. "I'm interviewing a candidate for Helen's job at a quarter past twelve, and I have a luncheon date at one," she said. "I wanted to cancel it, so that we could lunch together, but Miss Field won't let me. She's a terrible bully, you know. I think the best thing is for us to meet straightaway." Apparently there was an interruption at this point, for Margery added, not to Henry, "I know the early form has to be O.K'd today. I'll do it after lunch . . . well, tell Miss Manners it must wait until tomorrow . . . " Then, to Henry once more, "Shall I come along to your office?"

"I think that would be best."

Margery walked briskly into the little office, her big topaz earrings sparkling under her mink-trimmed hat, her dark brown suit and crocodile shoes as faultless as ever. She sat down and glanced at her watch.

"You will forgive me if I keep an eye on the time, won't you, Inspector?" she said. "I'm afraid my life is more than usually hectic, because I'm doing Helen's job as well as my own. I hope this girl will be suitable. I feel as though I had lost my right arm."

"I'm sure you do," said Henry. "I'll try to keep it short. You told me before that you are not a gossip, and I'm certain that is true. However, now that I've met your staff for myself, I would greatly appreciate your help."

"In what way?" Margery sounded on her guard.

"In assessing their characters."

"Well?" This time Margery's voice was definitely unfriendly.

Henry started gently. "Let's take Olwen Piper first," he said. "My impression is that she is clever but not very tactful; that she was extremely fond of Miss Pankhurst—almost to the point of hero worship—but that she has a toughness and resilience of character which can carry her through even a tragedy like this. I think she is headstrong and impulsive, and quite capable of violence. Whether she could or would commit a premeditated crime is another matter. What do you think?"

"I won't conceal from you, Inspector, how distasteful all this is to me," said Margery.

"Murder is distasteful," said Henry grimly.

They looked at each other steadily for a moment. Then Margery said, "Well. Go on."

"You haven't anything to add to my portrait of Olwen?"

"She's an idealist," said Margery. She seemed to find the words painful. "She's naïve as only a brilliant person can be. She never stops to consider whether an action may be inexpedient . . . politically or in any other way. She goes ahead and does what she thinks should be done, regardless of the consequences."

"Yes," said Henry. "A dangerous characteristic. She must have quite a few enemies."

"I wouldn't say enemies. She exasperates people, chiefly because she despises them. For instance, she won't accept that Teresa must occasionally feature a dress that she doesn't admire one hundred percent, if the manufacturer is spending thousands on advertizing with us. And then there was a terrible scene at the party after Nicholas Knight's last Collection, when he asked her what she thought of it, and she said that everything was either hideous or a direct pinch from Paris. I thought Nicholas was going to have hysterics. Perhaps it wasn't his best Collection ever, but one can't go round saying things like that. In her own sphere, I think she does make some effort to be a little tactful, but I honestly believe she's incapable of telling an actor or a dramatist that his work is good if she doesn't think so. It makes life very difficult. She's so . . . so unforgiving."

"That's very interesting," said Henry. "Now, what about Teresa Manners. Or rather, what about Mr. and Mrs. Michael Healy?"

There was a short silence, and then Margery said, "Well? What about them?"

"I have been told," said Henry, "until I'm sick to death of hearing it, that Helen was having an affair with Michael Healy. You yourself, if you remember, were the first person to draw my attention to it. Why?"

Henry rapped out the last word in a stern, policeman-like manner. If he had hoped to intimidate Margery French, however, he was due for a disappointment. She merely smiled slightly, and said, "Because I thought it would help you in your enquiries, Inspector. That is the right phrase to use, isn't it?"

"I don't think," said Henry, "that you told me the truth."

Margery regarded him calmly. "What an extraordinary statement," she said. "Why on earth should I lie to you?"

"I didn't say you lied," said Henry. "I said that you didn't tell me the truth. That is, not the whole truth. Now, I want to get this business of Helen's love life cleared up, once and for all, because it's confusing the issue." He paused. "I won't mince words, Miss French. Have you not known for some time that Michael Healy is desperately ill—dying, in fact? Weren't you aware that while you and Helen and Patrick all knew about it, neither Michael Healy nor his wife had any idea of the truth? Weren't you trying to gloss over a very serious and tragic situation in order to spare Michael and Teresa pain?"

Margery French did not answer at once. She was looking at Henry with what appeared to be perfectly genuine astonishment. Finally, she said, "I have no idea where you got hold of this extraordinary story, Inspector, but I can assure you that there's not a word of truth in it. There's nothing wrong with Michael that I know of, except perhaps slight strain due to overwork. If somebody has been spreading unfounded rumours . . . "

"This is not an unfounded rumour," said Henry. "It came directly from Helen herself."

"From Helen?"

"She told Mr. Walsh about it on the telephone the evening before she was killed."

Margery seemed unable to grasp the meaning of the words. "She told . . . ?" she repeated.

"She told Mr. Walsh that the man she loved was dying of cancer, that he did not know about it, and neither did his wife, and that . . . "

Suddenly, without warning, Margery slumped forward in her chair. Her face had gone deadly white under its protective layer of make-up, and her mink hat was tilted ludicrously over her eyes. Henry, who in spite of long experience had never been able to accustom himself to the sight of people who fainted under questioning, was somewhat shaken. He was on his feet in an instant, but before he could move Margery had opened her eyes.

"No . . . " she said, faintly. "Don't . . . I'm perfectly all right." She sat up straight, put a hand to her forehead, and automatically rearranged her hat. "Perhaps you would just get me a glass of water from the cloakroom, so that I can take a pill. I'm afraid I get these silly fainting fits occasionally. It's nothing to worry about."

"Of course—I'll get the water right away," said Henry. He was fascinated by the woman's courage. He could sense the sheer will power which had straightened up the small, slight backbone and ironed the tremor out of the slender hands. Mingled with his admiration, however, was a more reluctant thought—that here was somebody perfectly capable of committing murder if she considered it justified. The question was, would such an intelligent and civilized person ever feel entitled to take another's life? To this, Henry did not know the answer.

When he returned with the glass of water, Margery was sitting bolt upright, powdering her nose in a small handmirror. She smiled, apologized again, and quickly swallowed a pill from a silver pillbox. Then she said, "To go back to our conversation.

I assure you, Inspector, that this story is nonsense, and I do beg you not to spread it abroad. You can imagine how hurtful it would be, not only to Michael and Teresa but to the magazine. Why Patrick should have invented it, I can't imagine—but, as you know, he's a wild Irishman and he loves to spin a tale. Take it from me . . . I know him very well . . . "

"You certainly should," said Henry, grinning. "Although, of course, thirty-two years is a long time."

"So you know about that, do you?" Margery was completely self-possessed. "Of course, it was inevitable that you should find out. I do hope you will be discreet. It could be very awkward if it became common knowledge."

"I'm always as discreet as I can be," said Henry. "What interests me is why you should make a secret of it."

Margery hesitated. "I'll be frank with you," she said, at length. "Mr. Goring is very much against employing husbands and wives in the same office. When one of our fashion staff wanted to marry a man from the advertizing department last year, they were told bluntly that one of them would have to go. It's company policy."

"But what about . . . ?"

"Exactly. Teresa and Michael. That is a very special case, and I suspect that Godfrey isn't entirely happy about it, even now. I was determined not to lose Teresa, and I was equally keen to get hold of Michael, who had started to produce some of the most interesting work in London. Even so, I had to campaign for nearly a year before I got Mr. Goring's approval, and then I don't think he'd have done it if he hadn't been personally friendly with Teresa and her family. I had just won that battle when I—I met Patrick again. Shortly afterwards, my art editor resigned. I knew that Patrick was exactly the person for the job, and I knew that I could work with him, but I also knew that I could not possibly go to Mr. Goring and propose my husband for the job. So we agreed to let the past remain dead and buried for the time being."

Henry leant forward. "What do you mean, for the time being?" he asked.

"I'm very fond of Patrick," said Margery. "I always have been. This is a great secret, Inspector, but when I retire in March, Patrick and I are going to live together again. As far as the people here are concerned, I shall marry him. They need never know that we have been married all along."

"I see," said Henry. He hesitated. "Forgive me for saying this, but . . . I take it that Mr. Walsh is just as enthusiastic as you are about this project?"

"Of course," said Margery coolly. She studied her scarlet fingernails for a moment. "He's an irresponsible character, but I know what's best for him. He'll be far happier leading a sane, orderly life than pigging it in that terrible studio of his."

"I was most impressed by the studio," said Henry.

Margery looked up. "You've been there?"

"Yes. Last night."

"Then you know what I mean."

"Yes," said Henry, thoughtfully. He added, "Mr. Walsh was exceptionally fond of Helen Pankhurst, wasn't he?"

"In a purely platonic way," said Margery, a little sharply.

"Oh, yes," said Henry. "Yes, I'm sure of that . . . "

10

At twelve thirty precisely, Henry walked into The Orangery. The *maître d'hotel* recognized him at once, and approached, all smiles. Basking undeservedly in Goring's reflected glory, Henry experienced briefly the pleasures of the privileged. Deferential hands divested him gently of his raincoat, cigarette lighters appeared as if by magic before he had time to open his case, his chair was pulled back and his napkin flicked open and spread on his knee. Feeling fraudulent, but enjoying himself, Henry ordered a martini and then turned his attention to his fellow lunchers.

He could see only two familiar faces. Olwen Piper was eating at a corner table with a burly, grey-haired man whom Henry recognized from his television viewing as a currently popular novelist, wit, and player of panel games. The two of them were in the middle of an animated discussion, which had started smilingly enough. But as it progressed, Henry could see Olwen's mouth setting into a stubborn line, while the man passed from amused bickering to genuine annoyance. Evidently, Olwen's sincerity was causing her to put her foot in things yet again. She was probably, Henry thought, giving him her frank opinion of the latest bit of infantile but harmless nonsense in which he was engaged.

At a quarter to one exactly, Godfrey Goring came in. He

nodded to Henry, ignored Olwen, and made his way to his usual table, where he sat alone, engrossed in the *Financial Times*.

Just before one o'clock, Henry became aware of familiar voices coming from the table behind his own. The speakers were hidden from him—and he from them—by a looped curtain of tangerine velvet and a potted orange tree, but there was no mistaking the gruff, accented English of Horace Barry and the high, light tones of Nicholas Knight. Henry was intrigued by the fact that they had not come in by the front door, which he had under observation. He remembered the small staircase which ran down from Knight's atelier, and decided that there must surely be a direct way from it to the restaurant.

Barry was speaking, and he sounded agitated. "I am frank with you always, no, isn't it?" he demanded. Emotion seemed to have weakened his command of English. "Why you not so be frank with me, eh? Is it I pay you not enough?"

"I tell you, I haven't an *idea* what you're talking about. Not the *faintest*." Knight's voice rose, pettishly. "You've been listening to gossip from those terrible *Style* people. Even Godfrey was hinting the other night . . . don't think I wasn't aware of it . . . "

"Gossip, no." Barry's deep rumble was decisive. "I keep open my eyes and my ears, is all."

At this point, a diversion was caused by the arrival of the waiter, and the two men ordered their meal. As soon as the waiter's back was turned, however, Knight began again in an agitated squeak. "*Who* told you?" he demanded. "That's what I want to know. Who told you these *wicked* lies? As if it wasn't bad enough having my show next week, and half the fabric not arrived yet, and policemen all over the place . . . it's enough to give a person a breakdown . . . "

"Nobody tell me," said Barry. "*This* tell me." There was a smacking sound, as of a magazine or newspaper being placed emphatically on the table.

"That's American," said Knight, more calmly. "That has nothing to do with London."

"Listen, my friend." Barry cleared his throat, and began to read. " 'Are Paris designs being pirated? This is the big question raised by persistent rumours that some wholesalers are producing suspiciously accurate copies of Paris models without having bought the *toiles*, and before the official release date for photographs. This magazine deplores gossip, and thinks that the question should be brought into the open and thoroughly aired.' Then follows much about the high ethics of American wholesalers, et cetera . . . the lack of any sort of proof . . . then . . . ah, here . . . 'We are not denying that a few recent incidents in New York and London are difficult to explain away, nevertheless it is our opinion that wholesalers and designers in both countries can be exonerated, for one very good reason— the sheer impossibility of smuggling out of Paris a sufficiently detailed design to be useful. Granted the corruptibility of the occasional *midinette*, the great couture houses now have security checks of such severity that the smuggling of *toiles*—which has been alleged—would be, quite simply, a physical impossibility.' "

Barry stopped reading, and there was a silence. Then Knight remarked, "Well, what are you so worked up about? They say it's impossible, and we're exonerated."

"*They* say." Barry's voice was low now, so that Henry could barely distinguish the words. "*They* say it is impossible. But you see, I happen to know that it is not."

"What *do* you mean?" Knight's voice was an excited squeal.

"Not so loud," said Barry warningly. "We speak no more of this now. One thing only I say to you. I will have no scandals. I employ you, I use your name—therefore, your reputation is the reputation of Barrimodes. I do not accuse you. I do not question you. I say only—no more scandal, no more rumours, or . . . "

It was at this moment that Henry saw Veronica making her way across the restaurant, escorted by the bevy of smiling waiters who always seemed to materialize when she entered a public eating place. She waved cheerfully, and called out, "Hello, Uncle Henry! Sorry I'm late. I've been sleuthing for you."

At his corner table, Godfrey Goring looked up slowly from his newspaper to give Henry and Veronica a long, hard stare. There was no expression whatsoever on his face. Olwen Piper, however, reacted with more emotion. She broke off in the middle of a sentence to turn round and gaze with unashamed curiosity at Veronica. Her square-jawed face had gone very pink, and the look on it, while hard to define, might well have been anger.

Apparently unaware of the mild sensation she was causing,

Veronica dropped into a chair, and announced, ringingly, "Gosh, I'm ravenous. I've had a hell of a morning with that awful little queer upstairs."

Ignoring all Henry's warning signs, she buttered herself a piece of bread, took a big mouthful of it, and went on, "There's something fishy going on, Uncle Henry, you mark my words. I don't know exactly what it is yet, but I soon will."

"Veronica," said Henry quietly, "for God's sake, keep your voice down. Knight is sitting just behind you."

"Gosh, is he? Nicholas Knight in person? Where?" replied Veronica, as loudly as ever. Henry pondered gloomily on the strange quirk of nature that had allied extreme beauty with apparent feeble-mindedness in the person of his wife's niece.

"For heaven's sake, be quiet," he muttered. "Order your lunch and eat it and shut up. We'll talk in my office afterwards."

Veronica smiled. "Oh, very well," she said. "Anyway, I wasn't going to tell you today what I think I've found out, because I don't know for sure yet, but by next week . . . "

"Veronica!" said Henry sternly.

She picked up the enormous menu, and, in its sheltering shadow, surreptitiously winked at him. Henry was greatly relieved by the appearance of the waiter, which put an end to the conversation. He was also thankful when Veronica announced that she was not hungry, although his spirits sank when she went on to say that she thought she could just manage a plate of smoked salmon, and then maybe a liqueur soufflée. However, by dint of sticking to cold chicken himself, waving the wine list firmly away, and declining coffee, he managed to leave the restaurant with one and sixpence still in his pocket and his dignity unimpaired.

About halfway through the meal, Henry had noticed the cessation of Knight's and Barry's voices, and when he got up to leave he saw that their table was empty. Presumably they had departed through the same private door by which they had come in. Goring had left some minutes earlier, without as much as a glance at Henry or Veronica. Olwen was still arguing earnestly with her TV celebrity over endless cups of coffee, but she took time off to stare again at Veronica as the latter walked out. Again, Henry was uncertain what lay behind her expression. Anger? Apprehension? Exasperation? Perhaps a mixture of all three.

Back in the privacy of his little office at *Style*, Henry proceeded to give his niece a large piece of his mind. He dwelt at some length on her foolhardiness in getting mixed up in criminal matters, her lack of tact amounting to idiocy, and the possible unpleasant consequences which might ensue if she persisted in her present line of conduct. He demanded that henceforth she should dissociate herself from any kind of detection whatsoever, and he forbade her to appear in Nicholas Knight's show. He also asked her, several times, what she imagined her mother would say about it all.

Veronica listened penitently, with downcast eyes. When Henry paused for breath, she said demurely that she was very sorry, that she knew she had been silly, and that she wouldn't do it again. She agreed willingly to abide by all Henry's suggestions with the exception of quitting the Nicholas Knight show. "All the clothes have been fitted on me now," she explained. "I couldn't let him down at this stage. It wouldn't be professional."

Nothing that Henry could say would shake her on this point, but so gratifyingly chastened was her manner that he decided to let it pass, and went on to the subject of Paris and Rachel Field's suitcase. Veronica was indignant.

"I didn't touch her beastly suitcase," she said with spirit, "and if she says I did, she's lying."

"She doesn't say you did. She says you could have."

"Well, that doesn't prove anything."

"Look, Ronnie," said Henry, "I'm not accusing you of anything. I'm sure that anything you did was completely innocent. Nevertheless, if somebody did ask you to slip something into Miss Field's suitcase, you must tell me about it. I promise you won't get into trouble, and in a serious case like this, you mustn't have scruples about telling tales on other people."

"I tell you, I never went near the wretched suitcase," said Veronica. "I *was* in her room while she was packing, but I wouldn't have dared touch anything. You know the sort of person she is—everything beautifully wrapped up and packed in apple-pie order. When I pack, I just roll things up and stuff them in anyhow."

"Miss Field was called away in the middle of packing, wasn't she?"

"Yes. Teresa came and knocked on the door and asked her to go along to her room to check on something. She was away for about ten minutes."

"And all that time you stayed in Miss Field's room?"

"Yes."

"Nobody else came in?"

"Not a soul."

"Well," said Henry, "it certainly looks as though whoever ransacked Rachel's case didn't find what they were looking for. Unless," he added, sternly, "there's something that you haven't told me."

Veronica's big eyes grew even bigger, in exaggerated innocence. "Oh, no, Uncle Henry. I've told you everything."

"I hope you have," said Henry. "Now you'd better run along. I have some calls to make. Remember what I told you, and keep your nose out of trouble. Are you coming round to the flat for a drink tonight?"

"I can't. I'm going to the pictures with Donald."

Henry hesitated. He was more worried about Veronica than he wanted her to know. Yet he could hardly forbid her to go out with a young man against whom he had no definite grounds for suspicion, apart from a feeling that his evidence had not been entirely truthful. At length, he said, "Don't discuss the case with anybody, Ronnie. Not even Donald. Above all, don't tell him that you think you may have discovered something. Incidentally, what *was* all that nonsense you were talking at lunchtime?"

"Oh, nothing." Again the innocence was slightly overdone. "Just a very vague something. Anyway, you said I wasn't to meddle in . . . "

"If you've stumbled on something, you must tell me."

"No, honestly. It's nothing."

Henry was aware of conflicting pressures. As Veronica's uncle, he wished her to have nothing to do with the affair; as a policeman, he realized that she was extraordinarily well-placed for finding out just the sort of significant detail which could be invaluable. In the end he said, "Come and see us tomorrow and we'll talk it over then."

"I'm sorry, Uncle Henry. I can't. I've promised to go and spend the week end with Nancy at her parents' place in the country—you remember Nancy Blake, don't you? The girl I share my flat with."

"Well, that should keep you out of harm's way, at any rate," said Henry. "Till Monday, then."

"Till Monday," said Veronica. She put on her coat, kissed Henry's nose, and departed.

Henry made a phone call, and then took a bus to Onslow Street in Kensington, to the residence of Dr. Walter Markham.

Dr. Markham was a stout, fatherly man in his late fifties, who greeted Henry with an expression of worried concern on his normally jovial face.

"A great tragedy," he kept repeating, as he ushered Henry into the comfortable, leather-upholstered consulting room. "A great tragedy. Such a charming woman, and so young. And yet, which of us can blame her? If she saw fit to take her own life . . . " He sighed.

Henry was intrigued. Again the suggestion of suicide. "What makes you say that?" he asked.

"Well . . . " Dr. Markham hesitated. "I presume that the P.M. will have revealed her state of health . . . "

"You were her doctor," said Henry. "What was her state of health?"

Dr. Markham looked surprised. "I imagine," he said, "that she was suffering from an incurable cancer."

"You imagine?"

"I had better explain." The doctor settled back in his chair. "Miss Pankhurst was one of my registered patients. Fortunately, I saw little of her in a professional capacity. Occasionally, she would come to me if she had a cold or some such small ailment. Nevertheless, we were neighbours, and I think you can say that we were friends. About two months ago, she came to see me in a state of great distress." He paused. "She would not let me examine her, but she asked me, in confidence, to give her the name of the best cancer specialist in London. Naturally, I was very concerned. She maintained that she was asking on behalf of a friend . . . that is very usual. People who suspect they may be suffering from such a disease are often anxious to keep it hushed up until they know for certain. They do not wish to distress their family and friends unnecessarily. Helen confirmed my suspicions by being most insistent that I should tell nobody of her visit. In particular, she wanted to make sure that Miss Piper did not hear of it. Her flat-mate, you know—another patient of mine. There was nothing I could do except give her the information she wanted, and let her go. When I read of this tragedy in the papers, I naturally assumed . . . "

"Which specialist did you recommend to her?" Henry asked.

Dr. Markham looked uncomfortable. "I don't know whether I should . . . " he began.

"Doctor," said Henry, "there was nothing at all the matter with Miss Pankhurst, and she did not commit suicide. She was murdered."

"Good God. Murdered? What a terrible thing." The doctor looked really shaken. "But who?"

"That's what I'm trying to find out," said Henry, "and this information may help me."

"Well, since you put it like that . . . I advised her to go to Sir James Braithwaite. He's the acknowledged expert. In Wimpole Street, you know. My goodness . . . murdered . . . "

"Thank you," said Henry. "You've been very helpful. And please—keep quiet about all this. I've given you certain information in strict confidence."

"Of course, Inspector. Naturally. Murdered . . . what a tragedy . . . what a great tragedy . . . "

Sir James Braithwaite, Henry was informed by a crisp young brunette in a white uniform, was extremely busy and could see nobody until the end of next week. He had only today returned from a conference in Vienna, she added, and therefore had a lot of work to catch up on.

At the sight of Henry's card, the brunette opened her brown eyes very wide and looked scared. She asked Henry to take a seat in the waiting room, and disappeared, at what was almost a run, through a heavy oak door which led off the hallway of the solid Wimpole Street house.

Henry took a seat. He was alone in the waiting room, with only a bronze figure of Diana the Huntress and a pile of elderly magazines to keep him company, and he became more and more aware of the insistent ticking of the ormolu clock on the mantelpiece and the softly muffled roar of the traffic outside. If one believed, as Henry did, that buildings could catch and retain some echo of the events and emotions which they witnessed, then this must be one of the most tragic rooms on earth. The measure of human agony, apprehension, and despair which had flowed through it, he reflected, gave it a far better chance of being haunted than had a house which had seen a solitary, swift act of violence. In spite of himself, Henry shivered. He thought of Helen Pankhurst sitting in this same room, waiting . . . He thought of Michael Healy.

The door opened, and the brunette said, "Sir James can spare you a few minutes straightaway, Inspector." Henry got up and followed her into the consulting room.

The room was deliberately unclinical and reassuring. Its big bow windows overlooked a quiet garden, and the thin January sunshine, struggling to penetrate the white muslin curtains, gave an impression of light and warmth. Apart from two filing cabinets and a leather-topped desk, it might have been a pleasantly furnished drawing room. As Sir James Braithwaite rose from behind the desk to greet Henry, it was clear that he, too, radiated the same air of comfort and good cheer. He was a tall, handsome man with white hair, a smooth pink face which seemed to be always smiling, and blue eyes that twinkled behind horn-rimmed glasses. The sort of man before whom, one felt, insuperable problems would melt away to nothing. A man to be trusted.

"My dear Inspector," he said. "Please come in and sit down. What can I do for you? I trust your visit has no sinister significance?" The blue eyes sparkled merrily.

"It's very kind of you to make time to see me, Sir James," said Henry. "I understand you are very busy just now."

"Yes, I fear I am. I think Miss Bennett explained to you that I'm just back from a Vienna conference, and I know I don't have to tell you, Inspector, how things mount up the moment one's back is turned."

"When did you leave England?" Henry asked.

"At crack of dawn on Wednesday morning, by air," answered Sir James, with a wry smile. "That's the way life goes. I'd promised to speak at a professional dinner in Surrey on Tuesday night, and yet I had to be in Vienna for the opening of the conference at eleven on Wednesday. It was a two-day affair, but do you think I could slip quietly back yesterday evening and get a good night's sleep? Not a bit of it. Another dinner had been arranged for me in Vienna last night. I got back this morning, just in time to attend another luncheon here. Sometimes I feel I'm being turned into a sort of mountebank. My job is treating patients, not making speeches."

"So," said Henry, slowly, "you presumably haven't seen an English newspaper since Tuesday. You don't know that Miss Pankhurst is dead."

"Miss —?" Sir James leant forward, polite and puzzled. "I'm so sorry, Inspector. I don't grasp quite what you . . . Miss Pankhurst? Who is she?"

"The assistant editor of *Style*," said Henry.

Sir James gave a helpless little laugh. "I'm afraid all this is quite beyond me," he said. "My wife reads *Style*, of course, but it's hardly my line. Am I expected to know something about this young woman? I assume she was young. I imagine all fashion writers as being twenty-five and ravishingly beautiful."

"She was not, then, a patient of yours?" Henry asked.

Sir James shook his head. "I don't pretend that I can recall offhand every patient who has ever visited me," he said, "but I can tell you that she is not under treatment at the moment. There's a very simple way of finding out if she ever has consulted me . . . " He got up and went over to one of the green filing cabinets, where he flicked expertly through a series of cards. "No. I have never had a patient of that name."

"I think," said Henry, "that she may have used an assumed name."

Sir James sighed. "That is not unusual," he said.

"So," said Henry, "I've brought along a couple of photographs of her for you to see. They're not very good, but I hope you may be able to identify her."

Sir James studied the two pictures gravely. No trace of surprise crossed his face, but for several seconds he sat regarding the snapshots, frowning slightly. He said nothing.

"Well?" said Henry. "Do you recognize her?"

Without taking his eyes off the photographs, Sir James said, "Yes."

"Who was she?"

Sir James looked up and met Henry's eye squarely. There was no laughter in his face now. "You tell me," he said, "that her name was Pankhurst, and that she was unmarried. I knew her as Mrs. Charles Dodgson. She was not my patient, but her husband was . . . and still is."

Henry looked up. "Charles Dodgson?" he repeated.

"Yes," answered Sir James. "Is that name familiar to you?"

"It certainly is," said Henry. "Isn't it to you?"

"I have just told you that Charles Dodgson is my patient. Why are you smiling?"

"It's always pleasant," said Henry, "to encounter an informed sense of humour, even in grim circumstances."

"I'm afraid I don't understand."

"Never mind. It's not important. Tell me, what was your diagnosis of Mr. Dodgson's condition?"

"Really, Inspector, I hardly think that . . . "

"This is a murder investigation," said Henry. "You can speak absolutely freely."

"Murder?" Sir James looked up, startled. "I thought perhaps that . . . No. No, that would not have been in character. A very courageous woman, I thought. Even when . . . "

"Please," said Henry, "tell me your diagnosis."

"Mr. Dodgson," said Sir James slowly, "is suffering from a malignant growth in the stomach. At the moment, its effects are only such as to cause mild discomfort, but it is so situated as to be inoperable. Short of a miracle . . . which does sometimes happen . . . nothing can prevent it from developing in the usual way. I would give him a year to live."

"Have you told him so?"

"No." Sir James pondered. "In such a case, I always consult with a near relative as to whether or not the patient should be told. I first examined Mr. Dodgson on . . . wait a minute, I will check the date." He went back to the filing cabinet, and sorted through the cards. For a moment he looked bewildered, then he smiled. "Oh. Stupid of me. Mr. Dodgson's card is not here. I quite forgot. The circumstances were slightly unusual. Mrs. Dodgson—forgive me if I go on calling her that—telephoned me to make the appointment, but emphasized that she and her husband were both busy working people, and could only come to me on Saturday or Sunday. I explained that I spend every week end in the country—a vain attempt to preserve a private life. She said that this would suit her admirably. Her husband had no suspicion that he might be suffering from cancer, and she did not want to alarm him. She had already persuaded him to consent to a general medical checkup, and she could easily arrange for them to spend the week end near my country house. In this way, she could get him to come and see me informally, as it were, with no idea that . . . "

"Your country house is at Hindhurst, isn't it?" said Henry.

"Yes. Well, just outside, to be precise."

"I don't know when you first saw Mr. Dodgson," said Henry, "but you certainly examined him just over a month ago, on December 28th."

"That's right." Sir James looked surprised. "I remember it now, because it was during the Christmas holiday. That was his first visit."

"Mrs. Dodgson arrived first, probably by taxi, and spoke to you," said Henry. "I imagine that she asked you to keep your diagnosis secret from her husband, but to tell her. You replied that you wouldn't be able to give a definite answer immediately—tests would have to be made, and so on."

Sir James smiled. "This is wizardry," he said. "You seem to know more about it than I do. Go on."

"Mr. Dodgson turned up by car a little later, you examined him, and they drove off together. Correct?"

"Correct!"

"When did you next see him?"

"He came in for an X-ray a couple of weeks later. I was fairly sure of my diagnosis by then, but I wanted the X-rays to clinch matters. Mrs. Dodgson was not with him on that occasion. He was anxious about his condition, so I kept my promise, and merely told him that he had a stomach ulcer. He went off quite happy."

"Then," said Henry, "on Tuesday of this week the X-ray results came through, confirming your worst fears."

"On Monday evening, as a matter of fact," said Sir James.

"Sorry. On Monday evening. You telephoned Mrs. Dodgson, and asked her to come and see you."

"In principle, yes. In fact, it was she who telephoned me."

"Really? But why?"

Sir James smiled, a little sadly. "In cases like this," he said, "there is always the fear that the wrong person may answer the telephone if I call. Mrs. Dodgson was particularly anxious about

154

this. You see, she did not wish me to telephone her at her office. In fact, she was at some pains to discourage me from finding out where she worked, and yet, in the evenings, her husband would be as likely as she to answer the telephone. So I told her to ring me at Hindhurst on Monday evening, by which time I was fairly certain of having a positive answer for her."

"I see," said Henry. "So when she telephoned, you told her that you would like to see her as soon as possible. Naturally, you wouldn't want to break the bad news over the telephone. You explained that you would be in Hindhurst until Tuesday evening, and were leaving for Vienna on Wednesday morning."

"That is correct. The dinner I told you about was organized by the Hindhurst Cottage Hospital, where I work for a day each week.

"She replied," pursued Henry, "that she could come to Hindhurst and see you on Tuesday afternoon. This she did, and you told her the worst."

"Yes. That is all perfectly accurate. That is all I know. What happened then?"

"She returned to London," said Henry, "and started on an all-night working session for the magazine. All the other people concerned went home at about half past one, leaving her to work on alone. She was found dead the following morning, having drunk cyanide in her tea."

For a moment, Sir James was silent. Then he said, "And you are treating this as a case of murder?"

"Yes, I am."

Sir James nodded. "I am glad to hear it."

"Why do you say that?"

"Because, in the circumstances, you might be tempted to think of it as suicide, and I am convinced that you would be making a grave mistake." Sir James paused, considering his words carefully. "I am not a psychiatrist, Inspector, but it is my unhappy duty to have to break bad news—the worst possible news—to many people. I have come to gauge their reactions fairly accurately. Mrs. Dodgson behaved splendidly. She broke down when she first heard the truth, which is always a good thing. The sooner the inevitable emotional storm comes, the sooner the air is cleared. Then she pulled herself together and asked me a lot of highly intelligent questions. She wanted to know all about her husband's condition, and how she could best care for him and make his last months happy and comfortable. In short, her approach was constructive. I cannot believe that she went away and killed herself."

"She didn't," said Henry, positively.

"But . . . " Sir James hesitated. "There is this inconsistency in her name. Am I to take it that she was not, in fact, Mrs. Dodgson?"

"You are."

"Then—forgive me for asking this, but I am concerned with my patient—who *will* look after him?"

"Your patient has a wife," said Henry. "Whether she will be as sympathetic and sensible as Miss Pankhurst, I can't say. In the course of time I'll send her to see you."

"This puts me in a very delicate position," said Sir James, unhappily. "Does Mrs. Dodgson . . . the real one . . . know about . . . ?"

"I can't tell you that," said Henry. "Not for the moment. But I can tell you that she will come and see you, and that her name is not Dodgson either."

It was six o'clock when Henry left Wimpole Street. He went to the nearest phone box and put through a call to Olwen Piper at the flat in Kensington—the flat which had been Helen's. Olwen answered at once, and did not seem pleased.

"I have to be at the theatre by half past eight," she said. "It's not very convenient. I thought you'd have rung earlier."

"I can be with you by half past six," said Henry. "If you could spare me even half an hour . . . "

"Oh, very well."

Henry was looking forward with interest to seeing Helen's home. He knew already that she had not been rich. A couple of hundred pounds in the bank and the proceeds of a small insurance policy were all that her sister in Australia would inherit, apart from furniture and personal possessions. Henry guessed that, like many unmarried women, Helen had spent the bulk of her salary on clothes and on her apartment, and a quick look round was enough to convince him that he had been right.

The flat was on the seventh floor of a modern block, and was furnished with good, simple, contemporary pieces, bearing witness to excellent if somewhat austere taste on the part of the late occupant. There was a marked lack of the frills and knickknacks which often abound in a purely feminine household. A few pieces of clean-cut Scandinavian glass and pottery, and several reproductions of abstracts by Kandinsky and Klee, were Helen's only concessions to decoration; everything else was strictly functional.

Olwen greeted Henry brusquely. "I suppose you want to look around," she said. "I'll leave you to it. I have to change. Call me if you want me. I'll be in my room."

With that, she disappeared through an open doorway on Henry's left, beyond which he caught a glimpse of a small bedroom in a state of great disorder. Clothes and books and papers and gramophone records lay around in confusion. The contrast between Olwen's room and the rest of the apartment underlined the fact that this had been an oddly assorted ménage. Olwen shut the door behind her, and Henry began his tour of inspection.

Apart from Olwen's room, the flat consisted of a diminutive hall, a large living room with a balcony, Helen's bedroom, and a kitchen and bathroom. The living room did not occupy Henry for long; it was as neat and impersonal as a shop window, and he felt convinced that Helen would not have kept anything private there. He left it, and went into her bedroom.

Here, again, he noticed a certain lack of femininity. The studio bed had a navy-blue tailored cover, the dressing table was of plain, light oak, and bore the bare minimum of scents and cosmetics, although Henry noticed that they were of the most expensive and exclusive makes. The drawers in the austere, modern tallboy revealed neatly arranged piles of clean clothes and handkerchiefs, and the wardrobe was equally immaculate. Only a number of soiled handkerchiefs in the dirty linen bag testified to the fact that Helen had been an ordinary, vulnerable mortal with a bad cold in the head. Henry felt depressed. There was, however, one more piece of furniture: it was a small, roll-top desk, and it was not locked. Henry opened it.

The first thing that caught his eye was an unfinished letter, which lay on a pad of white blotting paper in the center of the desk. It was written in ink, in a precise, Italianate hand, and it bore no superscription other than the word "Tuesday." Henry picked it up and read it.

"I think I've got hold of the right stuff at last. It's not quite the same as one finds in Paris, but I've asked Teresa to bring me back a sample, so that we can compare them. I've practically made up my mind about the blue jersey dress—you know, the one Beth wanted to photograph. I'll let you know definitely in a few days' time, I hope."

Here the note stopped. Since it did not break off in mid-sentence, Henry guessed that Helen had not been interrupted while writing it, but had merely put it away to finish later—realizing, perhaps, that she would have to hurry to keep her appointment with the doctor. A large pin in the left-hand top corner of the paper secured something to the back of it, and Henry turned it over, expecting to see a scrap of dress material, for clearly the letter had been intended for Helen's dressmaker. He was mildly surprised, however, to find nothing except a blank sheet of writing paper pinned to the first one. He was on the point of replacing the note in the blotter when it occurred to him that he had no sample of Helen's handwriting—in the office she had worked exclusively on the typewriter. So he folded the paper and put it into his pocket.

Otherwise, the desk was as dishearteningly well-ordered as the rest of Helen's life. There were neat files of receipts, bank statements, and household accounts. There was a file marked "Letters to be answered," in which Henry found a note, apparently from an old school friend, urging Helen to spend a week end with the writer and her husband in Shropshire; a letter from a London store, informing Madam that the lamp shade she wanted was not available in yellow, and asking if blue would be suitable; and a card from the Electricity Board stating that, if convenient, their representative would call next Monday at 2 P.M. to inspect the faulty cooker.

Contemplating the contents of the desk, Henry felt chilled by the impersonality of it all. There were no invitation cards, no inane picture post cards from holidaying friends, no scribbled notes making or breaking dates. Above all, there were no love letters. Was it, he wondered, because she never received such communications? Or was it because she destroyed them?

Resolving to have a word with Olwen on the subject, he took a last look round the room, but it revealed no secrets. A small bookcase held some detective stories, two currently fashionable biographies, a celebrated but unscholarly account of archeological discoveries in Egypt, a complete set of A.A. Milne, and a couple of best-selling novels—one of them written by a university professor and the other by a self-confessed pickpocket. The lower shelf was stacked with back numbers of *Style*. "A middle-brow," Henry summed up to himself, "just very slightly raised."

In fact, of everything in the room, the most individual items were Helen's clothes. Henry was no fashion expert, but even he could see that the contents of the wardrobe revealed a strong and adventurous sense of colour, allied to a preference for simple, classic lines. There were no hats swathed in veiling or roses, no dresses in soft, pastel colours, and above all, no extremes of fashion. Henry found himself agreeing with Margery French's assessment. Helen had been a well-dressed woman—her *Style* training ensured that—but she played too safe to be the editor of a great fashion magazine. In spite of himself, the much-used word "flair" came to Henry's mind. He felt that he was beginning to understand what it meant.

Leaving the bedroom, Henry went into the white-tiled kitchen, and took a look at the garbage-disposal arrangements. To his depression, he saw that the apartment was fitted with a modern incinerator unit. Any correspondence which Helen had thrown away would be pulverized beyond hope by now. He went back into the hall and knocked on Olwen's door.

"Yes? What do you want?"

"I've seen all I need to see, Miss Piper," said Henry, "but I'd like a word with you when you're ready."

"Very well. I shan't be long."

A couple of minutes later, Olwen joined him in the living room. She had changed into a rose-pink silk dress, embellished with the softly draped ruffles which were all the rage, and she looked terrible. Any of *Style*'s fashion staff could have told her that one should not wear ruffles if one wasn't the type, fashion or no fashion, and that if one did wear them, it was disastrous to combine them with ropes of artificial pearls, a pair of bright pink satin shoes and a solid-looking white handbag. In fact, the fashion staff of *Style* were sick and tired of telling Olwen these things, since her reply was always either a defiant, "But I *like* pearls with it," or a vaguely-murmured, "Oh, really . . . yes, of course . . . " which indicated that her mind was miles away. As for Henry, he did not have the expertise to analyse Olwen's sartorial faults, but he knew a mess when he saw one. All the same, he made an effort, smiled, and said, "Ah, there you are. How charming you look."

"It *is* a pretty dress, isn't it?" said Olwen complacently. "Beth photographed it for Young Style a couple of months ago, on Veronica Spence. The picture was so lovely I felt I must buy the dress."

Privately, Henry lowered his opinion of Beth Connolly by several notches. He could not be expected to understand that, although the dress was identical, the resultant effect was a thousand miles away from the young, fresh drift of rose-petal pink which had floated across the pages of *Style*. It is a bitter burden that fashion editors have to bear, that their advice is generally only half digested by their readers.

"Well?" said Olwen, "What can I do for you?"

"First of all," said Henry, pulling out of his pocket the note he had found in Helen's desk, "can you identify that handwriting?"

Olwen glanced at it. "Yes, of course. It's Helen's."

"Good. I just wanted to be sure. Now, can you tell me if Helen generally received many letters?"

"I really can't tell you, Inspector."

"But surely you must . . . "

"Helen always got up first in the morning, and made coffee. I'm at the theatre most evenings, so I can afford to get into the office a little later, unless I'm specially busy. Helen was . . . well . . . secretive about some things. It became a routine that she always collected the post, and she took her letters into the kitchen and read them while the coffee was brewing. Anything that didn't need an answer, she put into the incinerator straight away— you know how tidy she was."

"What do you mean by 'secretive'?" Henry asked.

"Well . . . " Olwen hesitated. "One morning I was expecting rather a special letter, and I got up early and cleared the letter box and took her mail into her room to give her, and she was absolutely furious. As though I'd been opening her private letters, or something. Anyhow, there was nothing for her that morning except a couple of circulars, but she made me promise

I'd leave the post for her to collect in the future. It was strange, wasn't it? Not a bit like her."

"Very strange," Henry agreed. He felt considerably annoyed with Helen Pankhurst. Whatever intriguing correspondence she might have received, she had successfully obliterated all trace of it. Henry thought wistfully of those detective stories where a scrap of unburnt paper with a few significant words on it always seems to emerge from a pile of ashes in the grate. He'd like to know, he reflected grimly, what even Sherlock Holmes would have done if confronted with an electric incinerator. He became aware that Olwen was speaking again.

" . . . as soon as possible. You do understand, don't you?"

"I'm sorry. What were you saying?"

"Helen's clothes and things. I'd like to get them packed up and into storage as soon as I can."

"I can't see any objection," said Henry. He looked round the room. "I suppose all this furniture is hers. What will you do about that?"

"I'll write to her sister," said Olwen, "to see what she wants me to do with it. Of course, I'll have to refurnish completely, but for the time being I imagine I can go on using Helen's things." She glanced at her workmanlike wrist watch, which, on its stout black leather strap, did less than nothing for the rose-pink dress. "I'm afraid I have to go now."

"Me, too," said Henry. "Thank you for your help."

At the door, Olwen paused. "So I can pack her things up over the week end?" she said.

"If you wish."

"Thank you. You can't imagine how . . . how glad I shall be." For a moment, Olwen's voice broke. "It's her clothes. They're like ghosts . . . *doppelgängers*. I can't bear having them in the house."

"I can understand that," said Henry. "Right. Pack them up and get rid of them."

11

The week end was characterized by the coldest weather of a cold winter, and by a deep depression on Henry's part. He was pretty sure by now that he knew the identity of the murderer, but he had arrived at the answer by a combination of small clues and the instinct which he called his "nose." This did not give him anything like the solid proof that he needed, and besides, there were gaps that he could not fill in. Added to this, the situation of Michael and Teresa Healy weighed heavily on his shoulders. He could not make up his mind where his responsibility lay, and whether it was part of his duty to tell Teresa the truth. He even had misgivings about his own reconstruction of the case, and he frequently thought about what Donald MacKay had said, and wondered if he had been bamboozled by a group of experts into forming opinions which were in no sense his own.

On Saturday, to add to the general gloom, Henry went to Helen's funeral, which—with typical generosity and thoughtfulness—Godfrey Goring had organized. Apart from a genuine desire to pay his respects to the dead woman, Henry was anxious to see whether, in fact, the staff of *Style* had been correct in saying that Helen had had few friends outside her work.

It certainly looked like it. Margery French and Patrick were there, sitting together; so were Michael and Teresa. Godfrey Goring sat alone, looking suitably solemn. Beth Connolly was accompanied by a short, fair girl whom she introduced to Henry as Helen's secretary. The only other mourner was a stolidly built, motherly lady whom Henry had never seen before, and who turned out to be Mrs. Sedge, the charlady who had "done" for Helen for the past ten years. Henry made a careful mental note not only of who was there, but of who was not.

When the mournful rites were over, Goring suggested that they should all go back to Brompton Square for tea. He extended the invitation warmly to Mrs. Sedge and, after a palpable hesitation, included Henry.

It was not a happy gathering. Only Mrs. Sedge appeared to be enjoying herself. She was not in the least overawed by her surroundings, and her frank appreciation of tea and chocolate cake was refreshing. It was also obvious that she had been fond of Helen, and mourned her sincerely.

"A lovely lady," she said to Henry, extending her little finger conscientiously as she sipped from one of Goring's Meissen cups. "A really lovely lady, and a pleasure to work for. So considerate. Mind you, everything had to be done proper. No skimping the dusting or forgetting to scrub the underneaths of the saucepans. But what I always say is—you don't mind working hard if it's appreciated, do you?"

Henry murmured agreement, and Mrs. Sedge went on. "That Miss Piper, now . . . " She lowered her voice discreetly. "*Quite* a different matter altogether. Doesn't know the difference between clean and dirty, if you ask me. Of course, she's young yet. She wants me to stay on with her, but I really haven't made up my mind. It's not the same without Miss Helen."

"Still," said Henry, "I don't suppose you saw very much of either of them, did you? I mean, they were out at work all day . . . "

Mrs. Sedge looked at him pityingly. "That's not really the point, is it?" she said, gently rebuking. "Thank you, I *could* manage another small piece of cake. No, what I mean is, Miss Helen's room was always so neat and tidy, except that once, and then there was a reason. And she'd leave me my instructions, all properly written out. You knew where you were. But Miss Piper's room—well, you should see it, that's all I can say. *And* she doesn't like me going in there to tidy up."

Henry said, "Miss Helen sounds almost too good to be true.

I'm rather glad to hear she left her room in a mess occasionally."

"Only the once," said Mrs. Sedge. She smiled reminiscently. "Yes, the only time I remember in ten years. About a month ago, it must have been. I opened the door, and you could have knocked me down with a feather. Things were all over the place—papers and the like."

"Papers?" repeated Henry, interested.

"Well, when I say papers, I don't mean letters and things. Tissue paper. But then I might have known."

"Known what?"

"That there'd be a good reason," said Mrs. Sedge. "For once, you see, I'd gone straight into Miss Helen's room instead of into the kitchen when I arrived. And when I *did* go into the kitchen, there was a little note from her asking me not to touch her room that day, as she was in the middle of packing her things to go away. That's what I mean by considerate."

"To go away?" said Henry. "A month ago?"

"That's right. A business trip, I suppose it must have been. That was on the Monday. When I came again on the Friday, she was back."

"A little more tea, Mrs. Sedge?" Godfrey Goring appeared, charming and solicitous. Henry left him refilling Mrs. Sedge's cup, and went over to the other side of the room, where Michael Healy was talking to Beth Connolly.

Beth smiled quickly and rather nervously at Henry, and said, "It was nice of you to come along today, Inspector. I'm sure Helen would have appreciated it."

Michael gave Henry a cynical look. "All in the course of duty, I dare say, wasn't it, Inspector?"

"I suppose you could call it that," said Henry. "It's often difficult to draw an exact dividing line between duty and . . . " He hesitated. "Pleasure" did not seem to be the right word. " . . . and one's natural inclinations."

"How very perspicacious you are, Inspector," said Michael maliciously. "But of course, that's what we pay you for, isn't it?"

There was an awkward silence, during which Henry began to sympathize with Horace Barry's view of Michael. Henry himself, knowing what he did, was prepared to make every allowance, but even so, he had to admit that the photographer was an expert in the art of insult.

It was Beth who spoke first, with typical directness. "What a beastly, snide remark, Michael. I think Inspector Tibbett has been wonderful. It must be a hell of a job, investigating a murder in a madhouse like *Style*."

Immediately, Michael looked contrite. "I'm sorry," he said. "I . . . I haven't been feeling terribly well lately, and Paris is always a strain. As soon as I find myself getting bitchy, I know the time has come to take a holiday. I thought I might spend a few weeks in the Canaries when . . . when all this is over."

"I suppose I shouldn't ask," said Beth, "but how *is* the case going, Inspector?"

"Slowly, I'm afraid," said Henry. "I've seldom had an assignment where it was so difficult to get to the truth."

"Really? Why?"

Henry looked straight at Michael Healy. "Because," he said, "I'm up against extremely clever people."

Michael returned his direct gaze. "Have you found us obstructive or unwilling to talk, Inspector?"

"No," said Henry. "Everybody has been garrulous, frank, and anxious to help. That's just the trouble."

Michael gave a tiny smile. "You're pretty clever yourself, aren't you?" he said. And when Henry did not reply, he added, "Wouldn't it be much easier for everyone if you decided that Helen had committed suicide?"

"Yes," said Henry. "It would. It would also be untrue."

"How can you be sure?"

"I'm just clever enough," said Henry, "not to tell you that."

Soon after this, the party began to break up. Margery said that she must go, and offered a lift to the blonde secretary. Patrick at once cut in on this arrangement, claiming that the girl lived in his direction, and that he would not only take her home but stand her a drink on the way. Margery looked very angry indeed, but said nothing. Meanwhile, Teresa and Michael had volunteered to drive Mrs. Sedge as far as Sloane Square Underground Station, whence she could take a train to Putney. Henry was about to take his leave when Goring laid a hand on his arm, and said quietly, "Please, Inspector. Do stay and have a drink. I'd like to talk to you."

In the elegant drawing room, Goring put another log on the open fire, poured whisky for Henry and tonic water for himself, and said, "I'll come straight to the point, Inspector. I want to know what progress you are making on the case. It's no use telling me that I have no right to ask, because I think I have. The longer it drags on, the more unsettling the effect on my staff—and when people are unsettled they don't work well." He paused. "Margery came to see me yesterday. She says that efficiency is beginning to suffer in every department. For instance, Olwen Piper, who is usually the most meticulous of writers, let through a paragraph in her April copy which was not only inaccurate, but could have been construed as libelous. Fortunately, Margery spotted it when the proofs came through. When she spoke to Olwen about it, the girl got hysterical and said she couldn't concentrate on anything until the murder was cleared up. Then Teresa had been behaving very strangely—reorganizing the whole of the April fashion reportage quite unnecessarily, according to Margery. When Margery protested, Teresa snapped at her and reminded her that she wouldn't be sitting at her present desk much longer. Very distressing and most unlike Teresa. As for Patrick Walsh, he seems to have lost his grip completely, and is leaving everything to his assistant. These are my key people, Inspector. You can understand why I'm concerned."

"Yes," said Henry, "I can."

"Now," Goring went on, "I gave you my considered opinion when we lunched together, and I've seen no reason to change it. Frankly, I was disappointed at the outcome of the inquest. An adjournment merely prolongs the agony for everyone. It's perfectly clear that Helen killed herself. Can't you let it go at that?"

Carefully, Henry said, "It's for the coroner's court to decide, Mr. Goring. I can't possibly anticipate their verdict."

Goring gave Henry a faintly conspiratorial smile. "We all know," he said, "that the court will be influenced one way or the other by the police evidence. You can't hide behind the coroner's skirts, Inspector."

"I can assure you," said Henry, "that in a case like this, where there is an element of doubt, the verdict may well be a surprise to us all. We can only present the evidence as we see it."

"And how do you see it?"

Henry looked at Goring searchingly for a long moment. Then he said, "As you pointed out, Mr. Goring, you are in a very special position with regard to this case. I think that I am justified in taking you into my confidence, so long as you give me your word that nothing I say will go any further."

Goring looked pleased, and nodded with becoming solemnity. "I quite understand that."

"You know, of course," Henry went on, "that Miss Field's suitcase, which was in Helen's office, was rifled at some time during the night?"

"I had heard that. But I don't see what . . . might not Helen herself have done it, before she . . . ?"

"No," said Henry. "Helen collapsed over her typewriter, in the middle of typing a sentence; but the typewriter keys were covered with face powder from a box out of Miss Field's suitcase. There was powder on every key, except those on which Helen's fingers were resting. This, together with the fact that Miss Field's key to the building has disappeared, makes it virtually certain that somebody returned to the office later on, after Helen was dead, and ransacked the suitcase."

Goring considered this for a moment in silence. Then he said, "I am forced to agree with you, Inspector. Nevertheless, this by no means proves that Helen was murdered. Let us suppose that she committed suicide, and that later this mysterious person turned up and found her."

"And didn't raise the alarm?"

"They wouldn't have dared. They had no right to be there. They were bent on stealing something from the suitcase. Naturally, they were unnerved at finding a dead body in the room, which would explain the frantic haste with which the case was apparently rifled."

"That would sound convincing," said Henry, "if it weren't for the evidence of the fingerprints."

"What fingerprints?"

"The ones that weren't there. The Thermos flask had only Helen's prints on it, and the cyanide bottle had none at all. You see what that means?"

"That the person who poured out the cyanide was wearing gloves?"

"It's rather more complicated than that. We know that Ernest Jenkins, the darkroom boy, handled the Thermos earlier on, when he refilled it, so his prints would be on it—if it hadn't been wiped clean later on, after the cyanide was put in, and before Helen carried it along to her office. Then, Ernest also used the cyanide earlier in the evening, so his prints should have been on that bottle, too. If Helen had really poisoned herself, would she have taken the trouble to wipe the Thermos clean and then put her own prints on it, and would she have cleaned her prints off the cyanide bottle?"

After a long pause, Goring said, "So that is to be the police evidence, when the inquest is resumed?"

"That among other things. I hope to have a great deal more evidence by then."

"Well," said Goring, "in that case, I suppose we can only be patient. Dare I ask if you have a . . . a line on anybody?"

"Certainly you may ask," said Henry, pleasantly, "but I'm afraid I can't tell you."

"Of course not. I do understand." Goring hesitated, and then said, almost diffidently, "By the way . . . when the inquest is resumed . . . will the business of Helen and Michael Healy be dragged up?"

"Only if it's strictly necessary," said Henry. "I'd like to think that we shall be able to avoid it."

Goring looked profoundly relieved. "I'm thankful to hear that," he said. "It's the kind of publicity we want to avoid at all costs."

"But," said Henry, "I can't promise that it won't be mentioned later, in another court. At the murder trial, in fact. If the prosecution doesn't use it, the defence almost certainly will."

"Before a trial, there must be an arrest."

"Of course."

"It sounds to me," said Goring, "as though you were pretty confident of making one soon," he said.

Henry smiled, "I hope to," he said.

Suddenly, Goring said, "My wife tells me you called on her in Downley."

"That's right," said Henry. "I just wanted to clear her completely by establishing that she was in the country at the time of the murder."

"Clear her? My dear man, you surely don't connect Lorna with . . . ?"

"No, no. Of course not," said Henry hastily. "It was pure routine. In any case, she has a perfect alibi. She was playing bridge into the small hours that night with a host of witnesses."

Goring looked relieved. "That's good," he said. "I mean, in circumstances like these, one is always worried that one's family may be dragged in."

"Don't I know it," said Henry feelingly. He was heartily thankful that Veronica was safely out of the way, even if only for the week end. Then he added, "That's a lovely house you have at Downley, Mr. Goring. It must be sad for you not to be able to spend more time there."

"Work is work, alas," replied Goring. "Still, I hope to get down there later this evening, for what's left of the week end. It's lonely for my wife . . . I really must try to persuade her to spend more time in London."

"Mr. Goring," said Henry, suddenly, "what do you know about smuggling designs out of Paris?"

Goring looked completely taken aback for a moment, and then smiled. "You've been hearing rumours, have you, Inspector?"

"Yes, I have."

"Well . . . " Goring poked the fire. "I don't believe it myself, but these things are bad for the whole industry, and should be cleared up. I am naturally anxious to get to the bottom of the whole matter, but in my position, you understand, it's difficult . . . "

"Yes," said Henry. "I can see it is."

A few minutes later he took his leave. It was a raw, bitter evening, and Knightsbridge was totally devoid of taxis. He ended up by queuing for a bus, and arrived home chilled to the marrow.

Emmy was in the kitchen, preparing dinner. Since it was by far the warmest room in the flat, Henry was only too pleased to comply with her request that he should go in there and talk to her while she cooked. Standing as close to the blazing gas stove as he could without actually setting fire to his clothes, Henry told her about the funeral and recounted the gist of his conversation with Goring.

"I do feel sorry for him," said Emmy. "Poor man. He must be terribly worried. Henry, do you think—?"

She was interrupted by the telephone ringing. Henry went to answer it.

"Inspector Tibbett? This is Lorna Goring."

"How nice to hear from you, Mrs. Goring," said Henry.

"I'm sorry to bother you . . . I just wondered about that doctor in Hindhurst. My friend has been onto me again. Did you have any luck?"

Henry hesitated. "Yes and no," he said. "I found out who the doctor was, but he's a London man who happens to have a country house at Hindhurst. He works at the hospital there for a day each week, but I doubt if he would take on any private patients."

"Well . . . you never know. Could you give me his name, in any case?"

"I really don't think there's any point, Mrs. Goring," said Henry. "You see, you told me that your friend was looking for a G.P., and this man is a specialist."

"Oh. Oh, I see. Well, never mind, it was just a thought." Lorna paused. "How did the funeral go?"

"It wasn't exactly gay," said Henry. "Not unnaturally. However, your husband was very kind and gave us all a delicious tea afterwards."

"Ah." Lorna gave what sounded like a tiny sigh of satisfaction. "I don't suppose he happened to mention whether he was coming down here this week end, did he? He never lets me know. I've been trying to ring him, but he's out."

"In that case," said Henry, "he's probably on his way to you. He told me he was coming down this evening."

"This evening? Oh, that's good. Well, I won't keep you any longer, Inspector. So sorry to have been a nuisance. Goodbye."

Henry went back to the kitchen in a thoughtful frame of mind. Emmy was mashing potatoes.

"Who was it?" she asked.

"Mrs. Goring."

"Good heavens. What did she want?"

"I'm not quite sure," said Henry, "but I have a pretty good idea."

Henry had intended to take Sunday off, as a much-needed day of rest and refreshment, but he found he could not get the case out of his mind. He was markedly silent over the lunchtime beer which he and Emmy took at their local pub, and his lack of concentration on the dart board caused them to lose several games to notoriously mediocre players.

In the afternoon, instead of settling down to his usual session with the Sunday papers, Henry began making notes on the case. Whereas his official reports had been confined strictly to facts, these private jottings were basically character studies—Henry's personal impressions of people and their reactions. One character, however, eluded him. Helen Pankhurst herself.

Henry fell into a drowsy reverie. It was warm in front of the fire, and the dancing flames threw flickering shadows onto the walls. It was beginning to grow dark, but he did not put on the light. He thought about Helen. He had seen her just once, distorted and ugly in death. He thought of her as she had apparently appeared to the outside world—precise, tidy, dedicated to her work, and endowed with clinical good taste and complete emotional control; he contrasted this with what went on behind the "enameled intellectual shell" which Michael had talked about. He remembered that she worked among incredible confusion when under pressure; that she was capable of leaving her room untidy once in ten years. He tried to understand the real Helen—emotional, passionate, perhaps even violent, but above all vulnerable. And somebody had killed her.

People, Henry reflected, don't get themselves killed for nothing. It had been always one of his maxims that most murders were committed for love or for money. In Helen's case, the money motive seemed negligible. As for love—Helen had loved a married man. Henry went over in his mind the possible permutations of a *crime passionelle*. Her lover might have killed her for several reasons: if she had been unfaithful, if she had become an embarrassment, or if she was threatening to wreck a marriage which he had no intention of abandoning. His wife might have killed her out of jealousy. Another woman who also desired the lover might have struck at Helen. All these surmises seemed wildly melodramatic to Henry, and they were made somehow shabby and absurd by one incontrovertible fact. Helen had lived and died a virgin.

Somewhere, among the facts at his disposal, lay not only the truth but the proof. Of this, Henry was convinced. Somewhere lay the confirmation of what his "nose" told him. There was only one way to get to it. The long way. Go back to the facts. Tabulate. Analyse. Make lists. Make timetables. Henry reached for his notebook, but it was no use. Fatigue and warmth and a good lunch were too much for him.

Twice, Henry pulled himself up and jerked his eyes open just as his pen was about to slip through his fingers onto the floor. The third time, sleep was too strong for him, but since he had a bad conscience about nodding over his work, his subconscious employed the same, cheating tactics that it used when he was loth to get up in the morning. On those occasions, he would dream, vividly, that he was switching off the alarm, getting up, shaving, dressing . . . only to wake with a start to find himself still in bed and late for work.

So now, while Henry's physical self snored gently, his subconscious being sat alertly on the same sofa, making precise and penetrating notes. To his dreaming mind, the key to the mystery seemed to be within his grasp when he wrote "The Duchess of Basingstoke owns the cheetah," and the word sequence "Healy-Helen-Hell," which he wrote down several times, assumed enormous, metaphysical significance. He was not at all surprised to glance up and see that Helen Pankhurst herself had come into the room, and was standing by the fire in her fluffy white sweater and grey skirt.

"There you are," he said, slightly aggrieved. "About time, too."

"Your trouble is that you can't see things when they're right under your nose," said Helen, rather sharply.

"Don't bring my nose into this."

"It's so simple. I can't think how you missed it."

"Shut up and don't be so smug," said Henry, annoyed. "It's all very well for you. You're dead."

"If you're going to insult me, I'll go."

"No . . . don't go. Tell me. Please tell me . . . "

But Helen was walking away from him, towards the door. Henry tried to stand up and follow her, but in his dream his feet had become as heavy as lead, and he could not move them.

"Helen!" he cried. "Helen!"

"Whatever is the matter, Henry?" Emmy stopped in the doorway with the tea tray in her hands. On the sofa, in the dusky twilight, Henry writhed in uneasy sleep. "Helen . . . " he muttered. "Helen . . . "

"Come on, old thing. Wake up," said Emmy briskly. She switched on the light. Henry sat up slowly, rubbing his eyes.

"Must have dropped off," he muttered, shamefacedly.

"Worse than that." Emmy grinned. "You were talking in your sleep. Who *is* this Helen, anyway? I'm beginning to get suspicious."

Henry did not smile. "She's the girl who was killed," he said. "I've just had a dream about her. Tremendously vivid and real and . . . She seems to be impatient with me because I'm being dense about something."

"You've been brooding too much over this case," Emmy said, determinedly matter-of-fact. "What with Ronnie being involved and everything. And you had too much Camembert after lunch. You know that always gives you nightmares."

"Yes, I suppose that was it." But Henry could not get the dream of Helen out of his mind. He would be the last person to think of himself as psychic or clairvoyant, but something at the back of his mind was telling him that it was Helen herself who could help him now. Helen . . . her personality, her clothes, her office, her apartment . . .

He put his hand into his pocket and pulled out the unfinished letter that he had taken from Helen's desk. He unfolded it and read it again, not so much from any interest in what it said, as from a feeling that something as personal as handwriting might in some way bring him closer to her. He reread the note, and then, idly, turned to the second piece of writing paper which had been pinned to the back of the first.

When Emmy came in, a moment or so later, she found Henry sitting absolutely still, white-faced, gazing at a sheet of paper with a stunned expression on his face. It was, as Henry admitted afterwards, one of the most uncanny experiences of his life, and for a moment it took his breath away. For the sheet of paper which had been blank on Friday evening now had writing on it. Scrawled boldly across it, in the same hand which had written the other note, were the words, "See what I mean?"

It was some minutes later, when Emmy had gone out to get supper, that Henry lifted his head and said aloud, "Yes, Helen. I see what you mean."

12

Instead of going directly to *Style* on Monday morning, Henry went to Scotland Yard, where he handed over Helen's note, together with its mysterious addendum, to the handwriting experts for analysis. He then telephoned *Style* and arranged to speak to Teresa later in the morning, after which he put through a call to Paris and had a long talk with one of his opposite numbers at the Sureté, who also happened to be a personal friend. The French detective was much interested in what Henry had to say, and promised to investigate the matter at his end. He also agreed to purchase a certain small object and put it in the post to London.

At ten minutes to eleven, Henry was back in Earl Street, being greeted affably by the doorman, who seemed by now to have accepted him as a permanent member of the staff. Indeed, Henry was beginning to feel like one. He took the lift upstairs.

The door of the fashion room was open, and the usual pandemonium reigned. Telephones rang and typewriters clicked and there seemed to be clothes and jewelry everywhere. In front of a long mirror, a model in the briefest of underclothes was stepping out of one dress and putting on another. This done, she struck a pose. Behind her stood Beth Connolly, studying with half-closed eyes not—Henry was interested to notice—the girl herself, but her reflection in the mirror. When, later, he asked Beth the reason for this, she explained that the reflection gave a truer impression of what a photograph would look like.

By now, Henry had come to take semi-nude beauties in his stride. He went into the fashion room and said to Beth, "I have a favour to ask you. Can you get me a ticket for Nicholas Knight's Press Show tomorrow?"

"Yes, of course I can."

"And can you tell me the release date for this season's Paris photographs?"

"February twenty-seventh. That's when we—" Beth broke off as her secretary came up. "What is it, Marilyn?"

"Telephone, Miss Connolly."

"Oh, blast," said Beth. "Hang on a moment, Inspector. I won't be long."

Beth picked up the telephone. She sounded exasperated. "No, Nicholas . . . I told you before—I haven't the faintest idea where she is. She should have been here at ten for a job and she simply didn't turn up. . . . Well, I'm furious too, but what can one do? You know what these girls are like. . . . Yes, I agree, I wouldn't have thought it of Veronica, but it only goes to show you never can tell. . . . Of course I've telephoned her home. . . . Nancy doesn't know either. . . . Yes, I will, if I hear anything. Goodbye."

A cold hand was closing on Henry's heart. When Beth rang off, he said, "Can you come next door and talk, Beth?"

Beth looked slightly desperate. "Oh, dear," she said. "Will it take long? I've got a sitting, and everything has been bitched up because of . . . "

"Only a minute, I promise."

"O.K." To the model, she added, "Take that off, and put on the yellow, with the amber necklaces and the big straw hat. I'll be back."

As soon as the door of Henry's office was closed, he said, "What's all this about Veronica?"

"I'm very cross with her," said Beth. "She's let me down."

"What do you mean?"

"I had her booked for a sitting this morning, and she didn't arrive. I've had hell's own job finding another girl, and she's not really right for the clothes."

"But where can Veronica be?" Henry hoped that his voice did

not betray the degree of alarm which he felt.

"I suppose she's decided to stay down in the country. She told me she was going to Hampshire for the week end."

"She was going to stay with Nancy and her parents," said Henry. "I gather from what you said just now that Nancy is back."

Beth gave him a curious look, and then said, "I really wouldn't worry, Inspector. Nigel's having hysterics because she was due there for final fittings, and it's his show tomorrow, but I'm sure Veronica's perfectly all right."

"I expect she's just playing truant," agreed Henry, "but I think I'll have a word with Nancy all the same. If you do hear anything, you might let me know."

Nancy Blake answered the telephone in her deliciously husky, deep-brown voice. "No, she's not here. Who is it? . . . Oh, Inspector Tibbett, how are you? Haven't seen you for ages. . . . No, I've no idea, I'm afraid. . . . She went off on Saturday morning to stay with friends in the country. . . . No, she didn't say where. . . . What's that? My parents? Good heavens, no. I mean . . . Well, they're in India actually, that's why. . . . I think you must have misunderstood her. . . . All I can tell you is that she took a taxi from here on Saturday morning. . . . What? Let me think. . . . Yes, she was wearing her oatmeal tweed suit with a white sweater, and her bright red suede coat. . . . No hat. . . . Yes, she had her navy-blue leather suitcase with her. . . . Goodness, Inspector, it can't be as serious as that, can it? . . . I'm sure she's all right. . . . Yes, of course I'll let you know."

Henry rang off in an extremely troubled frame of mind. Two possibilities presented themselves, and neither was pleasant. For a start, Veronica had deliberately lied to him. Why? Was she off on some madcap scheme of her own, playing at detectives? Or had she planned an illicit week end with a boy friend? In either case, why hadn't she come back? Henry knew enough of his niece to realize that she had a strong sense of professionalism in her job.

He telephoned the fashion room, and left a message that he would be late for his interview with Miss Manners. He then rang Donald MacKay and told him brusquely to come to the office at once. He reckoned he might have to do a certain amount of bullying to get to the truth.

Donald looked distinctly apprehensive when he came in. Henry assumed a suitable intimidating expression. He did not invite Donald to sit down, but rapped out, "Well, Mr. MacKay. What is all this I hear about you and Veronica?"

Donald went very red, and said, "I'm afraid I don't understand, sir."

"Oh, yes, you do. Where is she?"

"I've no idea . . . I mean, isn't she at home?"

"She's missing," said Henry. "It may be very serious indeed. If you know where she is, or where she spent the week end, you must tell me at once."

"Missing?" Donald sounded really bewildered.

"When did you last see her?"

"On Wednesday evening. The day after . . . you know. We dined together."

"Don't lie to me," said Henry. "She told me herself she was going out with you on Friday evening."

Once again, Donald blushed painfully. "I . . . that is, yes. I mean, no. We had a date to go to the movies, but I had to cancel it. My mother was taken ill suddenly . . . my father rang me at lunchtime, and I got away early from the office and went straight down there. I didn't get back till last night. She's better now . . . my mother, I mean."

"Did Veronica tell you where she was proposing to spend the week end?"

"She . . . that is . . . no. I didn't see her. I telephoned her to let her know I couldn't take her out in the evening, and that was all."

"Where do your parents live, Mr. MacKay?"

"In Essex."

"May I have their name and address and telephone number, please?"

For a moment, Donald looked panic-stricken. Then he pulled himself together, and said with more spirit, "Certainly, if you insist, sir, but I do think it's rather impertinent. This can't have anything to do with Helen's murder."

"It may have something to do with Veronica's murder, if we aren't careful," said Henry, grimly.

"Good God. You don't really mean that?"

"I do," said Henry. "Come on, now. Your parents' address and phone number."

"Rabbit End Farm, Hockton, Essex. The number is Hockton 18. Their name, funnily enough, is MacKay."

"Wait here," said Henry. "I'm going to ring them now. And if I find you haven't told me the truth . . . "

"But I have!"

"We'll see," said Henry, picking up the telephone.

A gruff, amiable masculine voice with a marked Scots accent answered the phone. "MacKay here, Rabbit End," it said.

"This is Inspector Tibbett of Scotland Yard," said Henry. "Can you tell me, Mr. MacKay, when you last saw your son Donald?"

"Donald? The boy's not in any trouble is he? He was just telling us all about this murder . . . "

"No, he's in no trouble. Don't worry. I just want to know when you last saw him."

"Why, he was here until yesterday evening. He left on the 8:15. We hadn't expected to see him, but my wife had a bad turn on Friday . . . she suffers from her heart, poor lassie. I rang Donald, and he said he'd be down right away. He got here around teatime, and stayed the whole week end. She's better now, I'm glad to say. You never can tell with this heart trouble. Once, it'll blow over in a few hours, another time she'll be in her bed for weeks."

"I see. Thank you very much, Mr. MacKay. I just wanted to check . . . yes, he's fine. He's here with me now . . . yes . . . yes, I'll tell him . . . Goodbye."

He rang off and grinned at Donald. "I apologize," he said. "It seems you were telling the truth. Your father says to tell you that you forgot your toothbrush. He says not to bother to buy another, because he's sending it."

Donald looked relieved. He smiled. "Well, I'm glad you believe me at last," he said. "The question is—where's Veronica?"

"Precisely," said Henry. He was trying hard to keep his sense of proportion. After all, Veronica had deliberately deceived him, and had gone off on her own, voluntarily. Reprehensible though it might be, it seemed to rule out the possibility that she had been kidnapped.

At that moment, the telephone rang again. "Inspector Tibbett?"

purred a velvety, familiar voice. "This is Nancy again. You may as well call off your hunt for Veronica."

"Really? Why?"

"Because I know where she is. And when you said you might get the police onto her trail . . . "

"Yes, yes, get on with it. Where is she?" Henry was growing impatient. He liked what he knew of Nancy, but she could be maddeningly slow in getting to the point.

"She's at the White Hart Hotel in Porchester."

"Porchester? In the New Forest? Why didn't you tell me this before?"

"Well . . . " Nancy hesitated. "You see, she's not alone . . . "

"Oh, isn't she?" said Henry, ominously. He was thinking of an imminent interview with Veronica's mother, and not relishing the prospect. "Who is she with?"

"Donald MacKay," said Nancy.

"But . . . " for a moment Henry could find no words. Then he said, "How do you know?"

"Well, actually," said Nancy, "I've known all along. I didn't know what to say when you rang, so I called Beth—she knew about it, too, you see—and she said she'd been wondering whether to tell you or not, and eventually we decided that we'd better. Beth said you were so sweet, you'd be sure to understand."

"I understand less and less," said Henry. "One of the things I don't understand is how Donald MacKay contrived to be at the White Hart in Porchester and in his parents' home in Essex at one and the same time."

Donald, who had been contemplating the toes of his shoes, looked up, startled, and began to say something. Henry silenced him with an impatient gesture.

Nancy said, "Oh, that's easy. I can explain that."

"Can you, indeed? It should be interesting."

"Well, you see," said Nancy, "she got this telegram . . . "

"What telegram?"

"I'd better start at the beginning. I was out at a cocktail party on Friday evening, and when I got in, I found Ronnie very depressed. She told me that she and Donald had arranged to go to Porchester for the week end, and that he'd telephoned to say that the whole thing was off, because his mother was ill and he had to go down to Essex to see her. But then on Saturday morning first thing a telegram came. One of those night-letter things. I think it's still in Ronnie's room. Shall I get it and read it to you?"

"Yes, please do," said Henry. Putting his hand over the mouth-piece of the telephone, he said sternly to Donald, "Well may you look ashamed of yourself, young man. I shall have plenty to say to you in a moment."

"Are you there? I've got it." Henry could hear the crackling of paper as Nancy pulled the telegram out of its envelope. She read, " 'Mother better can get away Saturday meet me eleven-eighteen Porchester train Waterloo love kisses Donald.' "

Henry said, "Where was that handed in?"

"Just a moment. I'll look." There was a little pause. "That's funny."

"What is?"

"It was handed in at eight-fourteen P.M. on Friday evening—in London."

"Nancy," said Henry, "will you be a dear girl and get into a taxi straight away and bring that telegram to me here, at *Style*?"

"But I haven't got a stitch on!"

"Well, put something on. And hurry. This may be serious." Henry hesitated for a moment, and then said, "You still haven't explained why Veronica isn't back."

"Well, I suppose they decided to stay a bit longer. They were probably having a good time," said Nancy, reasonably.

"Donald is back in the office," said Henry.

"*Is* he? Gosh. Then where's Ronnie?"

"If I knew that," said Henry, "I'd be a lot happier. See you in fifteen minutes."

He rang off and turned to Donald. "I won't tell you for the moment what I think of you," he said. "That can wait. Mean-while, did you send Veronica a night-letter telegram on Friday night?"

"No. Certainly not."

"Who else knew about your mother being ill?"

"Everybody in the office, I should think. Father rang me here, and I asked Mr. Walsh if I could leave early to catch the four-forty from Liverpool Street. He said I'd have to ask Miss French, which I did. And I went down to the fashion room with some layouts and mentioned it in there. Beth was out, but everyone else must have known."

"And how many people," Henry went on, "knew of your original plan to take Veronica to Porchester for the week end?"

Donald reddened again. "It wasn't what you think, sir," he said. "I'm terribly fond of Ronnie. I respect her . . . "

"That's not what I'm talking about—for the moment," said Henry. "I want to know how many people knew, apart from Nancy Blake and Beth Connolly."

"I'm afraid most people did."

"What do you mean by that?"

"Well . . . you know Ronnie. Can't keep anything to herself. She was chattering about it all over the office."

"I see," said Henry, unamused. "So everyone in the place—except me—knew that you and Veronica were going off for what, in my day, used to be called a dirty week end?"

"Yes . . . I mean, no." Donald seemed to gain courage. "If you don't mind me saying so, sir, you really are awfully old-fashioned."

"In this instance, I'm not ashamed of it."

"No . . . you misunderstand me, sir. I mean, these days lots of people go away for week ends and holidays without sleeping together. Honestly. The fact that you assume that that's what we . . . well, I can only say that people must have been very loose-living in your day. Actually, I'm rather shocked."

"*You're* shocked?" For the second time, Henry found himself speechless. He also had a sneaking suspicion that, on this point if on no other, Donald might be telling the truth. "Well," he said, "that aspect of it can wait. The point is that you didn't go away together, unless your father was lying to me, which I doubt. You remained in Essex, while Veronica was deliberately lured away from home by a faked telegram; a telegram sent by somebody who knew all about your plans, which means, somebody from this office. You can go now, but don't leave the building. I'll probably need you again."

When Donald had gone, Henry plunged thankfully into a whirl of activity. At least, it helped to take his mind off the looming nightmare. First he broke the news to Emmy, and sent her off posthaste to Scotland Yard with a selection of photographs of Veronica. Then he telephoned the Yard and made sure that a description of his niece, and the clothes she was wearing, should be circulated immediately, and the matter treated as urgent. He set in motion a search for the cabby who had picked Veronica up in Victoria Grove, and despatched detectives to question the railway staff at Waterloo. Nancy arrived with the telegram, which was at once sucked into the maw of the police machine. Within a very short time, the operator who had taken it in would be traced.

More as a matter of form than anything else, Henry also rang the White Hart Hotel at Porchester. He was told that Mr. Mac-Kay had booked a double room for Saturday night, but had telephoned on Friday afternoon to cancel it. Nobody of that name had turned up, and there had been no sign of anybody answering to Veronica's description.

When he felt that he had done all he could in the matter of Veronica's disappearance, Henry turned to his long-postponed talk with Teresa Manners.

Teresa was sitting at her desk, looking as ravishing and as vague as ever. When Henry came into the office, a dark-haired girl whom he had not seen before was standing beside a rackful of dresses, displaying them one by one for Teresa's approval. For all her air of feyness, Teresa's judgments were crisp and to the point.

"Yes . . . very good. I like that. But we'll have to change the buttons. Plain large smoked pearl is what it needs . . . No, terrible. Out. It's last season's colour, and I will *not* have any more pleated skirts . . . Do come in, Inspector, I shan't be a moment . . . nearly finished . . . Ye-es, I suppose so . . . The suit's all right, but the shirt is all wrong. Get a plain cream shantung shirt with gold cufflinks . . . What in heaven's name is that horror?"

She raised her beautifully plucked eyebrows as the girl held up a bright green cotton dress.

"It's the one from Barrimodes, Miss Manners," she said. "I don't like it any more than you do, but you know how it is. We've simply got to use *something*. It was the best of a bad lot, honestly. You should have seen the others."

"The sooner Barry gets cracking with his Nicholas Knight range, the easier life will be for everyone," said Teresa feelingly. She inspected the offending dress with distaste. "Doesn't he make it in any other colours?"

"Eventually it'll be in blue, pink and yellow," said the dark girl, "but this is the only sample he's got at the moment."

"Blue, pink and yellow . . . Ye Gods . . . !" said Teresa in despair. She studied the dress through half-closed eyes, with the same expression of concentration that Henry had seen on Beth Connolly's face. At length she said, "Tell him that if he makes it in black, we'll use it. Not otherwise. Black with gilt blazer buttons. And make him rip that ghastly pocket off the skirt. It'll never be chic, but that way it'll be inoffensive."

"He won't like that, Miss Manners," said the girl gloomily.

"I know he won't," said Teresa, "but you'll just have to bully him. If he won't take it from you, get Beth to talk to him—he eats out of her hand. But get it into your head that we are *not* going to use the green. Over my dead body."

"Yes, Miss Manners. Well, that's the lot. I'll go and ring Mr. Barry straight away."

Pushing the dress rack ahead of her, she vanished into the Babel of the fashion room.

"That's one of my babies," said Teresa. There was affectionate pride in her voice. "She used to be a secretary, and I'm training her up as a fashion editor. She's going to be good. Well, Inspector, what can I do for you?"

Henry sat down, lit a cigarette, and said, "Miss Manners, what happened to the small parcel that Helen Pankhurst asked you to bring back from Paris?"

Teresa looked taken aback. "Goodness," she said. "I'd forgotten clean about it. That's how vague I am. You know what it was?"

"Yes," said Henry. He told her.

Teresa nodded. "I'm sorry about forgetting," she said, "but it couldn't be important, could it? A silly little thing like that . . ."

"It's possible," said Henry, "that it cost Helen her life. If things happened as I think they did. Where is it now?"

"In my . . . no, by God, it's not. How very odd. I'm certain I packed it, but now I come to think of it, when I unpacked my case on Wednesday, it wasn't there. If it had been, of course, I'd have remembered and told you about it."

"It wasn't there," said Henry, "because somebody took it."

"Oh, surely not. I must have left it at the Crillon. You know what a scatterbrain I am."

"Only in some things," Henry thought to himself. Aloud he

said, "I presume your case wasn't locked."

"No. I never bother."

"That's what I thought. And your case was in the darkroom all the evening—in fact, all night."

"Yes. But it's fantastic. You mean, somebody stole . . . "

"I think we can be more precise," said Henry. "And it wasn't exactly stealing. The somebody was Helen."

"Helen? Then where is it now?"

"My guess is that it doesn't exist any longer," said Henry. "Anyhow, never mind that for the moment. I just wanted to check with you to see if my assumptions were right. Now tell me something else. What are the mysterious rumours which are going round about Nicholas Knight?"

Teresa went very white, and Henry saw that her fists were tightly clenched. "Rumours? What rumours? I don't know what you mean!"

"I think you do," said Henry. "I mean, the stories about the pirating of Paris designs."

"Oh, that." Teresa seemed to relax a little. "That's just rag-trade gossip. It wouldn't interest you."

"But it does."

"Well, the simple truth is that Nicholas has an astonishing flair for recreating a Paris line, just by looking at a photograph of the model. He's not cheap, but his prices are nothing like as expensive as going to Dior or Monnier for the original. So lots of women get Nicholas to do them what he calls his 'Paris specials,' which cost considerably more than a dress from his ordinary Collection. He won't do them for everyone, just for favoured customers."

"Does he make a secret of it?" Henry asked.

Teresa smiled. "*He* doesn't," she said, "but his clients do. Naturally, they want people to think they've been buying in Paris, instead of getting a cut-price copy. In fact, we only heard of it quite recently here at *Style*. When rumours started going round, people began saying that the copies were so good that they must be made from original *toiles*. I think that's nonsense. What I think Nicholas *does* do is to get hold of photographs illicitly, ahead of the release date, but that's not a deadly sin. Anyhow, there have been a few awkward moments when women who'd bought the original model found themselves face to face with a Knight copy. But there was no scandal until a month or so ago, when the Duchess of Basingstoke turned up at a big charity affair in exactly the same dress as Felicity Fraser, the actress. The Duchess's dress was the real thing, which had been flown over that morning from Monnier's. Felicity's came from Nicholas Knight."

"And why," said Henry, "did that cause more scandal than the other encounters?"

"Because," said Teresa, "the Duchess was livid—not with Knight, but with Monnier, who had assured her that the dress was absolutely exclusive. She complained bitterly to him, and he confirmed, with a host of witnesses, that the model of her dress had never been allowed to leave the salon and had never been photographed. As soon as she picked it, after the original showing of the Collection, it was removed from the range, as it were, and kept under lock and key for her."

"What was Knight's explanation?"

"He says that somebody who was at the Press Show described the dress to him, and that he studied the cut from photographs of similar models."

"Would that be possible?"

Teresa shrugged. "I doubt it," she said.

"There are, of course," said Henry, "such things as miniature cameras disguised as cigarette lighters and so forth. But that would presuppose an expert photographer on the job." Teresa looked uncomfortable, but said nothing. "Oh, well," Henry added, "I suppose the truth will come out one day. It's just one thread in a complicated story. By the way, what was your room number at the Crillon? I think I'll just check up with them in case you did leave that little parcel there."

"I'm sure I . . . " Teresa began. Then her face lit up. "I know who might remember!"

"Who?"

"Veronica Spence. You see, I was very hectic on the last day, so she went out and bought it for me. Perhaps she has it still."

"I hope to God," said Henry, "that you're wrong."

He left Teresa looking bewildered, and made his way to the art department. Donald was working silently in a corner, intent on self-effacement. He started nervously as Henry came in, and then buried his nose in the layout he was preparing. Henry ignored him, and went over to the desk by the window, where Patrick was sitting and doodling on his blotter.

"Can you spare me a few minutes?" he asked.

"I suppose so," said Patrick heavily. He pushed back his chair. "This place gives me claustrophobia. Let's go and have a drink."

"All right," said Henry. "Where?"

"I know a dirty little pub round the back," said Patrick, brightening a little. "No fear of meeting anyone else from *Style* there. It's much too sordid."

The pub was shabby, comfortable, and deserted. Henry and Patrick installed themselves on an oaken settle, where Patrick ordered a large whisky, and Henry a tomato juice. Patrick looked at him with concern.

"That muck won't do you any good," he remarked. "Have something stronger."

"I don't like drinking on duty."

"You look as though you could do with a couple of stiff ones," said Patrick shrewdly. "What's up?"

"Veronica Spence has disappeared," said Henry.

"The pretty little model? How very odd. Where is she?"

"If I knew that," said Henry, "she wouldn't have disappeared."

"Ah. Yes. See what you mean." Patrick chuckled suddenly. "Probably found herself another boy friend to console her for her lost week end with Donald."

"You knew about that?"

"I should imagine everyone did. She was blabbing all over the office about it on Friday."

"Little fool," Henry said bitterly.

"Is that what you wanted to talk to me about?"

"No, but it's why I look as though I need a drink."

"What did you want with me, then?"

"Why haven't you told me," said Henry, "what you and Helen knew about smuggling designs out of Paris?"

Patrick looked considerably taken aback. "How did you know anything about that?" he demanded.

"I'm a detective," Henry answered. Paraphrasing Michael, he added, "That's what I'm paid for—to detect."

"Well, for a start," said Patrick, "I didn't tell you because I didn't know anything about it myself."

"What do you mean by that?"

"Helen came to me and asked me to get her certain things, and to try some experiments. I didn't know what for. It was only later on that I realized how they might be used . . . and then, of course, I kept my mouth shut."

"Why?"

"You think I'd incriminate my darling girl, after she's dead? Of course not. And besides . . . well . . . it wasn't really Helen's idea, you see. She was working on it for somebody else."

"And who was that?"

"X", said Patrick.

When Henry got back to *Style*, he found a message telling him to ring Scotland Yard. He sent out for a sandwich lunch, and picked up the telephone.

It appeared that reports were beginning to come in. The telegram had been sent from Charing Cross Road Post Office—one of the few in London which stay open late at night. The counter clerk was positive about one thing—it had been handed in by a woman. No, he wouldn't recognize her again; that was just why he remembered her, he added paradoxically. Pressed to elaborate this, he explained that she had looked so odd, all muffled up in a mackintosh and a big scarf and her hat pulled down over her eyes, and she'd spoken in a funny sort of whisper. She told him she had a terrible cold. Asked whether it could possibly have been a man in disguise, the clerk was emphatic. Not a chance, he said. Her hands were beautiful, with long fingernails painted red, and the one thing he *had* taken a good look at as she went out were her legs, and they were smashing. High-heeled shoes, too, with those dagger heels and pointed toes. You don't learn to walk in those unless you're born to it. Henry felt convinced. It had not been a man.

The taxi driver had been traced, and confirmed that he had picked Veronica up in Victoria Grove and dropped her at Waterloo. Of course he remembered. Wouldn't be likely to forget a pretty girl like *that*, with her bright red coat and that funny brown lipstick. She'd seemed very gay and excited, he said, and had chattered all the way. She'd also told him that she was going to Porchester for the week end with her boy friend. The last he'd seen of her was going into the station toward the trains.

On the other hand, the ticket collector at number ten platform was quite certain that she had not boarded the Porchester train. Certainly, there were quite a lot of people, but he was sure he'd remember if there'd been a beautiful girl like that. Besides, the taxi driver's evidence showed that she arrived at the station at eleven o'clock, when the barrier was only just open and very few people about. The station staff at Porchester Halt were even more emphatic that nobody had alighted from the train. It was a tiny place, and Veronica would certainly not have passed unnoticed. It seemed, in fact, that between the entrance to Waterloo Station and the barrier of number ten platform, Veronica Spence had vanished into thin air.

There was one other piece of information awaiting Henry. The handwriting experts had made a careful examination of Helen's letter, and gave it as their unanimous opinion that both sheets had been written by the same hand.

13

By that evening, ninety-nine percent of the population of Great Britain must have been aware of the fact that Veronica Spence was missing. Henry had decided that an all-out press, radio and television campaign was his only hope. At the same time, he was more than afraid that the whole thing might be too late. The girl had disappeared on Saturday morning, and it was Monday before the alarm had been raised. One fact only gave him hope. He, better than anybody, knew the characteristic tendency of murderers to repeat themselves, but Veronica had not been poisoned. The whole elaborate scheme of abduction suggested kidnapping rather than murder. However, Henry never lost sight of the fact that he was dealing with clever people.

He spent Monday evening at Scotland Yard, sitting by a telephone. Emmy was gallantly coping with Veronica's distraught parents, who had arrived from Devon to be greeted by a battery of photographers and journalists. Emmy, abetted by several stalwart policemen, had managed to get them safely into a taxi. Now, back at the flat, the three of them sat in a miserable, strained silence full of accusation and despair. In fact, it never occurred either to Jane or to Bill to turn on Emmy and say, "If you hadn't encouraged her to be a model, this would never have happened!" But to Emmy, in her guilt and misery, the walls seemed to be oozing with unspoken reproaches. The words screamed silently in Emmy's ears, until she longed to shout aloud, "Come on, then! Say it and have done with it! Say it!" It was not a happy evening.

Meanwhile, at Scotland Yard, news was filtering in. The publicity in the evening papers and on television had produced the usual crop of cranks, exhibitionists, and genuinely misguided characters, all of whose stories had to be patiently investigated. There was the unbalanced beatnik boy from Clapham who swore that Veronica was his discarded girl friend, whose throat he personally had slit with a flick-knife. There was the apparently demure spinster from Oxford who maintained that she had met Veronica in the Second Class Buffet at Waterloo, where the latter had confided to her that she was in fear of her life, as she was being pursued by a gang of international spies from Moscow. Unfortunately, the copy of the paper in which this lady had read the story contained a misprint, describing Veronica as carrying a vase instead of a case. When the spinster proceeded to describe the vase in great detail, her story was dismissed as improbable. Then there was the myopic but kindly old gentleman who insisted that he had sat opposite to Veronica on an underground train . . . the District Line, he thought . . . or was it the Central? . . . anyway he *thought* it was an underground train. When pressed, however, he was forced to admit that the young lady he had seen was wearing a dark blue suit . . . or was it green? . . . a fur hat and horn-rimmed spectacles. But she had such a *sweet* face, and he was almost sure she had a red suitcase with her. He was still talking to himself when a kind policeman led him gently out into the street.

The first sign of something genuinely interesting came in the form of a telephone call at about seven P.M. This was from a Mrs. Trout, of Surbiton. This good lady sounded neither cranky nor hysterical, and she was quite positive that she had seen Veronica in the Ladies' Cloakroom at Waterloo a few minutes past eleven o'clock on Saturday morning.

"I know the time, you see, because I was catching the 11:12 home after a visit to my oculist, and I wondered whether I'd have time to . . . em . . . powder my nose. I noticed her because she was so pretty, even with that funny new-fashioned lipstick, and then there was her bright red coat. I'm convinced it was her. We went into adjoining . . . em . . . conveniences. When I came out, there was no sign of her. The door of her . . . that is, next door to mine . . . was still marked 'Engaged,' so I presume she was still in there. I had to hurry off for my train. I didn't see her again."

"Did you notice anything else, Mrs. Trout?" Henry asked. "Anything that might give us a line on . . . "

"Well, I did notice that she looked excited. Flushed, you know, and smiling to herself. *That* girl's going to meet some young man, I said to myself."

"Nothing else?"

"No, nothing. I *do* hope you find her, Inspector. Such a lovely girl."

Following on Mrs. Trout's call, a detective was sent to interview the ladies' cloakroom attendant, a Mrs. O'Reilly, whom he found off duty, ensconced in front of the fire in a cosy bedsitter in the Waterloo Road. She was playing cards and swigging Guinness, and she greeted him cordially.

As luck would have it, Mrs. O'Reilly turned out to belong to the one percent of the British public who had neither bought an evening paper nor switched on a radio that evening, and who did not possess a television set. Consequently, the hue and cry had escaped her completely. She confirmed Mrs. Trout's statement at once, her sharp brown eyes twinkling as chirpily as a sparrow's under her thatch of grey hair.

"Shure, an' I saw the young lady," she said. "It's the one in the red leather coat you'll be meanin'. Now don't ask me what time she came in, dear, because I couldn't tell you. The middle of the mornin'—that's as near as I can say. I took her penny and showed her in, like I do for all the ladies, with a bit of a wipe-round to the seat, because you never know, do you? She had a suitcase with her, that I do remember, and she was as pretty as a picture. That'll be some model or film star or such, I thought."

"Did you see her leave?"

"Now, it's funny, isn't it, but I didn't. Of course, it's a busy time, Saturday mornin', with all the ladies tired from shopping and anxious to relieve themselves. She must have slipped out while I was attending to some other lady. I show them all in, you see, but they go out by themselves. Will you be taking a bottle of Guinness, Officer?"

There seemed little more that Mrs. O'Reilly could contribute, except that she recollected that Veronica had used the last lavatory on the left as you go in. The cloakroom was immediately cordoned off, causing great inconvenience to the feminine half of the traveling public, and Henry himself went along to inspect the last known spot where his niece had been seen. He had no real hope of finding anything interesting there, but it was something to do.

There was nothing remarkable about the particular cubicle which Veronica had used. It was as clean and as uninspiring as all the rest. In the rubbish rack on the back of the door were the usual assortment of used face tissues, pieces of cotton wool, and wrapping papers off chocolate bars. These were solemnly sorted out and inspected one by one. Suddenly Henry said, "That was Veronica's."

His sergeant looked at him in awed surprise, as though he had manifested supernatural powers. "How ever can you tell, sir?"

Henry picked up the soiled tissue. It was liberally smudged with the strange shade of sepia-brown lipstick which he had seen Veronica wearing at the *Style* studio. There were also several streaks of darker brown on it, and a trace of green.

"I can't be absolutely certain, of course," said Henry, "but I don't think that shade of lipstick exists in England yet. It would be a strange coincidence if another girl had brought one from Paris and used this same cubicle."

"Looks like she redid her make-up, then," said the sergeant. "Not that it helps us much. What we want to know is what she did next."

"Indeed we do," said Henry, but he looked thoughtful.

The trail seemed to end there, dead and cold. What had happened to Veronica in those few short yards between the ladies' room and the barrier of Platform Ten? The most likely explanation seemed to be that she had met someone—someone she knew, and who knew that she would be there. This person had spun her a story which had changed her mind about taking the train to Porchester. Since she imagined that she was meeting Donald at the barrier, the chances were that her acquaintance had offered her a lift to Hampshire, claiming that Donald was already in the car, waiting. This was, Henry reflected, the obvious explanation. There were two other possible alternatives, however, both of which filled him with even graver misgivings.

Back at Scotland Yard, Henry checked once more through the statements which he had taken during the afternoon. It was vital to establish the exact whereabouts at eleven o'clock on Sunday morning of all the people who knew Donald and Veronica's plans. He opened his notebook and made two lists of names—those with alibis and those without.

Donald MacKay headed the list of those whose movements were satisfactorily accounted for. While Henry did not seriously doubt the word of Donald's father, he had taken the precaution of getting the local police to check up. Donald was well known in the village, and there was ample confirmation from the railway staff and from neighbouring shopkeepers that he had arrived on Friday evening and stayed until Sunday. His father volunteered that he had got up early and gone for a long walk on Saturday morning and by twelve fifteen he had been playing darts in the local pub.

Donald's name was followed by that of Beth Connolly, who had been at her hairdresser's from ten thirty until midday, and had then gone straight on to lunch with a girl friend.

Teresa and Michael provided alibis for each other, which was less satisfactory. They had been at home, they said. In fact, Michael had stayed in bed until lunchtime. He had not been feeling well, and was dreading the ordeal of Helen's funeral in the afternoon. Teresa had pottered around the house, arranging flowers and writing letters. Their maid could confirm this, they said. Of course, she could not. The maid certainly believed that both of them had been in the whole morning, but she could not be sure. Michael had given orders that he was not to be disturbed, and she had not seen him between the time when she took up his breakfast at nine o'clock, and half past twelve, when he had rung and asked her to bring him a whisky and soda in his room; by which time, she agreed, he was up and dressed. Henry put a query beside both names.

The last two on the list seemed quite straightforward. Nicholas Knight and Horace Barry. Henry had included them, because he remembered that Veronica and Barry had both been at Knight's atelier on Friday morning, and sure enough both agreed at once that they knew all about the projected week end in Porchester. Equally, both denied that they knew anything about Donald MacKay or his mother, but Henry had decided to check, all the

193

same. It appeared that Nicholas had worked in the atelier from ten in the morning until five in the evening, sending out for a sandwich lunch. A dozen of his staff could confirm this. Horace Barry had been weekending with friends in Brighton since Friday evening.

The other list started with Rachel Field, who said that she had spent Saturday morning shopping for week-end provisions in Kensington High Street. The only shops which she could recall visiting were all large supermarkets, and Henry, thinking of the Saturday morning crowds, was not surprised that none of the staff remembered her. It proved nothing, either way. Unlike Veronica, Rachel was not a memorable person.

The next name was Patrick's. He had been at home, he said, painting. Apart from opening the door to the postman, who had delivered a parcel at about half-past nine, he had seen nobody. Margery French's account of her movements was equally inconclusive. She told Henry that she had taken a lot of work home, and spent the morning writing copy. There was one curious feature about her statement, however. She claimed that she had attempted to telephone Patrick's number several times during the morning, with the idea of arranging to meet him to go to Helen's funeral, and that she had received a persistent "engaged" signal. Eventually, she said, she had contacted the operator, who tested the line and informed her that the receiver had been left off its hook. She finally got an answer from Patrick, she said, at half past one. When taxed with this, Patrick merely replied that he frequently unhooked the receiver when he was working and did not want to be disturbed. It was an entirely reasonable explanation, on the face of it, but it still left room for doubt.

Olwen Piper had given a thoroughly unsatisfactory account of herself. She had started the morning, she said, by packing up Helen's clothes, but this sad task, together with the thought of the funeral in the afternoon, had preyed on her mind to such an extent that she decided to resort to her usual remedy of aimless walking. She had also decided that she could not face the funeral at any price. She had left the house about half past ten, and just walked. She didn't know where . . . round the streets. She was too upset to notice anything. At three o'clock she suddenly realized she was hungry, and took stock of herself. She found she had wandered as far as Kilburn. She had eggs and chips in a café, and took an underground home. By great good fortune, Henry located the café from her description, and the owner remembered her. This, again, proved nothing, either way. Mrs. Sedge, who had been working at the flat, confirmed that Olwen had left at half past ten, and had not returned when she, Mrs. Sedge, went home at noon.

The last name on Henry's non-alibi list was that of Godfrey Goring. Although the latter denied categorically that he had ever even heard of Veronica Spence, Henry reflected that he had been in the office on Friday, and should be checked. Goring said that he had spent Saturday morning at the office, working. Nobody else was there—the place was deserted. He had, however, lunched as usual at The Orangery, and this was amply confirmed. Here, again, however, there was a small inconsistency. The doorman at The Orangery maintained that Goring had not walked across the street from his office to lunch, but had driven up in his Bentley. Goring dismissed this by saying that he had left his car on a parking meter, and, realizing that time was running out, had decided to move it and to leave it to The Orangery to find him another space.

Henry studied his two lists carefully. Then, on the second one, he put small crosses by the names of Patrick, Margery, and Goring. That was to indicate the people who owned cars.

Then he settled down to think, with great concentration. He thought about Veronica, and the things she had said, and the soiled face tissue. He thought about the members of *Style*'s staff, and about the missing key and Nicholas Knight and Horace Barry, and the package that Teresa had brought back from Paris. Above all, he thought about Donald MacKay.

At a quarter to ten, he telephoned Donald's home number, and was told by the landlady that Mr. MacKay had been out since six, and she couldn't say where he was or when he would be back. Henry put on his raincoat and took a bus to Piccadilly. From there, he walked to Earl Street.

It was raining hard, and a cold wind blew up the narrow street, tossing stray pieces of sodden paper ahead of it. The *Style* building was dark and apparently deserted. Only The Orangery was warmly lit and inviting, but the commissionaire had wisely decided to take shelter inside, emerging only when a taxi drew up, bearing customers. The only human being in sight was the man with the basket of roses, who kept his lonely vigil on the pavement. From Nicholas Knight's atelier, two floors above, a light streamed out through uncurtained windows onto the rain-washed street below.

Henry walked up to the rose seller. "How much for half a dozen?"

The man's shabby raincoat was pulled up almost to his nose against the cold, nearly meeting the checked cap which he wore well down over his eyes. "Ten bob, guv'nor," he said, gruffly.

"I think," said Henry, "that it's time we had a talk, Mr. MacKay."

Before Henry knew what was happening, the man had picked up the basket of roses and flung it in Henry's face. By the time he recovered, the street was empty. Henry ran to the telephone box behind the *Style* building and put through a call to Scotland Yard.

"No," he said, "I don't want him arrested. Not yet. I want him picked up and followed. And you'd better alert the Essex police and tell them to look for . . . "

Back in Chelsea, Henry found Emmy sitting alone by the fire in a mood of acute depression and self-accusation. She had at last persuaded her sister and brother-in-law to go to bed, and was now drinking whisky in increasing melancholia. If only she had never encouraged Veronica to come to London . . . if only she had kept a stricter eye on her . . . if only . . . if only . . . It was with a tremendous sense of relief that she heard Henry's key turning in the latch.

Henry was able to reassure her a little. "I think there's a good chance that Ronnie is still alive," he said. "I don't want to raise any false hopes, but my theory is that for the moment she's just been put into cold storage, as it were. If I can play my cards right tomorrow . . . "

"Don't try to be kind to me, Henry," said Emmy brusquely. "Personally, I think she's been dead since Saturday. After all, the murderer didn't have any compunction in Helen's case."

"Veronica's case is quite different, Emmy."

"Henry, you must explain . . . "

"I can't," said Henry wearily. "I really can't, darling. I must go to bed. There's a lot to do tomorrow before half past two."

"What's happening at half past two?"

"Nicholas Knight's dress show," said Henry. "I have an invitation."

Emmy was almost speechless. "You mean you're going to spend the afternoon watching a fashion parade, while Veronica . . . ?"

"I think," said Henry, "that it may be a fairly unusual fashion parade."

14

First thing in the morning, Henry was at Scotland Yard. He put through a number of telephone calls, both to London and the country. He also gave certain instructions to his subordinates, and despatched a plain-clothes man to Somerset House to make some researches among the records there. He was pleased to find that a small parcel had arrived for him by express mail from Paris. He slipped it into his raincoat pocket. Then he went along to Wimpole Street, where he had a short, friendly talk with Sir James Braithwaite.

After this, he made his way to the offices of *Style*. Here, he first had a private talk with Margery French, and asked her if certain things could be arranged.

"It's not usual, Inspector, but I can fix it for you," she said, with her customary air of smooth competence. Henry noticed, however, that the dark rings under her eyes were more marked than usual, despite her make-up. He found—as did so many of her colleagues—that he had to keep reminding himself that this woman was ill, and about to retire on her doctor's orders.

Next, Henry went and spoke to Michael Healy. It was not an interview that he enjoyed, but it had to be done. After that, steeling himself, he had a long and painful talk with Teresa. Her distress was obvious, but Henry realized that, as he had guessed, she was not entirely surprised by what he had to say. He gave her what reassurance he could, and finally went off into the fashion room to pick up from Beth Connolly the heavily embossed card which invited Chief Inspector Tibbett to be present at the Press Showing of Nicholas Knight's Spring Collection that afternoon. Then, feeling in need of solace, he went and took a cup of coffee in one of the many Espresso bars in the neighbourhood, where he fell into pleasant conversation with a blonde sitting on the next stool. It was in a more cheerful frame of mind that he went back to the Yard.

He was gratified to be told that the result of the investigation at Somerset House was exactly what he had predicted, for it had been a long shot, deduced from frail evidence. Strengthened now in his conviction that he had solved the case correctly, he began to look forward to the afternoon with almost pleasurable excitement. It was at this point that an urgent call came through from the Essex police.

When Henry reached Nicholas Knight's *salon,* the *Style* team were already assembled there, although it was some time before the show was scheduled to start. A few other journalists and photographers sat on their tiny, uncomfortable chairs or stood in gossiping groups, but *Style* was in the majority, clustered together, as if in self-defence, at the far end of the long black and white *salon.* The room presented a very different appearance from the last time that Henry had seen it. Now, rows of gilt chairs lined three of the four walls, and down the whole centre of the room ran a ramp draped in black velvet, which burgeoned into a little apron-stage before disappearing behind the black curtains which, Henry knew, led to the atelier.

The salon had been liberally decorated for the occasion with huge sprays of mimosa, yellow and fluffy as newly hatched spring chickens, which had been flown over at great expense from the South of France. This idea, which had seemed brilliant to Nicholas at the time, was in fact proving unfortunate—for the dry, centrally heated atmosphere was causing the mimosa to shed clouds of fine dust onto those sitting beneath it, to the detriment of many a chic felt hat and worsted suit.

Henry paused at the head of the stairs, looking in through the open doorway. His interest was centered on the contingent from *Style.* They had turned out in force, and most of them looked nervous and unhappy. Indeed, the atmosphere of slightly frenetic excitement which accompanies any Press Show seemed here to be heightened to screaming pitch.

As usual, Margery French appeared to be the most composed of the group. She was wearing her mink hat with a dark red suit, and was managing to keep up an easy flow of conversation to the junior fashion staff with only the faintest trace of strain. Teresa, not surprisingly, looked wretched and sat by herself, a little away from the others. Henry saw Beth go up to her and say something. Teresa managed a small smile, and then went on doodling aimlessly on the back of her programme. She was evidently in no mood for conversation.

A little further down the room, Henry spotted an incongruous couple talking earnestly together—Rachel Field and Horace Barry. Rachel seemed more animated than usual. Her cheeks were slightly flushed and she was talking eagerly. About cats, probably, thought Henry.

As Henry still hesitated on the threshold, he heard a cheerful booming of masculine voices on the stairs behind him, and turned to see Patrick Walsh coming up with Michael Healy. Both seemed in high spirits. Henry surmised that they had lunched together, and lunched well, especially as regards liquid refreshment. Other people were beginning to arrive now, and the two men passed Henry, apparently without recognizing him.

Patrick went up to the Mayfair blonde, who was acting as doorkeeper. "Now, me darlin', we've no invitation cards and we're not pretending we have, but you're not the hard-hearted hussy who wouldn't take pity on a couple of poor, honest gate-crashers, now are you? And I can tell you, if you don't let us in, we'll break the place up, God's truth we will."

The blonde simpered delightedly. "Oh, Mr. Walsh . . . *of course* Mr. Knayte will be delayted . . . and Mr. Healy . . . we'd have sent yew cards if we'd *dreamt* yew'd be able to come . . . "

"You're new since I was here last," said Michael. He sounded slightly tipsy. "I must say Nicholas has surprisingly good taste in girls. What's your name?"

"Elvira, Mr. Healy."

"Ever thought of taking up modeling yourself, Elvira? I might be able to use you."

200

"Oh, Mr. *Healy!*" squealed the blonde, enraptured.

"Come and have a drink after the show. We'll talk about it."
The two men went in. Henry saw Teresa look up sharply.
Michael's appearance had obviously taken her by surprise, and
there was a terrible look of pain in her eyes as she watched him
come across the room to join the group from *Style.*

Henry decided that the moment had come to make his own
entrance; he was not looking forward to it. He approached the
blonde, who gave him a warm smile of recognition.

"Ah, Inspector Tibbett . . . that's rayt . . . Miss Connolly
telephoned . . . everything is in order . . . yew're over there
in the corner, with the *Style* people . . . may Ay tayk yewr coat?"

Henry surrendered his raincoat, and then went slowly across
the *salon.* He looked and felt grim and strained. He knew he
was the bearer of the worst possible news, but there was only one
course open to him. As for his own personal feelings, they were
numb. He felt the detachment of a man under a local anaesthetic,
watching dispassionately while a surgeon eviscerates him.

Margery broke off a conversation with Patrick to turn to
Henry and say in a friendly voice, "Ah, there you are, Inspector.
You're developing quite an interest in fashion, I see."

"Miss French." Henry's voice was quite steady, but it sounded
to his own ears as if it came from a great distance, "Miss French
—I'm afraid I have some very bad news. I think it's only fair to
tell you people about it straight away, before the official announcement. Veronica Spence has been found."

"Found?" Margery's voice faltered. Everybody else stopped
talking. Henry sensed that the whole room was holding its breath.
Almost in a whisper, Margery added, "Alive?"

"No," said Henry.

There was a gasp, almost a sob, from Beth. A moment of
terrible silence, and then everybody started asking questions at
once. Henry held up his hand, and said, "Please. I'll tell you all
I know, but it's not much. I got the message at lunchtime and I've
had no time to investigate. As most of you know, this is especially
painful for me, because Veronica was my niece."

There were murmurs of sympathy. The whole room was
listening eagerly now, and Nicholas Knight himself had broken
the unwritten law that a designer should never appear until after
his Collection has been shown. He came almost running through

the black curtains and down the ramp to join the group which clustered round Henry.

Henry went on. "The news came in a telephone call to Scotland Yard from the Essex police. She was found hidden under a haystack near Hockton. She had been strangled. They think she was doped first, so that she wouldn't put up any resistance."

"Essex?" It was Nicholas Knight who spoke, in a high-pitched, excited voice. "Whatever was she doing *there*?"

"The spot where she was found," said Henry, "is only a few miles from the home of Donald MacKay's parents."

"Donald . . . " Patrick began, and then stopped short. "Look here, Inspector . . . he spent the week end down there. I happen to know."

"So do I."

"And he didn't turn up to the office this morning. I thought he must be ill. God . . . the murdering little bastard. Have you got him?"

"Not yet," said Henry, "but we're close behind him."

"But how . . . how did he manage it?" Teresa spoke in a slow, wondering voice.

"I've decided," said Henry, "that since you have all been through the very unpleasant experience of being under suspicion, I owe it to you to tell you exactly our reconstruction of the case. The only redeeming feature of this tragedy is that at least we now know the truth, and everyone can relax and go back to work in peace." Nobody spoke or moved. Henry went on. "Veronica's murder was only too simple to arrange. As many of you know, Donald had arranged to take her to Porchester for the week end, but he had to cancel it because of his mother's illness. That was perfectly genuine, and at first it must have seemed to him that all his plans had been upset, but then he realized how he could carry them out with even less risk to himself.

"He went to Hockton on Friday evening, all right, but he slipped out of the house after his parents were asleep, and drove back to London in a hired car. Meanwhile, he had arranged for a female accomplice to send a telegram to Veronica, purporting to come from him, telling her that he could get away after all, and arranging a rendezvous at Waterloo."

In a small voice, Beth said, "Did you say a . . . a female accomplice, Inspector?"

"Yes, Miss Connolly." Henry looked straight at her. "A female accomplice who certainly didn't realize what she was doing. I hope she does by now."

"What happened then?" Margery French spoke quickly, impatiently, as if resenting the interruption.

"Veronica turned up at the rendezvous," said Henry, "where Donald met her with the news that he had a car and would drive her to Porchester. Once out of the station, I imagine he suggested coffee, and slipped the dope into her cup. He then hustled her quickly back into the car, where she soon became unconscious. He drove quickly to this remote spot in Essex, strangled her, and hid her body. He could reasonably hope that nobody would find her for months. It was only because certain suspicions made us alert the Essex police that . . . however, I can't go into all that now. MacKay went on to the village pub, where he played darts, and then went back to his parents' home for lunch. He had told them the night before that he intended to get up early and go for a long walk, and they, in all good faith, told the police that he had done so. They were also speaking the plain, unvarnished truth when they said that he had spent the whole week end with them. They really believed he had."

"Are we then to assume, Inspector . . . " The voice was Michael's, and it sounded light and heady with relief, " . . . are we to assume that Donald MacKay also killed Helen?"

"That would seem the inevitable conclusion, Mr. Healy."

"I hope to God you get him soon."

"We will," said Henry.

"But *for why*, Inspector?" Horace Barry spoke for the first time. "For why this MacKay kill first Miss Helen and then Miss Veronica?"

"That," said Henry, "is the crux of the matter. He was clever —almost too clever for me. He himself suggested that certain things I had been told about Helen were a smoke screen to hide another story, another man. I was far too slow in tumbling to the fact that the other man was Donald himself. He had fallen in love with Helen, with all the intensity of a young man who conceives a grand passion for an older woman, and she had finally and definitely turned him down. She had also told him that she loved someone else. Sooner than lose her, he killed her. And there were other reasons . . . I should have guessed that a man who would think up the ingenious idea that one supposed flirtation was being used as a smoke screen for another, would probably be basing the idea on something in his own life. And so it was. Donald was flirting with Veronica purely as a cover to hide his passion for Helen. Now Veronica was a bright girl, and she had worked out certain facts about Helen's murder, without carrying them to their logical conclusion, which would have given her the murderer's identity. She was foolish enough, in spite of all my warnings, to confide her theories to Donald, and in doing so, she signed her own death warrant."

"What had she found out?" Surprisingly, it was Rachel Field who spoke. "And what about my suitcase?"

"I can't go into all that now," said Henry. "It'll all come out at the trial. I've told you what I think you deserved to be told. Now I think we should get on with the show."

Margery French said, with a little shudder. "That poor child . . . Inspector, I think we should ask Mr. Knight to cancel the show."

"My dear Miss French." Henry was absolutely firm now. "I wouldn't dream of allowing the show to be put off. It would be grossly unfair to Mr. Knight, and Veronica certainly wouldn't have wanted it. You all know what a professional outlook she had. And let's be honest—isn't it true that most of us have known, in our hearts, that there was little or no hope of finding her alive? All we can do now is to get on with our work."

There was some demur, but Henry finally made his point. Nicholas, who looked understandably shaken by what had happened, made no attempt to go back to the atelier, but remained sitting with the *Style* group. The blonde receptionist, assisted by several minions, pulled the heavy black curtains, shutting out the daylight, and turned powerful spotlights toward the ramp. This idea of quasi-stage lighting for his shows was a gimmick which Nicholas Knight had established some years before, and which had become a tradition of the house.

The audience, still somewhat stunned by what they had heard, took their seats, and soft music began to play through concealed loud-speakers. The big double doors to the corridor were closed, and the blonde mounted to the stage apron and stationed herself under a convenient pink spotlight. She held a paper in her hands.

"Number Wan," she announced, in fluting tones. " 'Park Lane.' "

The girl called Rene, as lovely and apparently undernourished as ever, stepped out from behind the curtains, pirouetted on the rostrum, and began a mincing walk down the ramp, pausing every few yards in order to revolve gracefully. She was wearing a navy blue spring suit with an emerald green ruffled blouse. All around the room, notebooks were opened and pencils flashed. Work had started again, and the tragedy of Veronica Spence was already retreating into the background of consciousness.

"Number Tew. 'Lilac Time.' "

The Chinese girl slipped gracefully through the curtains and revolved elegantly, in a lilac velvet three-piece ensemble with an enormous white hat. There was a little burst of applause. With a quick, sure movement, she slipped off the coat to display the suit, and strolled down the ramp, dragging the beautiful silk-velvet coat after her in the dust.

"Number Three. 'Burnt Sugar.' "

The Show was under way. Henry watched with fascination, despite himself, as suits and topcoats gave way to spring dresses of various degrees of formality. Once he glanced at his watch, and was surprised that the time was slipping away so fast. It was obviously a successful show. Subtly, the atmosphere warmed. The applause became more frequent. Tiny, appreciative whispers ran round the room. Nicholas Knight, in the opinion of the experts, had pulled it off at last. He had arrived.

"Number Twenty-ayte. 'Ragamuffin.' "

This was Rene again, in a pink chiffon dress whose hemline was jagged, in the sophisticated manner of the rags worn by a pantomime Cinderella. There was a long burst of applause. Knight had really shown himself on the heels of Paris. In the half light, however, Henry noticed Teresa lean over and whisper something to Margery, who nodded, a little grimly.

"Number Fawty-wan. 'Peek-a-Boo.' "

As the show proceeded, the *salon* settled down to a relaxed atmosphere of enjoyment. Henry's remarks had been perfectly true. One did not have to be hypersensitive to feel the enormous relief brought by the removal of the load of suspicion which had bedeviled so many of these people for the past week.

"Number Sixty-six. 'Sugar Plum.' "

They had reached the evening dresses by now. "Sugar Plum" drifted by in a cloud of frosty tulle.

"Number Seventy-wan. 'Forget-Me-Not.' " A shimmer of blue and silver lamé flashed along the ramp, to enthusiastic applause.

The programme was nearing its end now, and the lights were dimmed for the entrance of the last model—the traditional finale, the wedding dress.

"Number Seventy-fayve. 'Sweet Mystery.' "

From behind the black satin curtains, illuminated by a single spotlight, stepped a model in what appeared to be a floating cloud of ethereal white. On her head she wore a coronet of artificial orange blossoms, which secured the long tulle veil covering her face. There was a strong burst of applause.

The girl seemed to float rather than to walk down the ramp. Then she paused, and with a sudden joyous gesture, threw back the veil to reveal her face. It was Veronica.

For a moment, there was a terrible silence in the *salon*, broken only by the relentless strains of Mendelssohn's Wedding March. In the half light, Veronica glided towards the far end of the ramp. Her face was grave and serene.

Suddenly, horribly, somebody began to scream. "Don't come near me! . . . Go away! . . . Take her away! . . . She's dead . . . I tell you, she's dead!"

Henry jumped up and pulled back one of the curtains, flooding the room with daylight.

It was Nicholas Knight who had screamed. He sat now with his face buried in his hands, as if trying to ward off the sight of Veronica, who was moving inexorably towards him. As she stepped gracefully down from the ramp and approached the *Style* group, Nicholas shrank back as though overcome by superstitious terror. It was not to him that Veronica addressed herself, however. It was to his next-door neighbour, Teresa Manners. From the protective camouflage of her bouquet, she brought out a small bottle of colourless fluid. This she proffered to Teresa.

"I came back to give you this, Miss Manners," she said. "It's what Miss Pankhurst asked you to bring from Paris. Of course, Miss Field is the person who can tell you all about it. She was telling me while I was helping her to pack at the Crillon."

Nobody, except Henry, was prepared for what happened next.

Nicholas Knight jumped to his feet and flung himself at Rachel Field in a paroxysm of hysterical fury.

"You lying, cheating bitch!" he screamed. "Making me think you'd killed her . . . and all the time you were working with them . . . you double-crossed me . . . you . . . " Choking with rage, he turned to Henry. "There's your murderess! There's the woman who killed Helen Pankhurst! I can prove it! I can . . . "

Rachel Field stood up. She was perfectly calm, and she looked at Nicholas with infinite contempt mingled with a strange sort of exasperated affection. "You poor little fool, Nicky," she said. "Didn't you realize from the beginning that it was only a trick to catch us?"

Before Nicholas could reply, the doors from the corridor opened, and the *salon* was suddenly full of dark blue uniforms. Henry said, "Rachel Field, and Nicholas Field, otherwise Nicholas Knight, I arrest you both for the willful murder of Helen Pankhurst. I must warn you that anything you say will be . . . "

The rest of the sentence was lost in uproar. Rachel had turned on Henry like a tigress. "It was me!" she screamed. "Leave Nicky alone! He had nothing to do with it! It was me . . . " It took two policewomen to drag her away. As for Nicholas, he was weeping hysterically as they led him downstairs to the waiting police car.

"Oh, Uncle Henry, how *horrible!*" cried Veronica, her composure suddenly shattered. She flung her arms round Henry's neck and burst into a flood of tears.

Henry patted her back encouragingly. "Take it easy, Ronnie. It's all over now. You were splendid. I was proud of you."

It was at that moment that Donald MacKay, looking white and exhausted, came diffidently through the curtains from the atelier. Gently, Henry disengaged his niece's arms from around his own neck and transferred them to Donald's. "I think," he said with a grin, "that you can probably do more good than I can. I should let her have a good cry and then buy her a stiff drink."

"I'll do that, sir," said Donald. Veronica did not protest. Indeed, she merely clutched Donald more tightly than ever when he picked her up, orange blossoms and all, and carried her out of the *salon*.

Henry turned to Michael and Teresa, who were sitting holding hands in stunned silence. "You two can go home now," he said. "You've got nothing more to worry about."

"But . . . " Teresa began.

"Oh, I was forgetting. Elvira has something for you. Elvira!"

The blonde sauntered up, unconcerned and smiling. She had in her hands a large envelope, marked "Photographs, with care."

"Elvira thinks they're all there," said Henry. "In future, I should take rather more care, as the label advises." He handed the envelope to Michael. "Now, if Miss French agrees, I think you should go back home for the rest of today. You've got a lot to talk about."

Teresa stood up. "I don't know how to thank you," she said to Henry. "Come on, Mike. Home." Unprotesting, Michael followed her out of the *salon* and downstairs.

Henry, feeling very self-conscious, climbed on to the rostrum. "Let's have some more light, Elvira," he said. Languidly, Elvira pulled back the remaining curtains. Henry addressed the audience, which was just beginning to recover from its shock. "Ladies and gentlemen," he said, "I can't apologize enough for putting you through such a harassing afternoon. I can only ask you to believe that it was the only way of bringing two criminals to justice. I don't have to tell you that the case I outlined against Mr. MacKay was pure fiction. He is not only completely innocent, but he has helped us a great deal. As have other members of the staff of *Style*," he grinned at Margery, "not to mention my friend Elvira, who has been a tower of strength, for no more reward than a cup of coffee."

Elvira simpered. "Delayted, I'm sure, Inspector," she said.

15

It was after ten o'clock that night when Henry eventually got home, but he found the flat ablaze with light and merrymaking. Emmy was dispensing drinks in celebration of a double occasion —Veronica's return from the dead, and the announcement of her engagement to Donald MacKay. Everybody was in high spirits, and Henry found it difficult to put the necessary degree of severity into his voice as he said to Veronica and Donald, "Well, I hope you two are thoroughly ashamed of yourselves."

"Ashamed!" cried Veronica with spirit. "I like that! You'd never have caught them without us, and you know it." She jumped onto the sofa and declaimed—"Model girl solves murder mystery. 'We were baffled,' admits Chief Inspector Tibbett of Scotland Yard . . . "

"We were *not* baffled," said Henry, piqued. "I admit that your ridiculous scheme was useful in the end, but only when I took charge of it. Heaven knows what would have happened if . . . "

"Henry," said Emmy, gently but firmly, "I think you had better explain to Jane and Bill and myself, before our brains burst. Ronnie keeps babbling about Paris *toiles* and invisible ink and horn-rimmed spectacles, and I can't make head nor tail of it. I don't think she can herself."

"You see," Veronica said, "I didn't know *who* it was. The

second person, I mean. That's why . . . "

"Maybe it would be best, Ronnie," said Henry, "if you let me tell it. You can correct me where I go wrong."

"You bet I will."

"I would like to start by saying," said Henry, "that I hope never again to have to work on a case with such a bunch of people."

"What's the matter with us, Uncle Henry? We're all so *nice*. And some of us are *intelligent*." She ruffled Donald's hair.

"That's just the trouble," said Henry. He took a drink, sat down, and said, "It's difficult to know where to begin. I suppose the right place is Helen's love affair with Godfrey Goring."

"With . . . with Mr. *Goring?*" Veronica sat bolt upright, her big eyes round with amazement. "But I thought it was Michael . . ."

"So did most people," said Henry, "except the people who really mattered. I very soon realized that there was some sort of conspiracy between Margery French, Teresa, Goring, Michael himself, and possibly Patrick to pull the wool over my eyes."

"Uncle couldn't pull the wool over anybody's eyes," said Veronica scornfully.

"That's the conclusion I came to," said Henry. "He wasn't part of this conspiracy, because Helen knew him too well to tell him the truth. He was an old and dear friend, and she longed to confide in him, but she couldn't trust him to keep his mouth shut, so she told him the situation without telling him the name of the man she loved. Uncle was one of the few people who were fooled into believing it was Michael."

"I thought all along it might be Goring," said Donald.

"You liar!" Veronica said affectionately. "It never even occurred to you."

"Actually, it was the most obvious solution," stated Henry. "They had been in love for some time, in fact. He found in her everything that his wife lacked—business sense, efficiency, tidiness, intelligence. There was one thing, however, that Lorna Goring had which Helen hadn't, and that was money. Of course, it was her fortune which had been poured into *Style*, although she didn't appear officially on the list of shareholders. Goring did not dare to leave her. More, she is a fiery and jealous woman and adores him. He did not dare risk her finding out that he was emotionally involved with a member of his staff.

"I think I ought to say, in fairness, that both Helen and Goring behaved perfectly honourably. They had no affair in the ordinary sense of the word. They loved each other deeply, and hoped to marry when Goring felt that the magazine was stable enough financially. Meanwhile, Goring spent the week in London—and some week ends as well, according to Lorna—and he and Helen spent most evenings together at his town house.

"Everything was fine until Olwen Piper came to share Helen's flat. I was surprised at first that Helen should have consented to such an arrangement, until I remembered that Goring had been on a prolonged trip to America when Olwen moved in, and that it was only supposed to be a temporary arrangement. However, when Goring returned, Olwen was firmly established, and Helen was, as Teresa said, too soft-hearted to throw her out. However, Helen realized she would have to think up some story to account for her frequent evenings out. She and Goring talked it over, and appealed to Michael and Teresa. I may say that Goring is an old friend of Teresa and her family, and they were the only people who knew about the affair.

"Michael and Teresa agreed quite cheerfully that Helen should use them as an excuse—say she was going to dinner there, and so on. What nobody reckoned on was that Olwen would develop a sort of schoolgirl crush on Helen, and grow violently jealous of the Healys. When she accidentally found the truth—that Helen had not been there to dinner as she said—she jumped to the conclusion that Helen and Michael were lovers, and tried to put a stop to it by circulating wild rumours. This put the Healys, Helen, and Goring all in awkward positions, but they decided to laugh it off. At all costs, the truth about Helen and Goring must not come out, for the sake of the magazine. Michael has the reputation of a philanderer—all right, so let people think he has added Helen to his list of conquests. In fact, Michael and Teresa tell me that they all regarded it as something of a joke. At first.

"But then something serious happened. A couple of months ago, Goring began to get worried about his health. He told Helen about it, but refused to go to his doctor, because he did not want Lorna to get wind of it and start fussing. Helen, who had a shrewder notion than he of what the trouble might be, at last persuaded him to go to a cancer specialist. They visited him together, calling themselves Mr. and Mrs. Charles Dodgson."

"What a strange name to choose," said Emmy. Then she added suddenly, "And yet it rings a bell. Wasn't it . . . ?"

"It was the sort of double-bluffing pun which would have appealed to both of them," said Henry. "As far as his affair with Helen was concerned, Goring was hiding behind the disguise of Michael Healy. Obviously, they did not want to give Michael's name to the doctor, so they picked on the name of another famous photographer."

"Charles Dodgson?" said Veronica, wrinkling her nose. "I've never heard of him. Which magazines does he work for? If he's so famous, my agent ought to ring him up and . . . "

Henry smiled. "He's been dead a long time," he said. "He was a pioneer of photography who became even more celebrated under a pseudonym of his own. Lewis Carroll."

"Alice in Wonderland?"

"That's right."

"Gosh, you are clever, Uncle Henry," said Veronica. "How did you find all this out?"

"By tracking down the doctor, who told me his diagnosis. Goring is dying of cancer, and has less than a year to live. At Helen's request, the doctor told her the whole truth, but to Goring he merely said that he had a stomach ulcer and should go on a diet."

"But how did you find out that it was Mr. Goring?"

"I admit," said Henry, "that when the doctor identified Helen as Mrs. Dodgson, I had qualms for a moment. The name seemed to point so obviously to Michael."

"So why were you so sure it wasn't him?" Emmy asked.

"Partly because I'm cussed," Henry answered. "When a lot of people start to ram a certain fact down my throat, I get suspicious. And Donald confirmed my suspicions by pointing out that the whole thing was phoney. Of course, when Helen was killed, it became doubly important to keep Goring away from any sort of scandal, so the ranks of the conspirators closed up. It wasn't very pleasant for Michael to be thrown to the wolves, but it was better than having the magazine fold up."

"Was that the only reason you decided it wasn't Michael?" asked Veronica. "Just pure cussedness?"

"Not entirely," said Henry. "I had a much sounder reason, and that was Michael's reaction when I told him that Helen was pregnant."

"Pregnant! Was she?"

"No," said Henry, "but at the time I thought she was. I put it to Michael, and he was completely shattered. He had always believed, correctly, that Helen and Goring were not lovers in the technical sense. But when I produced this bombshell, and accused him of being the father, what could he do? He was committed to his story, and he had to stick to it. He admitted the whole thing. Then I found out that Helen was a virgin.

"The only possible reason for Michael's behaviour was that he was covering up for somebody. But who? The answer was simple as soon as I heard that the doctor had put 'Mr. Dodgson' on to a diet for a stomach ulcer. As you know, that means light food and no alcohol. The only person who adhered rigidly to such a diet was Goring. He also qualified by having a rich wife. What was more, when Helen died, he was extremely upset and rattled, and he went out of his way to warn me not to believe anything Michael might say. He was determined that Michael should carry on the fiction to the bitter end, but he was terrified that, under stress, he might break down and tell me the truth."

"I feel terribly sorry for Mr. Goring," said Veronica seriously. "What will happen to him now?"

"His wife," said Henry, "is neither so scatterbrained nor insensitive as people imagine, and she's devoted to him. She, too, was worried about his health, and, in spite of all his precautions, she had more than a suspicion about his affair with Helen. As soon as I mentioned a doctor to her, she did her best to get his name out of me. When she was persistent about it, I gave her enough clues to find the name if she really wanted to, and I warned the doctor that he might hear from her. Sure enough, she ferreted him out and told him who she was. Sir James says that she was extraordinarily brave and sensible. She's going to leave with her husband next week for a cruise round the world. There's very little hope of curing him, but at least she will nurse him devotedly."

"All this is fascinating," said Emmy, "but it gets us no nearer Helen's murder or the invisible ink or . . . "

"Or *me*," put in Veronica. "Do get *on* with it, Uncle Henry."

"I'm sorry," said Henry. "I had to tell you all that first, so that you could understand what comes next. And the two are, in fact, connected. There was never any problem about how Helen was killed; the question was, *why*. For a start, I ruled out the possibility of suicide." He sketched briefly the arguments that he had already expounded to Goring. "So, Helen was murdered. And from this point of view, Rachel Field's suitcase was even more interesting than Helen's body. Somebody, in frantic haste, had ransacked that case, throwing everything onto the floor. Had this person found what he was looking for? Was there anything missing? There didn't seem to be. The light didn't dawn on me until Helen's funeral, when that nice Mrs. Sedge started talking about . . . "

"Tissue paper!" cried Veronica triumphantly.

"Now you've spoilt the point of my story," said Henry.

"I don't understand at all, Henry." Emmy's sister, Jane, put a timid oar into the conversation for the first time. "It's normal to use tissue paper for packing, isn't it?"

"It certainly is," said Henry. "Not for some young hooligans, perhaps," he added, with a meaning glance at Veronica, "but certainly for a meticulous person like Rachel Field. In fact, Ronnie told me that she wrapped everything up."

"If you'd only let me go in there, I'd have seen straightaway," Veronica said. "I mean, her hotel bedroom was a *mass* of tissue paper . . . "

"And there wasn't a scrap of it in Helen's office next morning," added Henry. "It sounded crazy, but Helen was apparently murdered so that somebody could extract the tissue paper from Rachel Field's case, and Rachel herself must be somehow implicated, because she never remarked on the fact that it had gone. Then two things happened. Some mysterious writing appeared on a piece of paper which had been blank before, and I remembered Emmy making a skirt."

"You're talking in riddles, Henry," said Jane, a little severely. Her farmer husband, Bill, had long since fallen asleep on the sofa, and now let out a ripe snore, as if in support of Jane's censure.

"I'd already gathered," Henry went on, "a certain amount about the world of high fashion. I knew that *toiles*—exact copies of a model in cheap cotton—could be bought in Paris from the designers at a great price. I knew, too, that some wholesalers

214

and designers—notably Nicholas Knight—had caused a scandal by coming out with copies apparently made from a *toile* which had never left Paris. I also knew that experts had ruled that it would be impossible to smuggle a *toile* out of a Paris atelier. Yet apparently it was being done. I asked myself what *could* be taken out of a workshop without arousing suspicion, and the obvious answer was tissue paper. Then I thought of Emmy cutting out from her paper pattern, and I saw the light."

"Now, wait a minute, Henry," said Emmy. "I'm not a detective, but I do know something about dressmaking. Do you suggest that somebody cut out a paper pattern of the *toile*, put in all the marking that it needs, and then walked out with it over her arm, simply saying airily, 'Just a few bits of old paper to wrap things in'? Come now."

Veronica was bouncing up and down on the sofa in excitement. "Aunty Emmy, don't you *see?*"

"Shut up, Ronnie," said Henry. "You can take over in a minute. No, Emmy, I don't suggest that. The *toiles* came out of the workrooms in the guise of perfectly plain, square, new sheets of tissue paper with no markings on them at all. In fact, these sheets were used to wrap certain garments taken out to be photographed by *Style*."

Emmy clapped a hand to her forehead. "Of course! What a fool I am. Invisible ink!"

"Got it at last!" cried Veronica. "And d'you know, I actually bought the ink myself!"

"You did? Don't tell me that *you* . . . "

"No, no. I bought it for Teresa, for Helen . . . "

"Ronnie!" Henry was stern. "Don't speak until you're spoken to." Veronica giggled. Henry went on. "The method of smuggling out the designs was beautifully simple, and only required the collaboration of one employee in each couture house. So far, our only sure proof comes from Monnier's. The girl would make an excuse to work late, and then trace a paper pattern of the pieces of a *toile*, together with sewing instructions, in invisible ink on white tissue paper. She would then mark the paper unobtrusively, and put it away. We know that Rachel Field was responsible for getting the dresses from the ateliers to be photographed by *Style*. The dress would come wrapped in this apparently innocuous paper. It was easy enough for Rachel to send it back wrapped in ordinary tissue paper, and keep the marked sheets for her own packing. Once safely home, she would send the sheets to Nicholas Knight, who had only to expose them to the heat of an electric fire to bring up the markings, and there were his Paris models. Of course, he couldn't expect more than a few *toiles* each season. His other copies he did, as he said, cut by eye from photographs. And here we must have a slight digression.

"It was clear that Knight was also getting Paris pictures ahead of their release dates. Where from? As soon as I saw a picture on his desk of Ronnie on the Eiffel Tower, I knew that it was *Style* pictures he was getting. Michael Healy had been making his own prints the night before, having sent his assistant home, and he took a brief case away from the offices with him. It seemed certain that Michael himself was supplying Nicholas with illicit photographs. I decided that he would only do so under pressure, and I remembered certain extremely catty remarks that Nicholas had made to me.

"In the end, I went straight to Michael and put it to him. He was nearly at the end of his tether, and told me the truth. Once, years ago, he had been mixed up in a nasty scandal with a crowd of notorious homosexuals. Knight knew this, and threatened to denounce him to Goring—not to mention Teresa—unless he supplied the photographs. I persuaded Michael to let me tell Teresa the whole story, which she took very well, and I told him he needn't worry about Knight any more. I also managed to get this season's pictures out of Knight's office for him. I don't think he'll have any more worries."

"All right," said Emmy. "My head's whirring, but I think I'm with you so far. You still haven't explained why Helen was killed, or who stole the tissue paper . . . "

"Nobody stole it," said Henry. "Its rightful owner collected it."

"Riddles again," said Jane, rather sharply.

"Once again," said Henry, "we digress. This time to the Duchess of Basingstoke's ball gown, which could not, as Knight claimed, have been copied from a photograph. There had been a scandal, and Knight, who is not a stable character, was getting worried. There's a tragic aspect to all this, too. He says now, and I believe him, that this was the last season that he and Rachel proposed to pirate designs. He was good enough to stand on his own, and today's show was a triumph. He's an immensely talented young man, but he wanted his success too fast."

"What I still don't see," said Donald, "is the connection between him and Rachel Field."

"That puzzled me, too," said Henry, "until I went back over the evidence, and realized that Knight was lying when he said he'd never met her before that night at Goring's. Everybody confirmed that he didn't go near her all the evening until he came up to her and Barry, and—as Barry said—'suggested they should leave and also said he would take Miss Field, as she lived in the same direction.' So, he knew her, and he knew where she lived, but he denied it. Why? Then I suddenly remembered a tiny moment while I was interviewing him, when I mentioned that I wanted to investigate the relationships between various people, and he nearly fainted with fright. That was when the thought came to me, suddenly, that they must be brother and sister. I sent a man to check at Somerset House, and sure enough, Nicholas Knight changed his name some years ago by deed poll. His real name was Nicolas Field."

Henry paused. "I know more about it now," he said. "I've spoken to both of them. They were born to parents living in respectable, white-collar poverty—the worst sort. Rachel is eight years older than Nicholas, and has been responsible for him since their parents died when she was sixteen and he was eight. She supported him, educated him, brought him up, and idolized him. When it became obvious that his talent lay in dress design, she sent him to art school. She took a job on *Style* to be closer to his interests. All the time, she was growing more and more fanatical about one idea. He should have his own salon. It would be the most elegant and sought after in London. He would make his name. He agreed with this in principle, but he realized that it would take years of hard work. When Rachel hit on the scheme for smuggling *toiles* out of Paris, he was only too keen to co-operate. Obviously, there must be no connection between them, so he changed his name, and they saw as little as possible of each other. Rachel provided the initial capital to start his *salon*. The Paris designs, plus Knight's own talent, did the rest. He landed his contract with Barrimodes, and success seemed to be in sight . . . and then things went wrong."

"What went wrong?" Emmy asked.

"First of all, the rumours, and the Duchess's dress. Then

217

Godfrey Goring, who wanted to stamp out the racket, and had a bright—and right—idea of what was going on. He could not do much about it himself, so he enlisted Helen's help. She in turn went to Patrick, who as an artist and art editor knew more about inks than she did. The letter which I found in Helen's desk was obviously intended, not for her dressmaker, as I thought, but for Goring. Attached to it was a sheet of paper on which she had written in the type of ink which appears only when subjected to heat. She said in the letter that it was not quite the same as the ink available in Paris, but that she had asked Teresa to bring her back a sample."

"That's what I bought," Veronica burst out. "I brought it back to the hotel and gave it to Miss Manners and—"

"And it disappeared out of her suitcase," said Henry. "Obviously, Helen, knowing it was there, took it herself and put it on her desk. That sealed her fate; that and the fact that she had accidentally opened Rachel's case and let some tissue paper spill out, and that she had put on the electric fire . . . "

"Henry! Go a bit slower," Emmy begged.

"All right. We're back at Goring's party. Patrick has had rather too much to drink. He hates Knight, and he shoots his mouth off, without really knowing what he's talking about. He says, 'Helen and I know what you're up to,' or words to that effect. This rattles Knight. As soon as they have dropped Barry, Nicholas and Rachel have a long and serious talk. He tells her to hand over the tissue paper, which he will burn, as it's too dangerous. She has to admit that it is still in her suitcase at *Style* . . . in Helen's office. Knight insists that she should go back and collect the case. After all, there's nothing suspicious about that. She can just walk in and say she's come to get her case. So they drive back to Earl Street and she lets herself in with her own key. Nicholas goes back to his flat.

"Inside, all is dark and quiet, except for the light from Helen's open door and the clicking of her typewriter. Olwen has just left. Helen is too absorbed with her work to be aware of extraneous noises. If she did hear the lift, she probably connected it with Olwen. Rachel gets to the office doorway and stops dead, in the shadows. What she can see is her suitcase, open, and the tissue paper escaping from it, with its markings showing clearly, having been brought up by the heat of the fire. And on Helen's desk, a bottle of the special invisible ink from Paris. Personally, I doubt if Helen had even noticed what had happened to the tissue paper, but she would have in the morning. Rachel knows that the game is up. The years of working and struggling and cheating and scheming to make Nicholas Knight famous . . . were they all to end in disgrace and prison? Then, I think, she thought of the Thermos, and the cyanide. She slipped along the corridor like a shadow, put the poison in the flask, wiped it, and walked back down the stairs. It must have been from the mews at the back that she telephoned Knight, and told him what he must do.

"He was to watch from the window of his bedroom, which looked straight into Helen's office. As soon as Helen was dead, he was to slip across the street, let himself in with the key which Rachel would give him, and remove both the tissue paper and the ink bottle. He was to throw the key away, for there must be absolutely no contact between them for some time. It would be too dangerous to try and send it back. She intended to report the loss of the key much later on, when the hue and cry had died down.

"To do Nicholas credit, he did exactly as he was told. He must have been in a terrible state of nerves, and I don't blame him. It must be quite an ordeal, even for a balanced person, to go and burgle a room which contains the body of someone he has helped to murder, and whom he has just watched die. It's no wonder that he simply grabbed the tissue paper out of the case and left everything else scattered all over the floor. Nevertheless Rachel, who is a perfectionist, was very angry next day when she saw what an inefficient job he had made of it. He had drawn attention to her suitcase. If he'd repacked it and shut it, we might never have got at the truth."

"How do you know all this, Uncle Henry?" Veronica demanded. "Have they confessed?"

"They've filled in the details," said Henry, "but I had guessed the broad outlines. Rachel gave herself away."

"How?"

"It was bad luck on her," said Henry, "that Beth asked to borrow her key so soon after the murder. Not being able to produce it, she was forced to admit that it was lost, and also to maintain that she hadn't noticed it was missing. Now she kept it on the same ring with her house keys, and it was a big, heavy thing. I couldn't believe that she wouldn't have noticed its absence at once. Then, she was upset when I told her that the murderer must have come back to rifle the suitcase. She knew perfectly well that her case had been ransacked. She'd even seen it, and her only emotion was anger. The second time I mentioned it, she was frightened because I told her that I knew the murderer had come back to the building later. By that time, I was pretty close behind her, and she knew it. My trouble was that I hadn't enough proof. The crucial paper patterns had been burnt, and the ink destroyed. I had no case that would stand up in court. It was at this point that my charming but nitwitted niece decided to take a hand." He bowed to Veronica. "Will you go on from there?"

"Not nitwitted at all," said Veronica, spiritedly. "Jolly bright, I call it. You see, I'd bought this ink in Paris . . . of course, Miss Manners didn't know what it was for or how important it was, or she'd never have let an idiot like me have anything to do with it. It was just a commission that Miss Pankhurst had asked her to do, and she was busy, so she sent me to get it. I never connected it with the murder at all, until I went to Nicholas Knight's for fittings. Then I suddenly remembered that last time I was showing for him, just after the last Paris Collections, I'd seen them making one of what he calls his Paris specials, and I'd seen bits of paper with those funny ink marks on them, and something clicked! I wanted to tell Uncle Henry, but he was beastly and wouldn't let me, so I thought, 'I'll show him. I'll do it alone.' When I say alone, I mean with Donald, of course."

"You mean, you talked the poor boy into it," said Veronica's mother. She had not brought up four attractive daughters for nothing.

"Well, I did rather throw him to the wolves," admitted Veronica, "but you didn't mind, did you, poppet?"

Donald was looking at her with the expression of a young man who does not mind hell, fire, or high water so long as a certain basic situation remains unchanged. Jane sighed. "Go on, then. What did you do?"

"Well." Veronica put her head on one side and looked serious. "You see, I was certain Knight was involved, but I knew he must have an accomplice, because he never went to Paris. So I had this idea. I went round saying very loudly in the atelier and all over the place that I knew his guilty secret. That would get round fast enough—dress houses are marvelous places for gossip. Then, I decided to disappear. Dramatically. I'll hide somewhere nice and quiet, I thought, and Donald can watch Knight's place like a hawk, and the accomplice is bound to turn up, because neither of them will know what's happened to me, and each will think that the other has *taken steps*."

"A sillier idea," remarked Henry, "I have seldom heard. Didn't it strike you that after your disappearance Knight and his accomplice would be less likely than ever to communicate with each other? When I found poor Donald stationed on the pavement outside Knight's atelier . . . "

"I paid the flower seller ten quid for that," Donald remarked morosely.

"Isn't he marvelous?" cooed Veronica. "He didn't complain once. Anyhow, it worked."

"Only," said Henry, "as I have already pointed out, when somebody with a little sense took over. Anyhow, tell us how you actually did it."

"Well—we were going to Porchester to disappear, but then Donald's mother got ill, so we thought up a much better plan. He went down to Essex on Friday to sort of soften them up for the blow. Then I went and sent myself a telegram on Friday evening, and acted so *suspiciously* . . . I hope the man remembered me. I couldn't have done more if I'd stood on my head."

"It wasn't your head he remembered," said Henry. "It was your legs."

"Anyhow, the telegram came on Saturday morning, so I showed it to Nancy, to make sure she knew. Then I put on my full Paris war paint and my red coat and made myself really conspicuous. I bet the taxi driver remembered me."

"He did," said Henry.

"Well, then I got to Waterloo, and I went into the Ladies'. And while I was safely locked in the john, I changed into my old navy blue suit and my rabbit hat, and I took off all my make-up and put on a pair of gorgeous horn-rimmed spectacles that Donald bought me at Woolworths."

"So it was you," said Henry.

"Who was me?"

"There's a dear old gentleman," said Henry, "to whom Scotland

Yard owes an apology. He swore he traveled on an underground train with you, and he described exactly what you were wearing. Nobody believed him."

"Wasn't that lucky?" said Veronica, with a brilliant smile. "He must have thought you very dim."

"Not so dim as all that," said Henry. "I did realize that you'd changed in the cloakroom and disappeared deliberately. You left a face tissue covered in that terrible brown lipstick and your mascara, which you'd obviously rubbed off very thoroughly. That, together with the strange fact that everybody noticed you go in and nobody noticed you come out . . . "

"I thought it was pretty clever," said Veronica, who did not suffer from false modesty. "Well, I simply took a tube to Liverpool Street and a train to Hockton, and had a lovely week end with Donald's parents, who are honeypies."

"But when all the hue and cry broke out . . . ?"

"They didn't recognize me," said Veronica happily. "Not from those awful pictures from *Style* that were published everywhere. I tried to keep them away from the newspapers as much as possible, of course. I think, actually, they were just beginning to get a bit suspicious when you telephoned."

"Telephoned?" Jane sounded bewildered. "You mean, you knew she was there, Henry?"

"I've told you how I reasoned it," said Henry. "I knew she'd disappeared on purpose. It seemed an obvious place for her to be."

"Uncle Henry was *furious*," said Veronica. "I thought the telephone was going to explode. Anyhow, the nice policemen from Chelmsford came and smuggled me out. We phoned Uncle Henry at Scotland Yard to say we were on the way, and then we drove like a whirlwind to London, with me hidden on the floor under a rug, and the siren going. It was divine.

"When we got to Scotland Yard, Uncle Henry asked me if I knew Elvira at Nicholas Knight's, and of course I did. He said he'd been in touch with her, and she was prepared to smuggle me in through the back staircase that leads up from The Orangery, and to take the bottle of ink from him and put it in my bouquet. Then he told me what I had to say and do . . . and . . . well, that's it."

"Lots of people helped me at the last moment," said Henry. "Elvira was wonderful, and Margery French made sure that the

Style people all got there early, and arranged to bring Rachel Field along, which was unusual—her secretary doesn't normally go to dress shows. I wasn't expecting Michael and Patrick, but it seems that Margery begged Patrick to come along and give her moral support, and that he was lunching with Michael anyhow. So we staged our little drama and, as I had hoped, it was too much for Knight's nerves. What would have happened if we'd had two people of Rachel's calibre to deal with, I don't like to . . . "
He looked round, with the sudden, curious sense that he had lost his audience. Donald was kissing Veronica with a fervour which indicated that neither of them would be interested in anything else for quite some time. The others were all asleep.

"Oh, to hell with it," said Henry. "I'm going to bed."